A Mourning of Remembrance

By Stephen Tiedman

To my father, Dennis Tiedman. Like the main character Bernie, you could fix anything. Unlike Bernie, however, it was your mind that was strong and your body let you down. Miss you every day, Dad.

Table of Contents

Contents

r 1

Chapter 1

Writing Entry for Friday, January 30

I am supposed to be writing about myself. I do not prefer to do that. Mr. Kubach says it will help me discover myself. Quite frankly, Bobby Shultz "discovered" himself in the locker room and got in trouble last week. I pointed that out to Mr. Kubach and received a reprimand. Mr. Kubach is my 'special needs' teacher. I put quote marks around special needs because there is nothing special or needy about being in this ridiculous class.

What good is writing about myself going to do? It is not like writing about myself will magically open my mind to the world around me and intake everything that has not been shoved in already. I tried explaining that to Mr. Kubach. He would not listen even though I thought I presented a well thought out rebuttal of the information. I cited my sources. He still said I had to keep this log about myself. I asked what happens if I do not do it. Failure was his response. How do you fail special needs class? By not being special or needy enough?

Given little choice, I have decided to keep this log. However, I am not going to write about myself. Instead, I will write about my grandfather. Mr. Kubach did not say what I had to write. My grandfather is a part of me, biologically speaking of course.

I have a feeling that this assignment was just a way to keep me busy and stop "being a paperweight" as Mr. Kubach likes to say. "Being a paperweight" is when a kid sits around and does not do anything. I probably could write down anything, and it would not matter. My guess is that he will not even read this assignment. I am still going to write about my grandfather though. Thinking about him makes being in this school somewhat tolerable. Sometimes.

Bernard Trevor Pierce was born February, 21 1940 in Ann Arbor, Michigan. Nothing like starting at the beginning, right? Hackney, I know, but I have to start somewhere. His parents were Frank and Gayle Pierce. I have never met them because they died before I was born. Makes it hard to meet a person, right? Ann Arbor is not too far from here. Grandpa took me there to see where my great-grandparents were buried. He knelt by the stones, and I stood and waited until he was finished. Then we went for ice cream. It was a nice day partly because it was just my grandfather and me and partly because my father was not there. That was when I was seven and before my grandfather had to stop driving.

My grandfather served in the Army from 1957 to 1961. Perhaps I will write about his time there. He has shared many stories about that time, and if I have to keep writing these ridiculous entries, then I will write about them.

I have ten more minutes of writing, so I want to concentrate on one story. It is the earliest memory I have of my grandfather.

I was four years old, and my favorite toy was this Batman car that went everywhere with me. I think I must have rubbed the paint completely off that thing. My sister had been born the week before and there were people constantly coming over to look at her, which I never understood why. All she did was cry and suck on my mother. Big whoop. I did not like all those people tromping in and out of my house. Some were family, but that still bothered me. To make matters worse, my parents were paying more attention to the baby than me.

I walked into my parents' room where my sister was staying and saw both my mother and father making fools of themselves over the bassinet. I did say that I was in the room, but either they did not hear me or they ignored me because neither of them turned around. I got angry and then threw the one thing I could–my Batman car. Now this was no Hot Wheels car. This toy had it all. It could fit a six inch action figure, fire missiles, and other inappropriate things a toy should not do for a four year old. The car sailed over my parents' heads, hit the wall behind the bassinet, and then broke into several pieces, showering down on baby Pauline. She started to cry, but I did not notice that all that much. What I really noticed was my precious car was broken, and the person responsible had been me. My father whirled around, yelled and then scooped me up. The entire time he was carrying me, I was trying to squirm out of his grasp to go see how bad my car was. I was put in my room and then yelled at some more. I assumed it was the usual stuff about *why did I do it* and *the baby could have been hurt*, but I was not paying attention. Finally my father realized I was too hysterical to listen, or he tired of yelling because he left, shutting the door.

At four, I knew that I could not leave that room when I was in trouble or else I would be sent back longer. Normally it wouldn't be an issue being placed in my room for a timeout, but that was when I had my Batman car. I must have screamed for what I thought was an hour when the door finally opened and my mother came in. She held what was left of my car in her hands. My precious car was in three pieces. The cockpit door had broken off, one of the wheels was off, and it was missing one of two fins on the back. Sitting next to me, she put her arm around me and told me that I needed to be patient with my new baby sister and my parents. She gave me a hug and told me I could come out of my room. Then she left. I picked up my broken Batmobile and started to cry again. Another person entered my room; it was my grandfather.

He asked if I was having a rough day. Like it was not obvious enough. Then he looked down at my broken car. He said that my Superman car was all broken. I did not bother to correct him. He took the pieces from me, gave me a hug, and then left. I followed him out to the living room where my grandmother, father, and mother, who was holding Pauline, were. I watched as my grandfather grabbed his coat and said he would be right back. Grandpa and Grandma Pierce lived like ten minutes away. Grandpa came back an hour later with my Batmobile. He had fixed it. The broken wheel was back on, along with the fin and cockpit. The car even rolled better than before it was broken. That was the first time I learned that my grandfather could fix anything.

End of Entry

+ + +

School can be agony at times for most students. It is just a fact of life. No student enjoys every minute of the day at school. Those that say they do are just fooling themselves. For some students, just about every minute of school can be excruciating. So it was for Gavin Pierce. He was sitting in his resource class at St Clair Shores High School. It was the last class of the day for the seventeen year old young man, but it was also the longest.

He was sitting at a table by himself, trying to concentrate on his work at the moment. One could tell that he was succeeding in his concentration because there was very little writing on the algebra work. Had it been history work, Gavin would have sped through it, but it was Algebra II and intolerable. Occasionally, Gavin's eyes would look up at the digital clock that was above Mr. Kubach's desk, and then a look of disappointment would cloud over his face. Time not only came to a standstill in Kubach's class, it seemed to go backward.

Mr. Kubach was a portly teacher who specialized in special education. He had been a teacher for 22 years and most of it in the Detroit area. The students knew all of this because he had told them on the first day, even if they had him the year before and the year before that. For Gavin, as teachers went, Mr. Kubach wasn't that bad, but that was because he didn't teach a particular subject. He managed some of the resource classes where the students with special needs were placed to help with homework and organization. The room wasn't the size of a normal classroom at the high school and had tables instead of desks in it. Gavin was one of only a few students that had a table all to himself. It was how he preferred to work. Most of the other students in the room annoyed him. When someone sat down at his table, he would move to the furthest point away from that student. Most students had gotten the point and left him alone as much as space allowed.

Gavin looked down at his Algebra II again and then flipped his pen away. Frustration crossed his face as a black cat crossed a superstitious person's path. He looked up at the time and was equally disappointed again.

"Algebra kicking your butt?" Mr. Kubach asked from behind and then put his ample weight into the empty chair next to Gavin.

"No, but I am not doing too well with it. Whoever thought of mixing numbers and letters should be dragged out into the street and beaten past an inch of his life," Gavin said, not bothering to look over at the teacher. Mr. Kubach gave a chuckle and then peered at the problem that was stumping the young man. He pointed out some variables that Gavin had missed and soon the problem was solved. Without looking again, Gavin said, "Thanks. One down and nine to go."

"They are pretty much the same. Just different letters," Mr. Kubach said, standing up. "I'll come back and see how you are doing."

Gavin proceeded to the next one and then looked at the time. Five minutes had passed. There were still 20 to go. Does time pass any slower than when one is at school and the end is so close, but yet so far? Being Thursday, Gavin still had one more day to go before the blessed weekend, but that was for tomorrow. If he dwelled too much on the obstacles that the next day held, he would go crazy. For now, it was satisfactory for Gavin if the next twenty minutes would just pass without incident. The algebra problems were just that, problems. Concentrating on them was not going to pass the time. For Gavin the only thing that would pass the time would be to think about one of two things, his grandfather or boats. Since it was Thursday, it would have to be boats.

Lake Saint Clair is connected to Lake Huron by the Saint Clair River which allowed boats to access the great lake. St. Clair Shores had many docks and was a great access to the waterway. Every Tuesday and Thursday, Gavin would go down to the closest dock and watch the boats.

The boats varied in style, sometimes from moderate sized freighters to beautiful sailboats. It was the sailboats that Gavin paid close attention to. When there was a sailboat out on the lake, Gavin would watch it for quite some time. Being the second of June, there should be some sailboats out on the water.

School ended June 11, and that date couldn't come any faster for Gavin. Some school districts were done with the school year by the end of May; that was a fact that Gavin would bring up many times with anyone that would listen. June 11 and freedom.

Gavin kept on pretending to work hard on his homework but not too hard. If it looked like he was concentrating too much, Kubach would think he needed help and be over again. Just the right balance was needed to keep the teacher from coming back.

Gavin looked up and saw that Kubach was helping Cindy Hessler, a portly girl that was also short. Gavin wasn't short himself, but close to six feet tall, nor was he portly but just the opposite. He had been told that he actually needed to put on weight to get to his correct weight size. It wasn't like he didn't eat; it was just the fact that he couldn't put on weight. His father told him that when he got older, his metabolism would slow down and the weight would catch up.

The bell finally rang, and Gavin shot up like a missile leaving a silo. Quickly gathering his belongings and barely hearing Kubach wish the class a good day, Gavin left the room in route to his locker. The halls of the high school quickly filled up creating an obstacle course for Gavin to maneuver around through. He mostly kept his head and eyes down, not wanting to look anyone in the face. They were less likely to acknowledge him by doing that.

His locker was on the other side of the building, and he was halfway there when a voice from behind him nearly stopped him in his tracks.

"Hey, looks like someone let the squirrel out of its tree!" The voice belonged to Jordan Offterberg. Jordan was in the same grade as Gavin and had gone to school with him since grade school. He had been annoying Gavin since then as well. Not every youth with a form of autism has a thorn in his or her side like Gavin had, but sadly, many did. There is a saying that kids can be cruel and when they sniff out someone different, they can be merciless. Some antagonizers mature over the years and some even feel bad about the torment they have caused, but not Jordan Offerberg. He determined back in first grade that he didn't like Gavin and set out to make his life miserable. To Gavin's credit, he had gotten used to the razzing and could ignore it. Ignoring the jerk was what he was trying to do now.

"Going to collect some nuts? Why? You're already nuts!" Jordan yelled out and laughed his ridiculous donkey laugh. Gavin moved on and soon was out of Jordan's torment range. Gavin knew it could have been worse with Jordan, but it still didn't make it any less annoying. Gavin turned down another hall and heard no more from Offerberg. Had Gavin raised his head, he would have seen the various posters on the walls of the hall advertising clubs and other school events, but he kept his head down, missing it all.

"Gavin!" Another voice called out from behind. It was not Offerberg again because this voice was female. It seemed he was popular this afternoon. Gavin recognized the voice as belonging to Sophie Kline. He had known Sophie since middle school. She was a good head shorter than Gavin and had a slim frame. Her auburn hair was in a ponytail and when Gavin turned around, he saw her smiling at him. Gavin found her to be a pretty girl, and it seemed like she liked him with how she always seem to greet him in the hall. "How was your day?"

"It was a day," Gavin answered and for a moment his eyes caught her blue eyes and then his immediately dropped to the floor. He stood there for a bit then seemed to remember something. "How was yours?"

"Government was tough today. Werner assigned some essays on the functions of the Senate that don't make sense. Did you understand them?"

"Yeah, I was done with mine before the period was out."

"Would you be able to help me?" Sophie asked. "Do you have time now, or do you have to get home? If you're worried about missing the bus, I can drive you home."

"I do not have to go home, but I do not have time," Gavin told her without lifting his head. Then, since he felt it needed no explanation, he said, "It is Thursday."

"Oh, maybe another time," Sophie said, clearly sounding confused.

"Yeah, sure," Gavin said and then kept walking in the direction he was originally heading. He heard Sophie call out *goodbye*, and Gavin raised a hand in response. If he kept getting interrupted, he was not going to make the bus in time. He would not be taking his normal bus, but the one that dropped off closest to the pier. That bus left at 3:40, which gave him five minutes.

Arriving at his locker without any more problems, Gavin took out his key to unlock his lock. Gavin's locker did not have the typical combination lock because it gave him such a hard time. The key lock was much easier for him to get open. Gavin dumped his books and work into the locker where it landed on the pile already there, shut it, and then left for the bus. It was warm out so no jacket was needed, and he didn't take his homework because he never did school work at home. Homework meant something different to Gavin.

Bus 56 was where it was supposed to be and some students were getting on it. Gavin hoped he wasn't too late to get his usual seat. His usual seat was in front of the bus, away from the annoying kids that sat in the back. The front seats of the bus were usually open as it was when Gavin climbed aboard the bus.

"Must be Thursday," said the driver, a plump African-American woman with a friendly demeanor when one didn't rub her the wrong way. Gavin had never rubbed her the wrong way, so she had no issues with him. "Can't believe your parents let you go to the Nautical Mile by yourself."

"They know I will be home by seven," Gavin said as he climbed the steps. Carla laughed as the two of them had gone through this many times before. When Gavin first started this routine, he had to explain to Carla why he wanted to ride her bus and not his usual one. She had also asked if it wouldn't be easier to get his driver's license. Gavin had told her he wasn't ready to drive. She thought that was funny, especially living in Detroit. He reminded her that he lived in St. Claire Shores, where yes it was a suburb of Detroit, but it wasn't officially a part of it.

"Go take your seat, honey." Gavin did just that. He sat in his seat and scooted over so he could see out the window and not have to talk with the people around him. He hoped that if someone did sit next to him that it would be Toby. Toby wasn't his friend, he was just a kid that rode the same bus. What was great about Toby was the fact that he didn't try any idle chit-chat with Gavin. Toby would sit down without even *a howdy* and not try to talk about aimless things. Some kids liked to yap on and on about pointless subjects. Gavin would then have to tell the kids that he didn't care which would make them mad. There was none of that with Toby.

The bus started to fill and sure enough, it was Toby that sat next to Gavin. The seat sank down from the young man's weight, but that was the only way Gavin even knew Toby had sat down next to him. Gavin had no idea what grade Toby was in or why he smelled like Pine Sol all the time; he never asked.

Once the bus was ready to leave, just about every seat was filled and the bus was loud. Carla bellowed to keep it down and the volume did drop a few decibels. The door closed and they were on their way. Gavin had gotten used to the bounciness of the bus a long time ago, and it was so familiar that it was like an old friend. Gavin didn't take the bus in the mornings because his father drove him to school. No matter how bad a day Gavin had, the bounciness would let him know that he was heading home where he would have a few hours of peace before his dad got home himself.

The usual sights passed by, and Gavin knew exactly how far the Nautical Mile was from those landmarks. Once the bus got on Jefferson Avenue, it would stay on that street. Gavin's destination was five miles to the south, and the bus would pass by another one of his favorites, St. Clair Shores Public Library. The library was located on the lake and even had slips for boats. Gavin would often go to the library as well. Traffic was about average on Jefferson, so it took about fifteen minutes to arrive at the stop. The stop was right by St. Clair Shores Park. Toby got up to let Gavin out, Carla said her usual *goodbye and be careful*, and then Gavin was out.

Anything that dealt with school was behind him for the day. What lay before him was the park and its two fountains. The fountains were currently working and water was spouting from them. There was a small pedestrian bridge that crossed the pond and led into the Nautical Mile itself.

The Nautical Mile was on Jefferson Avenue between Nine and 10 Mile roads. The area is home to 27 marinas that have over 2,000 boating slips, making it one of the biggest spots in the city to hold personal craft. Also on the Mile, were numerous restaurants, shops, and other entertainment venues.

Gavin knew all this information because once he adopted a place, he liked to look up as much information as he could. The library that he had passed earlier was very helpful, as well his family's computer at home. Gavin liked to know the history of the places he lived in or went to. It would sometimes annoy his little sister when he talked about the history of a location.

A few years back, his parents took the three Pierce children to Disney World. Before going, Gavin spent time looking up the history of Disney World and knew so much that his father said Gavin probably knew the place better than Walt Disney himself. Gavin then told his father that since Disney World had opened in 1971 and the man himself had died in 1966, that he actually *did* know more about the place. His siblings were even less impressed whenever he would chime in with a bit of history about whatever park they were at in the resort. By the end of the trip, no one was listening to Gavin's history lessons. That didn't stop him from saying them though.

From the park, Gavin had a choice of where to go. Since he wanted to see the boats, he kept heading east to where some of the marinas were. From there he could see the boats in their slips and then continue walking until he got to the shore. He started passing slips which held boats of various types. His eyes passed over the typical fishing boats and would linger when he saw a sailboat. Many of them were sloops, or smaller sailboats. Their masts were tucked away, but he could still tell what type of rigging they used. Some had the Bermuda style, while others had the two-sail rig. He wouldn't get to the slips that held the schooners until further down the marina because of the size needed to hold the much larger boat.

It took Gavin 20 minutes to get to the shore because he had stopped to look at some of the boats that were being prepared to take off. Most of the people on the boats ignored Gavin, but some would wave. He did return the waves because it was rude not to.

Gavin could hear the shore before he arrived at it. He could hear the water lapping against the rocks, and he found it soothing. He had been out to the shore when the wind was strong and the noise was much different and more violent with the waves crashing, almost as if they were trying to break the shoreline apart.

Looking out on the lake, Gavin saw plenty of boat traffic and quite a few sailboats. Many were of the smaller, sloop size, but there were a couple bigger ones. Three years ago, Gavin had seen a three-mast schooner with five tiers. It was a rare sight since most of those boats were used as passenger cruise ships. These ships was the type that explorers would have used when exploring the world. Gavin had even been lucky enough to go on it when it had docked. It had been part of a promotional program for the cruise line.

Gavin hadn't seen a schooner like it since. The schooner had attracted a lot of attention, but Gavin still came even with all the people that had lined the shore and marinas to see the beautiful sight. He stayed mostly on the fringes in order avoid the crowd as best he could. He the schooner it right away on the horizon and couldn't believe the size. As it neared, he still couldn't believe how big it was. The ten main sails were white along with the ones in the front. Gavin's eyes never left it until it made its final approach to dock.

There was a cool breeze off the lake that felt good against Gavin's skin. He was wearing his usual tee-shirt and jeans. Once school ended, he would switch to his baggy, canvas shorts which were currently waiting for him in his closet. His shirt had an image of a sailboat on it. He would try and wear it at least once a week on one of his trips to the Mile. Gavin wished he could have brought his binoculars to see the boats on the lake better, but he didn't want to bring them to school because they were expensive. He had saved up a long time for those Nikon eight by forty pair. There was plenty of time in the summer to bring them along for viewing.

Gavin lingered at the show for another half-hour or so and knew he would have to make his way back. The five thirty bus would be arriving and he needed to be on it. The bus ride would take about half an hour and he would arrive home a little after six. His dad would be getting home about then as well. His time on the Mile was done for now, but tomorrow was Friday. On Fridays he would visit his grandfather at the nursing home. That was Gavin's second favorite thing to do.

Chapter 2

Writing Entry for Friday, February 6

I love sailboats. That would not surprise anyone that knows me. Perhaps what would surprise people is that I have never sailed on one. It is not because I am afraid to, I am not. It is because my father is deathly afraid of them. He will not get on one nor will he allow me to get on a sailboat or any other boat. I never knew the reason why until my grandfather told me. It was after I asked him why my father would not let me go on boats.

I was helping with yard work at my grandfather's home (my grandmother had passed away three years earlier) and after I asked that question, Grandpa became very quiet. At first I did not think he was going to answer me. Then he did.

First he dug out his wallet. It was a tattered, beat-up old thing. My dad tried getting him a new one, but Grandpa said his old one would be just fine. Usually when Grandpa dug out his wallet it meant I was going to get some money. Initially I thought he was going to pay me so he would not have to tell me the story. Instead of money coming out, he took out a picture.

Even before I saw the front of the picture, I could tell it was old. The back was yellow and creased. He handed it to me, and I saw a much younger-looking Grandpa and Grandma. The two had four children with them. I recognized my father right away because I had seen pictures of him when he was a kid. In the picture, my father looked about seven or eight. I saw a young Aunt Jenny. Since she was a year younger than my father, she would be six or seven, and my uncle Will would have been one in the picture. The fourth child I did not recognize. It looked to be a little girl of around two. My grandmother was holding baby Will, while my grandfather held the mystery two-year-old. Aunt Jenny and my father stood one on each side of their parents.

My grandfather told me that the picture was taken a day before the accident. I asked who the little girl was and was told she was my Aunt Naomi. I told Grandpa that I did not have an Aunt Naomi, but he said that I did. Except she died when she was two. I was stunned. Here I was, all of ten and I was just finding out that I had an aunt that had died when she was two.

Grandpa told me that it was a boating accident. It was on July 7, 1972. It happened right out on Lake St. Clair, where I like to watch the sailboats. It started out as just a normal family excursion, except that my grandmother did not go out on the boat because she did not want to take little Will. Grandpa said she wanted to keep Naomi back as well, but Grandpa insisted that the little girl would have fun sailing.

I was then shocked to hear that my grandfather knew how to sail. It was a rented sloop that was used that day. It had the normal two sail rig, not hard for my grandfather to operate at all. They brought a lunch along since they would not be back until later that afternoon.

Everything was going well until after lunch when Grandpa noticed some storm clouds on the horizon. He played it off as no big deal, but started to turn around and head back. The wind was no longer with them, so the sails were brought in and the motor was started. The storm moved in quickly and Grandpa had the three frightened kids move to the center of the boat. There was no shelter on the boat, but all four were wearing life jackets. Back in 1972, it was not a law that children had to wear them, but Grandmother would not allow any child of hers to be on a boat without one.

I'm giving the brief version of what happened out there, but my grandfather gave me the long version. We were sitting on his lawn as he told me the story. My attention (for once) stayed right on Grandpa as he told the story.

The winds picked up and waves started to toss the little sloop around. By then they had made it to St. Clair Lake, but still had a ways to go to get to the shore. The engine started to sputter, and Grandpa went to work on it right away. I could see my grandfather deftly working on the small motor of the sloop, complete with his usual cursing. He said he got it going again, but the storm had fully moved in. Along with the high winds, it was pouring rain. The boat capsized, tossing Grandpa and his children into the lake. It was chaotic enough, but the situation became even more so as Grandpa struggled to find his children in the torrent of water.

He found Aunt Jenny first and grabbed hold of her life jacket. After frantically calling for the other two, he spotted my father and swam over with Jenny in tow. Once he arrived at my father, he started to look for Naomi. That was when my father held up an empty life jacket that Naomi had been wearing. It had not been properly tightened and she had slipped out from it. Grandpa had learned later that my father saw Naomi and started to swim to her when the jacket slipped off and she went under. My grandfather dove under water after telling Jenny and my father to hold hands, but could not find his two-year-old daughter. He wanted to keep searching, but knew he had to get the other two back to shore. He had his other children grab a hold of his jacket and made the long swim to the shore.

From the time the boat capsized to the time he arrived at the shore, a half an hour elapsed. It took two days of searching the lake until the body of my aunt was found. Even though he was only seven, my father blamed himself since he had a chance to save her. No one else in the family blamed him, but that did not matter. My grandfather also blamed himself for what happened. He said it was a rough time after the boating accident. He had not been on a boat since.

My grandfather was silent after he was done telling me all this. At first I thought he was going to cry, and it would have been the first time I ever seen him do so. He did not cry, but I think it was close. He told me he had not told that story for a long time but felt that I should know why my father would never set foot on a boat again. Hearing Grandpa tell this story did not stop me from being interested in sailboats though. It just helped me understand a little bit more.

End of Entry

+ + +

The sun broke through the blinds, spilling into room 122 of Lake View Manor Assisted Living Complex. The room was of decent size, with a single bed under the window, a dresser on the opposite side, a desk with a chair, and tan carpet on the floor. A bathroom was across from the room, along with a doorway that led to the small living space.

The bathroom could be accessed from both the bedroom and the living space. A form slept on the bed and stirred every now and then. This was Bernard Pierce, Gavin's grandfather. He rolled onto his back and his eyes opened. At first he just laid there, as if trying to remember either where he was or who he was. His legs then swung off the bed and he stood. He turned his body some and a loud crack came from his back. A small grunt escaped his mouth and then he headed to the bathroom to do his morning ritual. Once that was done, he headed back into the bedroom to get dressed for the day.

As he was putting on his pants, he stopped and looked at a calendar on the wall. The days were marked off, not because he was counting down to something, but to let him know what day it was. The nurses would cross off the days during their evening rounds. Bernard, or Bernie as he was known at Lake View, was not in assisted living for any complications with his body. His body was healthy for a 75 year-old man. It was because of his mind. He had Alzheimer's.

He was diagnosed with it three years ago and moved into the assisted living facility a year and a half after the diagnosis. He thought he was doing fine, but his children disagreed, especially after the car accident. He had only been slightly confused, even though he had driven that stretch of highway many times. A wrong turn was taken and he found himself on the wrong side of the highway. He didn't realize it until the oncoming traffic came at him. He then swerved into the ditch and hit a retaining wall. That was the last time he had ever driven a car. His son said he was lucky that he hadn't killed anyone, and Bernie supposed he was right. That still didn't water down the indignation of the entire situation.

He had to stop living on his own after the fire. It was a minor one, but it was enough. He left the burner on and a hot pad too close to it. It caught on fire, along with some nearby curtains. He was able to put it out with the fire extinguisher, but the neighbors saw the smoke coming out of an open window and called the fire department. The fire was contained by the time they arrived and there was only minor damage, but his son Michael was told about it. That was that. His three remaining children ganged up on him and now he was living at Lake View.

Lake View Manor was not a dump by any means, and it shouldn't be with the amount Bernie was paying to live there. His children said that Bernie could afford it, why not treat himself? Bernie had taken over at the garage he worked at and made a profitable business out of it. He had expanded to two other garages around the area, no small feat in the Detroit area.

Bernie ended up selling his garages about seven years ago. None of his children wanted to take the business over, and Bernie could see the writing on the wall. The time to sell was then, before the price went down. He made well over seven figures on that sale- not bad for a high school dropout.

He used to remind his son Michael of that every chance he got since Michael was an assistant principal at a high school.

On the dresser in his room were plenty of pictures, mostly of himself with his family. There were some days when the nurses would find Bernie sitting on the edge of his bed looking at those pictures and saying the names of the people in them. More often than not, he would remember them all. That wasn't always the case though. There were a few times when he would see a person in the picture and have to stop and recall who he or she was.

That was usually one of the grandchildren he didn't see too often. He had six grandchildren, three of which lived in St. Clair Shores. The other three were his daughter Jenna's children and they lived in Boston. His son Will never got married or had children. Of the three grandkids here, he saw Gavin the most.

Bernie saw that it was Friday and started to put his shirt on. One could see he was thinking about something and then a smile came on his face. It appeared he had just remembered that Friday was the day Gavin came to visit him. Gavin would often come with the rest of the family when they visited on weekends, but he came alone on Fridays. Bernie looked forward to seeing his grandchild; it helped break up the monotony.

There was a knock at the door in the living area, so Bernie finished putting on his shirt. He walked out into the small living area, which consisted of a television, a small couch and an easy chair. Opening the door, Bernie saw one of the nurses standing there. If he didn't open the door after the second knock, the nurses would enter on their own.

"Good morning Mr. Pierce," the nurse, Melanie, said in an overly chipper voice. "I just wanted to let you know that breakfast is being served just in case you might have forgotten."

"Oh, thank you, Melanie," Bernie said. He actually had forgotten about breakfast. The time was eight–thirty, and he usually went to breakfast by eight. He had slept in, which he was doing more often. How many times in the last week had he overslept and someone had to come search for him?

"You want to make sure to come down right away. Breakfast will stop being served at nine," Melanie said in her perky voice. She turned and then started to walk down the hallway. Bernie watched her for a moment; she was an attractive young lady.

He went back into his room to make sure he was ready to go to the dining area. Looking in the mirror, he saw a man of 75, still with his hair but gray now. His face was well wrinkled. If he had ever seen how he looked now when he was 20, he wouldn't have believed it was the same person. His shoulders slumped some, nowhere near the height of six foot two anymore. When did he get so old? When does anyone get old? Bernie seemed satisfied with his appearance and left his room.

The dining hall was a short walk away and when he arrived, he saw it was sparsely populated. Breakfast started at six-thirty and the busy time was around seven to eight. The food was in the kitchen and residents had to go back there, say their name, and then received whatever food was on the list that they could eat. Since Bernie had no restrictions, he was free to sample whatever was on the menu. He chose some scrambled eggs, bacon, and coffee.

"The usual, huh?" said Justin, the young man that usually was the one who served up breakfast, as he smiled from behind the counter.

Bernie just nodded and smiled. Was that his usual? Did he order it all the time?

Bernie took his tray and went over to where the beverages were. He poured himself some black coffee and then headed out into the dining area. He saw that Howard and Carl were still at a table and headed over.

Howard Grotts and Carl Klineman were two of his friends at Lake View. Howard was in his eighties and was mobile only with a wheelchair. He had lost both legs in Vietnam, where he had been a career soldier up until then. Carl Klineman was in his late seventies and had suffered two strokes and one heart attack. He mentioned many times that he was surprised he was still alive.

"Look who it is! You youngins think you can sleep in all the time!" Howard shouted out when he saw who was approaching their table. "About gave up on you."

"I just couldn't decide if I wanted to see your ugly faces this morning," Bernie replied back as he sat in one of the empty seats.

"Another burn from Bernie!" Carl said in his whispery voice. His last stroke had affected his speech pattern some, but those who hung around Carl long enough got used to it.

"Hey, Bernie, what day is it?" Howard asked.

"Friday," Bernie responded. It was a daily ritual when Bernie would show up. "My grandson is coming today."

"That calendar sure is coming in handy," Carl said and then coughed. He coughed about a dozen times a day. "Wish one of my grandkids came on a regular basis."

"I doubt mine even remember what I look like," Howard said and took a sip from his coffee mug.

"I doubt they would want to," Bernie said, causing a laugh from the other two.

"Damn, Bernie! You're having a good day!" Howard exclaimed. "Two days in a row now!"

"Yup, I'm on a roll," Bernie said and took his own sip. He grimaced from the taste, which he did every time he tasted the facility's java. "What they do, go out to the lake and get this crap?"

"No, that would taste better," Carl said. "You think we would get used to this swill by now."

"Not me. It's like I'm tasting it for the first time every time," Bernie said with a smile. He was having a good day.

"Yeah, joke about your condition. That's real classy," Howard said, but he was smiling.

The three of them would be at the table trading insults for another hour or so before going off to find something else to do.

***

Boxes were carefully stacked along the north wall of Michael Pierce's small office. Most of his personal belongings were currently residing in those cardboard boxes. Whatever was remaining out in the open were items that he would not be taking with him.

It was Friday afternoon with about 15 minutes left to go in the school day. Most of the students and faculty were excited about the impending weekend, but Michael knew he would be coming in over the weekend to get ready for the end of the year some more. He was currently one of the assistant principals at St. Clair High School, which was the same one his son attended.

His position at the school was coming to an end because he had gotten a job as principal at Fraser High School, which was five miles away in another suburb of Detroit. The district was much smaller than where he was at now, but it would be his first principal's job. Michael had been waiting for four years to get into such a position and was determined to do a great job in order to move up.

He had started out as a high school math teacher in the area after attending Wayne State University, which is located right in Detroit. Michael had not wandered far from where he was born. He could have moved away from the area like his siblings, but then there wouldn't have been anyone to watch over his parents, now just his father.

As he was looking forward to becoming a principal, he was going to miss where he was at. He had attended the school as a student, taught there for a while as a teacher, and was finally part of an administrative team. Two of his children had also attended the school. His oldest was now in college, and Gavin was currently attending the school. His youngest was two years away from high school.

Michael had told his wife that he wished he could stay there at least one more year for Gavin, but when the opportunity arose, both he and his wife agreed he had to take it. Gavin would be fine for a year at the school. They had done well with handling Gavin and his uniqueness.

Gavin wasn't a disruptive student by any means; he was actually the opposite. Without proper motivation, Gavin would just sit at the desk until the period was over and move on to the next class. Michael and his wife had tried everything to get Gavin to work. Rewards and punishment did not work to motivate Gavin, although there was one motivation that Michael had thought might. It was one that he did not want to grant. His son liked sailboats, of all things. At first Michael had thought it was just a passing fancy, but if it was, it was taking a long time to pass.

While they lived at home, Michael would not allow any of his children to be on a boat. They asked why, but he never told them. His oldest and youngest soon got the point and didn't make an issue out of it. Gavin, on the other hand, would not let go. Suddenly, Gavin stopped asking and never said another word about it. Michael wasn't sure exactly what happened, but he wasn't about to ask. It was unwise to bring up a topic that Gavin had ridden to death when he had finally stopped dissecting it. Gavin still kept pictures and models of sailboats, but at least he stopped asking to go on one.

Michael knew about Gavin's excursions to the Nautical Mile on Thursdays but did not condemn them. Michael also knew he was probably being unfair pushing his fear on his children, especially when that fear started when he was seven. Perhaps moving away earlier would have helped him deal with that, especially moving somewhere where there wasn't a body of water, but responsibility kept him tethered to St. Clair Shores.

With his father at Lake View Manor, someone had to be around to make sure he was being treated right. The place was expensive, but his father was well cared for. When his father was diagnosed with Alzheimer's a few years ago, Michael did some research and realized that his father would have to be placed somewhere soon. It was a few months after that diagnosis that he moved his father into the residential home. Lake View specialized in dealing with Alzheimer's, among other issues the elderly have.

Michael visited his father on weekends and called at least once during the week to check on him. Gavin went on Fridays and sometimes Wednesdays to see his grandfather. That made Michael feel good about his son. Gavin was never asked to go; he just did.

Gavin always got along with his grandfather. Michael's father was one of the few people Gavin would look in the eyes. Sometimes Gavin wouldn't even look Michael in the eyes, but he would always with his grandfather.

Michael knew his father would never get better and it would only be a matter of time before his mind really started to deteriorate. There were medications to help with the erosion, but they only worked for so long. His father's mind would keep getting worse until he entered what was called the severe stage where his mind wouldn't even be able to do the daily items that his body needed to do. Then his body would start to shut down and then death.

Michael kept his two siblings up on what was going on, but they did not visit as regularly as Michael would have liked. Now was the time to see their father when he could still recall who they were. Michael noticed that his father was forgetting some information, but he still recognized family and friends. He had his days, but thankfully the good ones far outweighed the bad ones; that wouldn't always be the case. He told his brother and sister that, but still they only visited once a year.

It is not like their father could visit them. At this point he could, but Michael really didn't want him leaving on an extended trip. What would happen if he had one of his bad days when his mind grew foggy and forgetful? When his mind grew foggy and forgetful? His father would completely be relying on whoever took him on the trip, and that person had better be ready for what was to come.

Michael knew the only person that would even think about taking on that responsibility was himself. He loved his brother and sister, but his sister had her own family and his brother was too wrapped up in himself to tackle that sort of venture. His father never really mentioned that he wanted to go anywhere. Michael would sometimes take him out for the day and bring him to the house, but that was all.

Sometimes the responsibility wore on him, but he tried not to let it show. Michael knew this summer would test his stress level with getting ready for the coming school year as a principal, but luckily that was the only thing he had to worry about. His oldest son was staying at Michigan State University where he was going into engineering, his youngest daughter had friends to hang around with, and Gavin, well was Gavin.

Gavin mowed lawns in the summer, which surprisingly he didn't have to be motivated to do. He mowed a total of ten lawns and would do about two a day, keeping a schedule. Rainy weather would sometimes get him behind schedule. When it did, Gavin would just mow the lawns he missed on the next good weather day. Gavin actually made some good money mowing lawns, and Michael and his wife opened a savings account for him. As far as Michael knew, Gavin had never taken anything out of that account. Michael wasn't one of those parents that continued to check into his children's accounts, even though his name was on them was as well. That was one area he did not have to worry about with Gavin.

Michael's summer was going to be dedicated to getting ready for his new job. Even the family vacation was going to wait. Every summer the family took a trip for at least a week. Sometimes it might be camping at one of the state parks around the state, and sometimes it was bigger like the Disney World trip a few years back. Michael had talked it over with his wife, Nancy, and both agreed they could wait until next summer for a vacation. Michael was thankful for having time to get ready. He would finish up at St. Clair Shores High in the middle of June and then go to Fraser High and get to work there. Michael had an idea what was waiting for him at his new job, but time, thankfully, was on his side.

Chapter 3

Writing Entry for Friday, February 13

My grandfather's favorite story to tell is how he met my grandmother. He tells it all the time to anyone that will listen. He says it was fate, if one believes in that kind of thing. Grandpa was 20 when he met the girl that would be his wife. Her name was Belinda Marie Kiles. She was 19 at the time and attending Wayne State, my dad's alum mater. My grandmother was studying to be a teacher, which she was for four years until her first child was born. Women's rights were sketchy back then I guess.

Grandpa had dropped out of high school and was working at a place called Al's Repair Shop. He was already the best mechanic there. He started at Al's when he was 16. He knew a little about mechanics when he was hired but was a fast learner; much faster than when he was in school. I have already written that my grandfather can fix anything. He is a little shaky with electronics but given time can eventually repair it. It is because of his ability to repair that he met my grandmother (and I guess the reason why I am here too).

It was July 16, 1960, a Saturday. The weather was a scorcher according to my grandfather. He was returning from the lake where he had been goofing off with some friends. They had been boating of all things. Grandpa's car was a 1955 Dodge Royal Lancer convertible. The majority of the car was white, but the trim at the top was red. It looked like a sweet ride. I am not into cars, but I think this one looked pretty darn cool. I have seen pictures of it, and my grandfather looks happy next to it in every one of them. He had to give it up when he started having children. I guess Grandma gave up her job, and he had to give up his car.

Grandpa did not buy the car new. He actually bought it from the previous owner after the owner smashed it up in an accident. After the shop closed, Grandpa would work on repairing the Lancer until it looked new again. He had spent just about every evening over a course of three months working on the car. The parts were from other wrecks of the same model. The car had only been road ready for two days when he met Belinda.

It was late afternoon, and Grandpa was returning back to his little house he shared with two other friends. His parents had not been happy that he had dropped out of school but would have let him stay living with them. Grandpa did not want to, so he moved in with some friends. The two friends he moved in with were former high school buddies that went to college in town. They were not the ones that he had just been out on the lake with. Unlike me, my grandfather had a lot of friends. Grandpa had the top down and the breeze blew his thick hair around.

My grandfather was a looker when he was younger. I know that is a weird thing for a grandson to say, but it is the truth. The thing about Grandpa was that he did not go out to meet girls. I guess it was different back then. Grandpa said there were dances and other get togethers where young people could meet. Not like today where one could have a complete relationship over the Internet. Being a dropout, Grandpa had stopped going to high school dances, and not being in college, Grandpa did not go to those functions. He figured that the right girl would come along sooner or later. He was a few miles out of St. Clair Shores when the right girl came along.

My grandmother's car, a 1947 Chrysler Town and Country, left her on the side of the road. Her car was a tank, and I do not mean that in a good way. The thing was huge, and if it were to hit a car made today, I am betting that whatever it hit would be pulverized. Her car was also not in good shape. She had gotten it at a discounted price but had been having issues with it from the very first day.

Grandpa said he almost passed her by but decided to play Good Samaritan and pulled over. He says it was the best decision of his life. He pulled in behind her and got out. She was sitting on the driver's side in the grass, in tears. She had been out there for a half an hour and no one had stopped. Grandpa told me he never understood why a driver did not stop, not with how pretty she looked in her sundress. Even though he already knew, Grandpa asked her what the matter was, and she quickly dried her tears with her left hand. She told him that her car broke down and then went on to say that she just had the thing fixed. Grandpa just nodded as he listened. They swapped names and that was when Grandpa heard the name of the woman he would love for the rest of his life. He then told her to wait. He headed back to his car, retrieved his tool box which he always kept there, and then returned to Belinda's car. He popped the hood and got to work.

The whole time he was working on the car, Belinda hovered around like she did not know what else to do. It took Grandpa 20 minutes to identify the problem and 15 more to fix it. He told her something was wrong with the fuel pump. The engine was not getting enough fuel to run. He said he fixed it, but it would only be temporary and that she would have to get a new one. When he told her that, she looked like she was going to cry again. She said she had just sunk 20 dollars (a lot back then I guess) and really could not afford to put more in. Grandpa told her to bring it to Al's Repair Shop on 23rd Street. He said he would do it for a fraction of the cost and that they had a part that would fit. Grandpa said that her face had a look of pleasant surprise on it when he told her that.

She asked if she could give him anything for what he had done; she said she had some cash on her. Grandpa said there was only one thing he wanted from her and that was her phone number. He told me he felt very brazen in asking her for that, but she smiled and wrote it down on some scrap paper in her purse. They said their goodbyes and Grandpa watched her climb into her Chrysler, start the engine up, and drove off with a wave of her hand. Grandpa was still smiling as he got into his own car to go home.

He called her two days later. That following weekend they went out on a date. The rest is history.

End of Entry

+ + +

The lawnmower's engine chugged along as Gavin pushed it across Mr. Lipkinsky's lawn. He was close to finishing and then would take the weed eater to touch up the rest.

School had been out for three weeks, and Gavin couldn't have been any more grateful. He had three months of not sitting in a boring classroom, dealing with idiots, and listening to how he needed to get to work. True, he only had one more year of public education, but he had no idea what he was going to do after that. With his older brother, it was expected he would go to college, and with Gavin, it was the same. The only thing was Gavin didn't know if he wanted to go on with schooling.

The last strip of long grass was done, and Gavin turned off the lawnmower. The lawnmower was over ten years old, and Gavin had gotten it at a good price because it wasn't running. That had been three years ago, and his grandfather helped him get it working. Grandpa had even taught him enough small engine repair skills to keep it running.

The houses that he mowed were all within decent walking distance from his own house. It was the one time that he kind of wished he could drive. He was more than above the driving age, but every time his father asked if he wanted to take the test for his driver's license, he shook his head no and would not talk about it. There was no logical explanation for why he did not get his license; he just didn't want to do it.

Gavin bagged the grass and put the bag with the other three he had collected from Mr. Lipkinsky's. The bags were loaded on a wagon that just had ropes for sides. The recycling for grass was three blocks away, so Gavin would haul the wagon over there and then come back for the lawnmower which would be loaded up on the wagon along with the weed eater to haul back to his house.

This summer he had 11 lawns to take care of. He had expanded his business to helping with planting and other aspects of lawn care the owners did not want to take care of themselves.

He had even helped Mrs. Jones with where to place her flowers in her flower garden. Mrs. Jones was 80 and lived two houses down from him by herself. She seemed to be in good shape for her age and was sharp in the mind as well. Last week Gavin saw that her flowers were not doing so well and suggested putting them in a different spot and arrangement. Mrs. Jones was skeptical but finally relented. Gavin moved them, and they have been flourishing ever since.

His mother had once told him he had a green thumb. When she did say that, Gavin looked and told her his thumb was not green but the normal color. He found out later that it wasn't supposed to be taken literally.

"All done?" a voice said from behind. Gavin turned his head and saw Mr. Lipkinsky walking out from his house. Mr. Lipkinsky had to weigh close to three hundred pounds and waddled more than walked.

"Yeah, I am," Gavin said, his eyes not meeting Mr. Lipkinsky's. If the portly man noticed, he didn't say anything.

"Looks great as usual. Can I pay you for next week too? I won't be around at all."

"You can wait until the following week," Gavin said as he looked at his shoes. "I would not want you to pay for work that has not been done yet."

"It's okay, Gavin. I know you will do the work. You always do," Mr. Lipkinsky said and then handed Gavin a 20 dollar bill. "I'll see you in two weeks."

"Thanks, Mr. Lipkinsky," Gavin said and raised his head because he knew the big man was walking back to his house.

Gavin folded the bill and put it in his pocket. He would be going to the bank on Friday and would put it into his account. Not all the money would go into his bank account, but the majority of it would. He would keep some to have as spending money, namely when he had lunch at a restaurant at the Nautical Mile. Usually it was just a hotdog from one of the stands there, but sometimes he would treat himself and eat at the Ram's Horn where he had his usual cheeseburger and fries. The Ram's Horn had the best cheeseburger and fries. They were so good that it didn't even bother Gavin to eat alone at the sit-down restaurant.

Today was Wednesday, so Gavin would be heading over to Lake View to visit with his grandfather once he was done cleaning up. Trimming the weeds didn't take too long but hauling the grass took the longest.

By the time Gavin arrived home to take a shower, it was already three in the afternoon. He had the house to himself as he got ready. His father was at his new school getting ready for his new position, his mother was at her real estate job, and his sister was over at friends. He liked it when the house was quiet; it gave him time to just relax and think about things.

After his shower was complete, he went into his room to get dressed. His room was sparsely decorated and was a pleasing light blue color. He had two pictures of sailboats up on his wall and a model of one on his dresser. He would have had more decorations that related to sailboats, but knew he would be pushing the issue with his father.

Selecting a blue tee-shirt and cargo shorts, Gavin put them on and grabbed his wallet. He had just enough money in his wallet to pay for the city bus to and from the stop by Lake View. Gavin never carried more money than he needed for the day.

The afternoon was still beautiful out as he left and headed for the bus stop a few blocks away. The bus driver was the same as usual and greeted Gavin as he got on. Gavin selected a seat toward the front and hoped no one would sit next to him.

Riding the city bus wasn't like riding the school bus. He had less control who sat next to him. Just last week some woman in her fifties sat next to him and talked the entire trip even though Gavin didn't look her in the eyes or really respond. He was quite thankful when his stop came. Today he was in luck, as no one came to sit next to him before his stop came.

His grandfather's care facility was close to the shore, which didn't make the name of the place a lie. One could see the lake from the home. From his grandfather's room, the lake was not visible and Gavin had often wondered if that was on purpose. Did Grandpa still blame himself for the accident that happened all those years ago? The accident was still preying on his father, so why not Grandpa?

Gavin had to cross the street to get to Lake View, but the street wasn't so busy that he had to worry about being run down. The home's sign stood out front and depicted a lake with a sun over it. Was the sun setting or rising? Gavin thought with the residents in the place it had to be the former. He opened the glass door and a chime rang out. Gavin cringed when he heard it even though he should be used to it by now.

"Good afternoon, Gavin!" a female voice belonging to the receptionist, Isabelle Granger, said. He didn't have to look over to know who the voice belonged to. "Is it Wednesday already?"

"Yeah, all day long," Gavin said. It was a routine they had and would repeat every Friday when he came in. "Is my grandfather in his room?"

"Yes he is, dear," Isabelle said, and Gavin thanked her and headed down the hallway.

Room 122 was on the left side of the hall. When Gavin arrived, he knocked and waited for a reply. He heard his grandfather's muffled voice telling him to come in and he did so.

His grandfather was sitting in the easy chair that was in front of the television, which was currently off. He was holding some pictures and staring intently down at them. Once Gavin walked further into the room, he looked up and gave his grandson a nod.

Gavin walked over to the chair and looked down at the pictures. The one that was showing was of his grandmother when she was around 30 or so. She was holding a baby, which Gavin thought was his father. His grandfather flipped to another one and again it was a youthful Belinda. This time she was standing in front of a stream with mountains in the background.

"Where was that taken?" Gavin asked. He had never seen the picture before. It was in black and white, and his grandmother looked even younger. His grandfather didn't answer right away, just stared at the picture some more.

"That's Belinda," he said and Gavin said yes it was. "She was my wife for 30, no 40 years."

"Yes, Grandpa," Gavin responded. It actually had been 41 years before Belinda passed away, but 40 was close enough. "Was that picture taken before you two got married?"

"No, no. After."

"Right after?" Gavin prodded gently. "Honeymoon?"

"Honeymoon? We went to some mountains, so yes," his grandfather said. "Colorado! That's it!"

"See, you remembered," Gavin told him. He found that sometimes his grandfather needed a little prompting to remember. Sometimes he did recall what he was searching for, but sometimes he didn't.

"I can't believe I couldn't remember that. A man shouldn't forget something like that."

"It is okay, Grandpa. I forget to put the toilet seat down all the time and my sister falls in."

"That's different. And it's her own damn fall for not looking before she squats." Gavin laughed out loud. Grandpa had meant *fault* not *fall*, but it still worked. Gavin didn't correct him.

"Did you have a good time in Colorado?" Gavin asked. He had never been to the state; the mountains really did interest him.

Again his grandfather didn't answer right away. Gavin was about to tell him that it was okay that he didn't remember when his grandfather said, "We rented a cabin there. Don't know if the place is still there, but it was a nice place back then. No, I didn't have a good time; I had a great time!"

"You want to finish looking at your pictures?" Gavin asked.

"No, I can do that later. Chess in the socialist hall?" The chess games were in the social hall. Lake View was not socialist as far as Gavin knew.

Wednesdays were their chess days, although Gavin didn't get upset if it didn't happen. Some Wednesdays his grandfather just wasn't up to playing the game. It was actually Gavin who taught his grandfather to play. On his good days, his grandfather could keep up with Gavin.

"You ready for me to beat you again?"

"Like to see you try," his grandfather said and the two got up to go to the hall.

***

The door shut gently, and Gavin had gone for the day. Bernie sat back down in his chair but did not turn on the television. He picked the pictures up from where he had put them down for chess. Gavin beat him in chess and was quite nice about it even though Bernie had made some stupid mistakes. He realized his mistakes after he made them and couldn't believe that he had actually made those moves in the first place.

His grandson taught him how to play about three years ago. It was after he had come out about his ailment. Gavin asked if he wanted to learn to play chess to help keep his mind sharp. At first Bernie had been resistant, but he decided to give it a try. It turned out he liked the game, and it did keep his mind working. But over the course of the last few years, it was becoming harder and harder for him to remember where to move the pieces and mistakes like today's were happening more frequently.

After the game today, they stayed in the social hall and talked about Gavin's mowing job and what his parents and sister were up to. Bernie was glad to hear that the lawnmower was still running and that Gavin was taking good care of it. He was proud of the boy and all that he had accomplished.

Michael was worried about Gavin, but Bernie really wasn't. The kid was different, but not in a bad way. He had his quirks, but who didn't? He was a good, respectful kid. Bernie wasn't just saying that because he was his grandson. The others at Lake View liked Gavin as well. They thought it was strange that he wouldn't look anyone in the eyes, but they got over it. Bernie had never seen Gavin treat any of the other residents with anything but respect. There was nothing strange about that.

Going back to the pictures, Bernie went to the next one which showed his wife Belinda sitting in that convertible he owned when he was 20. What kind of car was that? He should know this because didn't he spend a lot of time working, restoring it? Faces were still familiar to him, but the other details were becoming harder to recall. How soon would it be for faces become like the small details? Gavin had helped him remember the location of his honeymoon, but he knew he would forget it again. He wanted to hold on to the memories, but his condition would not allow it. He wanted to remember every tiniest fraction of his life with Belinda, all the good times and even the bad.

Luckily, there wasn't too much bad. The accident with Naomi had been probably the worst. Would he forget that too? He knew that he was in the mild stage but felt he was slipping into the moderate stage where he would be forgetting more things from his past and be unable to learn new things. Can't teach a dog new tricks, he thought, especially one with Alzheimer's.

Bernie turned to the next one and it revealed a smiling Belinda with a different car, the car they had gotten after Michael was born. He had to sell his other one. This car's type too, he could not recall. He had worked on automobiles his whole life and now he couldn't even remember the ones he owned. Would he remember them if he sat there long enough? Was it important? He felt that it was.

Taking the two pictures out, he held one in each hand, the older one in his left and the newer one in his right. He went back and forth between the two. He looked closer and saw a Ford emblem. A 1965 Ford Galaxy. That was it. They had bought it brand new; it was the first new car either of them had owned. For a while they only needed one car because Bernie's work was only a few blocks away.

That left the other car. He took the picture out and started to look for clues. There were no emblems that stuck out like on the Ford, but the look was so distinctive that his mind screamed 'Dodge.' A 1955 Dodge Lancer! How he had loved that car and hated having to give it up, but it was for his family. Bernie sat back and felt tired after finally remembering the make of the two cars. There was a knock at the door.

"It's open!" Bernie shouted, not wanting to get up. At the door was one of the caregivers, whose name escaped Bernie's mind. She had only started at Lake View last week, so he didn't beat himself up about it too much. She was in her early thirties and had a plumpness about her that was almost appealing.

"Mr. Pierce, we were wondering if you were coming down for dinner?" Bernie looked at the clock and saw that it was six. Where had the time gone?

"Aw, hell, I forgot again," he said and struggled to his feet. He had forgotten the pictures that were in his lap and they scattered to the floor.

"Let me help you," the nurse said and she knelt down along with Bernie to pick the photographs up. She lingered on one and said, "She's very pretty. Was she your wife?"

"Yes, she was," Bernie said, his voice was faint. He knew that someday he would forget about Belinda, photographs or not. His mind would deteriorate to the point where everything and everyone would be unfamiliar. Someday he would forget about all the people he loved. How was that fair?

Chapter 4

Writing Entry for Friday, February 20

When my grandfather was three, he almost died from Pertussis. For those that do not know what Pertussis is, it is commonly known as Whooping Cough. A cough almost killed my grandfather. Had it succeeded, I would not be here in this class writing this.

Grandpa was three when he caught Pertussis. Vaccines for the disease did not come out until later in the 40s, so Grandpa was not protected. Back then Pertussis was the leading killer of children, now it's probably cars or rabid squirrels. Grandpa says he does not remember the ordeal; he only knows what his parents told him. He had to be admitted to the hospital and was there for several weeks. I guess it was touch and go for a while if he was going to live or not. It had to be pretty darn scary for a three-year-old to be in a situation like that. I see pictures of kids in hospitals sometimes smiling and I wonder why. They would have to be feeling just awful.

Grandpa even spent his fourth birthday there and was not given presents because they would have had to be destroyed due to the contamination factor. How unlucky can a kid get? Grandpa said after that scare, any time he got a cold and coughed, his mother would panic and take him to the hospital, sure that he was going to die.

My grandfather laughs after he tells that story about the time he almost died. It is not a hysterical, 'I am crazy' laugh, but a low chuckle. He said life is a very fragile thing, and something small like a cough can even alter it.

He is right. How would life have changed had my grandfather died? Yes, I would not be here, nor would my siblings or father. My aunt and her children would be gone, as would my uncle. All those people that had their cars fixed by Grandpa would have to have them fixed by someone else. And who is to say that that person would do the job that my grandfather did? Perhaps that person makes a mistake that Grandpa would not have done and the car blew up, killing the driver and his family?

This is all speculation, keep in mind. Now if my grandfather dies, the life I know will still remain, minus one of my favorite people of course. Is there a point in a person's life when he or she has accomplished everything that he or she will do to make a difference in people's lives? Is it when a person dies, or sometime before? Does the body just linger, not knowing that its usefulness has long since past?

I think that is when a person truly dies, when he or she no longer is meaningful to other people. Perhaps that is why people have children and make friends, to be meaningful to someone. My grandfather is meaningful to me, so he is still alive. What happens when his body dies? He will still mean something to me, so is he still alive? I suppose in memory he is, but memory fades.

I do not know how this turned so deep and depressing. I think I have written enough to fool Mr. Kubach.

End of Entry

+ + +

Fourth of July was loud and obnoxious. Gavin disliked the holiday despite the historical ramifications. It was because of the fireworks. People might find them pretty to look at, but they sure weren't fun to listen to. Up until 2011, it was illegal in the state of Michigan to own and shoot off fireworks unless one had a special license, which was given to professionals. The law was changed, allowing anyone to buy certain types of fireworks. The people rejoiced by buying and then firing off the small explosive devices.

Gavin was never a fan of loud, abrupt noises anyway, but fireworks were the worst. Why couldn't the state have kept the ban? It was bad enough that there were areas in Detroit that had issues with guns, but to allow such things as fireworks in the hands of just anybody, what were they thinking?

His father said it was because of money. The state could make a lot of money from the sales, and they were. His father didn't like fireworks either, namely because of the negative impact they had on schools. Students would sometimes try to sneak them in and light them off, causing quite the disturbance. If caught, those students were suspended and could be up for expulsion, but that was not a big deterrent as it should have been.

There also was a student that had gone to St. Clair High (before Gavin had gone there) that had messed around with fireworks and lost a hand. That was right after the ban was lifted. The 17 year old had wanted to go into auto mechanics, but with only one hand, that was unlikely.

This Fourth of July, Gavin was inside waiting for it to be over. It was ten o'clock at night, but the fireworks were just getting started. His parents and his sister went to watch a professional show, but Gavin had no interest in going. Had they gone to watch the show that was at the Nautical Mile, Gavin might have been tempted. Of course they had not, but instead they had opted to go to one that was farther away from the lake in another suburb. It was the same suburb where his father was going to be principal.

His father had been spending nearly every day at the school getting ready for the upcoming year. Gavin himself was trying not to think about his upcoming senior year.

Gavin actually had spent very little time with his father this summer. People probably would say that he was growing apart from his father, but they were never really close in the first place. It was a blessing to Gavin that his father was putting his full concentration into his new school because it meant less time harassing Gavin about what he is going to do in the future.

He had passed all his classes, though with some it was close. Gavin knew what he had to do to pass. His father wasn't happy about the grades, but he didn't go on his usual rant about getting good grades for college. Perhaps his father finally came to the realization that Gavin probably was not going to go on to college. Just what he was going to do was still a mystery, but Gavin still had a year of high school to figure that out.

Before he holed up in his house against the fireworks, Gavin had spent part of the day out on the Nautical Mile and at Lake View. It was Saturday, so he didn't mow and with it being the Fourth of July, he thought he would take a trip to Lake View. His parents and sister were going to go the following day.

Nautical Mile was okay. There were a lot of people, so he didn't stay as long as he would have liked. The Fourth was a busy time for the Mile. Some people arrived early to get a good spot for the fireworks show.

Immediately after the Mile, he headed over to Lake View where he found that his grandfather was not having a good day. He had been warned even before going into the room. The nurses had to get him up and pretty much help him get dressed and ready for breakfast. Then they had to go find him for lunch.

When Gavin got into the room, his grandfather was sitting in his easy chair with some more pictures. It seemed more often that his grandfather was spending his time siting in his chair with photographs, and trying to recall family members and friends. Gavin wondered if he just spent all day sitting in that chair looking at photographs. If that was the case, why wouldn't the staff do anything about it? Gavin wondered if he should tell his father about his worries. Of course, would his father do anything?

Many times his father said that Lake View was the best care facility around, and from what Gavin had seen of it, it was. Gavin had never heard his grandfather complain about the place other than the usual gripes of having to be in a home. Grandpa had friends at the home and the staff seemed friendly enough. No, Gavin doubted that his grandfather just sat in his chair all day looking at pictures.

Another firework went off outside, startling Gavin, his thoughts of his grandfather slipping away. This one sounded like it was coming from next door, but Gavin doubted 85-year-old Paul Olsen was shooting off fireworks. Gavin had no desire to go to the window to see the nuisances. He could go to bed but knew that sleep would not come to him while the noise was going on outside.

Gavin went to the computer and turned it on. The Pierce family computer was in the living room. It was not allowed to go into any of the bedrooms because his father was worried that they would look up porn or go on chat rooms and meet with pedophiles. Gavin didn't bother to tell him that chat rooms were old and no one went on those any longer.

After firing up the computer, Gavin went to Internet. He was searching for general information on the Colorado Rockies. He wished he had more information, but that was all he had gotten from his grandfather.

Right away several sites popped up about a professional baseball team. He changed the parameters and found sites with maps and other bits of information about the area. He clicked on images and saw a lot of pictures of mountains. Gavin had only seen mountains from afar, and they didn't look all that impressive. The mountains in the pictures looked better, and they slightly intrigued him.

Gavin went back to the web page and found a site on a place called the Rocky Mountain National Park. Was that where Grandpa stayed? It had been many years ago, so the place he stayed at may not even exist any longer. He decided to click on the site and see what it had to offer. Gavin stayed on the page for quite some time, especially when he found a section on the history of the park. His interest so piqued, he didn't even hear the fireworks which were now shooting off outside at a more constant pace.

"What are you looking at?" a voice said from behind, startling Gavin almost more than the fireworks. He turned around and saw his twelve year-old sister standing right behind him. How had she gotten so close without him knowing? "Oh, it's just mountains."

"What did you think it would be?" Gavin asked as he closed out of the page.

"Dirty pictures of girls," Pauline told him. "Then I could tell Dad and get you in trouble."

"Sorry to disappoint you, Paul," Gavin said. Calling her Paul only made her mad.

"Maybe I'll tell him anyway. I'll tell him you were looking at naked women with big breasts," she said, and Gavin clicked out of the Internet. He turned around and saw her smiling. He couldn't tell if she was kidding or not. "And I will tell him you were drooling."

"He can check the browser history and see that I wasn't. Even Dad knows how to do that," Gavin said as he stood up.

"You're no fun. You didn't even come to the fireworks show. It was really neat! They had several go off at the same time creating the American Flag."

"So Mom and Dad failed, uh?"

"What are you talking about?" Pauline asked as Gavin turned to face her.

"Mom and Dad said they were going to try and lose you there with all the people in hopes that someone would take you with them."

"Shut up, you jerk!" Pauline shouted and marched down the hall to her room.

Gavin's parents came in after his sister had left. His father was getting close to being 50 and his mother was 45. His father's hair was slowly going gray, but it was not receding. He was lucky to get that from his father. If his mother was getting gray hair, Gavin couldn't tell because it was still auburn like it always had been. She could have dyed it, but if she did, she did a good job at mixing it in.

"Quiet evening?' his father asked.

"No, the fireworks were too loud," Gavin said.

"Oh, yeah. Those," his father said. A silence settled over the room and his mother broke it by saying she was going to get ready for bed. She gave Gavin a hug and left. Gavin rarely gave hugs, but he had stopped stiffening when he was given one. "What are you planning for tomorrow?"

"I have to mow two lawns to make up for today," Gavin said. "If there is time left over, I might go see Grandpa."

"Again? You're spending a lot of time with him lately," his father told him. "Not that there's anything wrong with that, but wouldn't you rather hang out with friends?"

"I am fine with how I spend my time," Gavin said, his words sounding stiff. Surely his father had to know that Gavin's friends didn't number to very many. And the one friend he had, his father didn't approve.

"All right then. Don't let the fireworks keep you up too late," his father said and followed his wife down the hall.

Gavin's room was downstairs; it was the only one that was in the basement. It had belonged to his older brother, and when Brent went off to college, Gavin took it over. He liked it because it was the only bedroom in the basement and had a bathroom close by. His parents had told him he could have it as long as he kept the bathroom clean, which he did.

There was also a family room downstairs that had a 42-inch flat screen and entertainment center. Gavin would watch television, but not as much as an average teenager might. Gavin thought about going down to watch while he waited for the fireworks to end, but he knew there would be nothing on worth watching. He ended up deciding to just go to bed. The room downstairs would provide some barrier against the raging fireworks outside.

Since he only wore an old pair of running shorts to bed, it took him only a few minutes to get ready. He lay on his bed in the dark room and thought about his grandfather. He couldn't get the image of his grandfather sitting in the chair all day looking at pictures out of his head.

* * *

He awoke with a start. His body was full of sweat and twisted in an uncomfortable position. At first he thought he was back at Vietnam with how hot he was. The lone sheet he had started out the night with, was entwined around his legs and body like a snake that was trying to squeeze him to death. The room held a dull light, and Bernie thought it had to be around five in the morning, half an hour before he had to get up and get to the motor pool to start his day shift. What would he be working on today? Standard Jeep? Armored Personal Transport? Bernie doubted it would be a tank; those were worked on at other camps, not in Saigon. Getting positioned in Saigon was a stroke of luck. The front was far off from where he was stationed, so the chance of having to be a part of a battle was slim.

Bernie struggled out of his sheet. His body didn't want to move very well. It felt stiff and there were aches in his joints that no 23 year-old should have to endure. The blanket finally relinquished its grasp on him, and he managed to swing his legs off the bed. He was wearing striped pajama bottoms, not his Army green shorts that he slept in. How did that happen?

For the first time since waking up, Bernie looked around his room. It was not the tent that he shared with several other soldiers, but a bedroom. The dresser across the way had a clock on it that read 5:15 and several framed pictures. He was not 23, but 75. Vietnam was a long time ago. The disoriented feeling was lifting off him like a mist, but he remained on the bed.

How had he thought he was at Vietnam? It felt so real.
He hadn't thought about his time in Vietnam for quite some
time. He had been lucky that he hadn't been a part of any of
the battles. His skills as a mechanic got him stationed in
Saigon, where he worked on the generals' jeeps and other
support vehicles. It was a memory that had escaped him for
quite some time. The fact that it had invaded and took over
scared Bernie some. This had never happened before, at least
not that he could remember.

Breakfast wouldn't be served for another 45 minutes,
but Bernie didn't want to go back to sleep. Instead he got up
and got ready for the day. When he was done, he went into his
small living space and turned the television on. Lake View had
basic cable, and Bernie started to flip through the channels. He
stopped on the History Channel which had a program on the
Civil War. When the television was on, he would normally
watch the History Channel. Sometimes the channel had on
pointless programming, but other times the programming
interested Bernie. He always did prefer his history course in
school. It was the other courses that he didn't do well in.

The same stack of pictures was on the floor where he
left them the night before. Yesterday was the Fourth of July,
but Bernie, like most of the other residents, didn't stay up to
watch fireworks; some did and went outside to watch those that
were fired off over the lake. Bernie picked up the stack and
just held it.

There were more pictures of the life he shared with his
wife, but they were at Michael's house. When he moved into
Lake View, a lot of his belongings were sold, but the
mementos were kept in boxes at Michael's. It was depressing
thinking the bulk of his life was residing in cardboard boxes.
The pictures he had brought with had been his favorites, but
now the memory of when and where those pictures had been
taken was fading. The images were starting to be like
something seen in a picture frame. He wanted to hold onto
those memories, but he started to realize that that was probably

not going to happen. The Alzheimer's was getting worse. The medication he was taking wouldn't help; it would only help for so long and then its effectiveness would be gone.

He pulled out the photo of Belinda standing in front of some mountains. His wife looked so young, so fresh with life. The mountains stood tall behind her, but Bernie couldn't remember where the picture had been taken.

He closed his eyes and tried to think. Had this been the first time he had forgotten where or had he forgotten many times before? It had been their honeymoon, a honeymoon that took three years of waiting to take. That much he remembered. There was something else about the honeymoon that seemed like it had once been an important memory, one of such profound emotion, that he could not remember. It dealt with his wife that was obvious. He also thought it dealt with a location in the mountains, but that was all he could recall.

How can a man forget something like that? Especially with a wonderful woman like Belinda was. A small part of him was glad that she wasn't here to see him go through this. Of course if she had still been alive, he wouldn't be at Lake View but at his home where he belonged.

Why did he feel that he has gone through this before? The mountains in the background almost seemed to mock him as he tried to remember. He sat there for another 40 minutes until he gave up. He wanted to rip the picture up, but knew he would regret that. Having so little of Belinda left, Bernie didn't want to destroy any more. Soon his memories of her would be destroyed and that was bad enough.

Chapter 5

Writing Entry for Friday, February 27

My grandfather is a veteran. He was drafted into the Army in 1961, which was the same year he married my grandmother. That was why they got married. He actually wanted to wait until he returned from overseas, but my grandmother was quite insistent on doing so before. Maybe it was for the benefits if he got killed there, but I never understood why they just did not wait. Grandpa had to leave a week after having a quick marriage ceremony but did see his bride one more time before being shipped off to Vietnam.

The plane ride overseas was the first he had ever been on. The plane ride back to the States was the last one my grandfather ever went on as well. It was not like he had a traumatic time like others over there, it was the fact that he had to be separated from the woman he loved.

My grandfather was stationed at Saigon, where he worked in the motor pool. It seemed my grandfather's skills as a mechanic became evident during training and the Army decided to put them to use. About the smartest thing the Army ever did.

My grandfather soon was repairing vehicles for generals and other top officials. By the end of his two year service, my grandfather was a Motor Sergeant, and had he stayed, would have been placed in charge of the biggest motor pool in Vietnam.

Once my grandfather's term was up, he was discharged even though his higher-ups wanted him to stay on. There was no way that was going to happen; he had a lovely young bride waiting at home that he had not seen for two years.

My grandfather didn't talk much about his time in Vietnam; he said there was not much to talk about. He said the only difference between there and here was the fact that, over there, he slept in a tent and it was hot. Otherwise his work was pretty much the same. On occasion, my grandfather would tell stories about his time there, but that was usually after he had a few beers.

He is not a big drinker, but does like a beer now and then. My father does not drink at all and when he sees my grandfather having alcohol, he gets that 'I do not approve' look on his face. Hell, I do not think my father approves of anything that might loosen a person up, not that I ever experienced that with alcohol before.

One of my grandfather's favorite stories to tell is the time he ended up driving a lieutenant around in a jeep he had just repaired. The lieutenant sounded like a real jerk (I will not use the name my grandfather used since this writing is for school), and when Grandpa told him he just worked on the vehicles, not chauffeured them, the lieutenant pointed at his rank and said there was no choice. My grandfather could have made a stink about it, but he had no pending projects, so he went along.

The lieutenant ended up having my grandfather drive him first to an officers' club and then to a brothel. Now from what my grandfather heard, the best brothels were in Thailand where a lot of soldiers went during their R&R, but Saigon had quite a few for the guys that were stationed there. My grandfather said he never went to one before and that the only woman he ever slept with was my grandmother. I was 15 when he told me that, and it was after he had quite a few beers.

My grandfather had to wait outside in the jeep while the lieutenant was in the officers' club. When he came out, he was somewhat intoxicated and had to be helped into the jeep. My grandfather thought he would drive the pointy-headed lieutenant back to the camp but the lieutenant wanted to go somewhere completely different instead. He wanted to go to a brothel.

I hope I do not go into explicit detail about what brothel is to you, because that is one area that I do not want to discuss. I will say it once: a brothel is where a man will pay for sex. Why a man would want to do that is beyond me.

My grandfather told the lieutenant that he did not know of any brothels and the man responded that that was bull squat (again not what he really said). He said that my grandfather being a lowly enlisted man should know where one was. Again my grandfather said he did not, but the lieutenant insisted he did. So my grandfather thought and then remembered a place that had been talked about by some of the other men. He thought he knew the general location of this place and put the jeep into motion.

They arrived at the area where it was supposed to be and Grandpa stopped the jeep in front. There were Vietnamese women standing outside, some talking to Vietnamese men and American soldiers. The soldiers looked young as they looked at the building. The building itself looked dirty and not the kind of place a sober or sane person would go into. The lieutenant asked if this was place, as if he could not see the prostitutes flashing themselves outside, and my grandfather said yes.

The lieutenant then said my grandfather could come in too, but Grandpa replied he would wait outside. The lieutenant laughed and then questioned Grandpa's sexuality. To my grandfather's credit, he was not mad at the question but calmly told the lieutenant that he was on duty and wanted to make sure he was available when the man was done. That was accepted and the lieutenant strolled off.

My grandfather then watched the man whom he had taken a great distaste to right away stroll up to the place, and he was immediately surrounded by three women. My grandfather said the women had a lot of makeup on and looked like they were in their forties, which probably meant they were in their fifties after the makeup was scraped off. It did not seem to bother the lieutenant as he made his selection and went inside.

The lieutenant came out about 40 minutes later, all disheveled. His uniform had been buttoned quickly because it was off center and not completely tucked in. He climbed up into the jeep with a smile on his face. He said that he had the time of his life, that the prostitute he had been with was quite the expert. He told my grandfather that he would never forget the experience.

My grandfather knew that the man would not forget the place, not for quite some time. The reason my grandfather knew of the place was because when he arrived in Saigon, he was told to avoid the place at all costs. Sexually Transmitted Diseases ran rampant in the place and a person was sure to get one there, protection or not. Grandpa was quite surprised that the lieutenant was not given the same speech when he arrived at Saigon. Perhaps he was the same way with the 'tour guide' as he was with Grandpa.

STDs are the gifts that keep on giving and one which the lieutenant did receive; my grandfather found that out two weeks later when the man came up and hit Grandpa. He claimed that Grandpa knew about the place and purposely took him there. There was no denying it; it was true. The lieutenant wanted Grandpa thrown in the brig (a jail for soldiers), but that didn't happen. People just laughed when the lieutenant told them what happened and they kept telling him he deserved it for being so stupid. It must be nice to be able to tell people the truth. The lieutenant swore he would get my grandfather back, but that did not happen because the guy was eventually transferred without making good on that threat. The lieutenant was left with a burning sensation, and my grandfather was left with a fun memory to share with his 15 year-old grandson.

End of Entry

+ + +

The work was stacking up as the impending school year was on the horizon. It was the end of July, and Michael felt he was way behind where he should be. Classes didn't resume for students until September third. Faculty were expected back August 29th to work on professional development. Teachers would be given some time to get their classrooms ready, although the time would be limited and most teachers would come in on their own time to work.

Michael had his staff list ready to go; there were a few people that had left for various reasons and the positions had to be filled. He still had to finalize a couple of things with the new hires, but he was fairly pleased with the people he'd hired.

The past month he had spent getting used to his office staff and talking with some of the faculty that would trickle in to do various tasks. Fraser High School didn't have summer school, so the building was fairly quiet. There were still boxes in his office, but a lot fewer than when he moved in. He was slowly making the transition. There had been principal meetings to attend, along with some other ones that required his attention.

He was currently in his office working on the computer. He was looking over the demographics of the students coming in. Orientation for the incoming freshman was just two weeks away, and Michael wanted to make sure everything was ready. Of the 150 freshman, about 75 would show up for the orientation. The ones that did not show up would have to be contacted about the information that was missed.

"Michael," a voice said from behind, and he turned around. The head secretary, Patty Junkins, was standing at the open doorway. Patty was in her late fifties and was a godsend. She had worked at the school for 20 years and Michael was her third principal. Patty knew more about the school than anyone and had been a huge assistance to Michael. "It's getting to be close to five. You made mention of going to visit your father after work and picking up your son."

"Thanks, Patty. I'm about finished for the day," Michael said. He had told her his plans for the afternoon and then lost track of time. It was Thursday, and Gavin would be visiting his grandfather. Usually he would just take the bus home, but Michael decided that today would be a good day to see how it was going and drive his son home.

The sun was shining as Michael walked to his car in the parking lot. He had his own parking spot, and his maroon Buick Verano sparkled in the light. He had just run it through the car wash the day before because he didn't have time to wash it by hand. He could imagine what his father would say to that. His father believed that a person should always wash his or her vehicle because that was part of owning a car. That might be good for his dad who had been a mechanic, but Michael was short on time and needed to cut corners when he could.

The interior of the car was hot; it was 85 outside. After starting his car, Michael turned the air on and waited for it to cool down the car. Traffic was brisk as he drove out of the lot and toward Lake View.

It was a nice day out; he wondered what Gavin and Pauline had done today. Gavin had his mowing job, and Pauline had probably gone over to a friend's house and goofed around. He hoped she spent some time outside, enjoying the beautiful day.

At least with Gavin, Michael knew where he was. He could set a watch by that kid. Having a routine could be a good thing, but sometimes Michael wished his son wouldn't be so rigid. He was too young to depend on a daily routine. Life sometimes did not allow for routine. Events had a way of happening, and a person had to learn to adjust to them. As a principal, Michael knew when a routine was necessary and when to go off one. He had to expect the unexpected in his line of work, but he also needed to embrace the routine of things.

It took Michael 15 minutes to drive to Lake View, and when he pulled into the parking lot, it was 5:20. There weren't many cars in the lot, and Michael figured most of them belonged to the employees. Francine was standing guard at the receptionist desk and waved to Michael as he came in.

"They should be in your father's room," Francine said, still smiling. Michael doubted the red-headed woman ever stopped smiling. "Dinner's going on now."

"Thanks. I won't be long," Michael said and made his way to his father's room. The door was closed, but he tried it and found it open. He found his father and son sitting on the small couch that was in the living room, looking at pictures. His son looked up when his father walked into the room.

"Forget how to knock?" Michael's father said, not even bothering to look up.

"Should I?" Michael said with a fake smile on his face. "What are you two doing?"

"Just looking at some pictures," Gavin said. Michael noticed his son's eyes went back down. Michael walked over and saw that the photos were of his father and mother. Some were when they were childless and others when their children were young. There was even a picture of Naomi in there.

Michael had not seen a picture of his dead sister since he was a kid. He realized that he hadn't looked at any pictures from his childhood for quite some time. His parents looked so young, and now when he looked at his father, he realized just how old he had gotten. His father still had a full head of hair, but it was all gray now. His once tall frame now slouched some. Then there was that tired look on his face that sometimes had a mix of confusion with it.

"Just reminiscing?" Michael said and even though the easy chair was open, Michael remained standing. "So how was your day, Dad?"

"Same as always. Nothing changes in this place."

"It's a nice place, Dad," Michael said and sighed. He did not want to have this conversation again.

"I'm not saying that, Mikey," his father said, and Michael had to bite his tongue to keep from saying anything. He hated being called Mikey, and his father, who was the only one that called him that, knew it. "I am just getting tired of seeing it all the time."

"Dad, they have bussing to events around the city. Go on one of those."

"That's not the same!" his father said, his voice elevated some. Michael saw Gavin look at his grandfather and then look back down. Michael felt he was missing something but wasn't sure what. "I want to go to the Rockies!"

"What?" Michael asked, shocked. "What do you mean you want to go to the Rockies?"

"The Rocky Mountains in Colorado!" His father kept his eyes on Michael, and Michael stared back.

"I figured that, Dad. What I mean is, why?"

"Because I'm sick of this place and want to go on a trip!"

"Dad, let's not be having this conversation in front of Gavin," Michael said, hoping it would curb it for a while.

"Why the hell not? He's an adult now. He's a part of my life. Hell, he's probably more a part of my life than you are! At least when he visits me, he wants to be here!"

"That's not fair, Dad," Michael said, purposely keeping his voice down. He didn't want any of the staff worrying about an argument coming from the room. "I wish I could visit as much as Gavin does, but it's just not possible. And when I do come, I come to see you because I want to."

"Michael, I'm sorry I said that. I've just been having a hard time lately," his dad said and then went through the pictures, as if searching for one. He stopped and then held a picture up. It was a photo of himself and Michael's mother, taken on their honeymoon. "There have been more days when I look at this picture and can't recall where it was taken. I know that it's my wife with me and that it was our honeymoon, but the location escapes me. Gavin has found me several times sitting in this chair holding this picture. He's been nice enough not to mention that he has done it many times before."

"Grandpa, it is okay," Gavin said and Michael had almost forgotten that his son was in the room.

"No, it's not okay. I know what is happening to me and it is not reversible. How much more time until I start forgetting who I am with? Or you? Or Gavin?"

"I don't know," Michael said and then sat down in the easy chair. He wished he could tell his father that it would be fine, but he knew it wouldn't. He had done his research. "I wish I could help you, Dad, but I can't."

"You can. Take me to the Rockies. I want to go there one more time and see if I can remember for the last time. I want to walk in the same area where I took your mother on our honeymoon. I want to see if I can remember every moment of that wonderful time."

Michael was silent for a moment. His father looked at him with hopeful eyes, much like his childhood dog looked at him in hope of food. He wanted to tell his father that he would, but there was no way. School started in a month and there was a lot to do from now until then. A trip to Colorado would take some planning, and then there was his father. Taking him on a trip of that magnitude would be difficult as well.

"Dad, I can't this summer. Next summer I might be able to swing something, but with my new job and all, well, you know."

"Yeah, I know. I know that by next summer it will be too late. My condition will worsen by then, and it will be pointless. Pointless because I won't even remember the wonderful woman I was with. It will be like seeing it for the first time. Hell, I probably won't even know you by then. No, it has to be now," his father said. Gavin's head had gone up again, and he was looking at his grandfather. "I know that your brother and sister would never do it. They wouldn't be able to do it. But you could. Please, Mike. I have to go there when I still can hold onto any scrap of memory."

"Dad," Michael started to say but couldn't finish. He saw two tears come out of his father's eyes. He had only seen his father cry two times in his life. One had been at Naomi's funeral and the other was when Michael's mother died. He didn't see any possible way he could do it, but he said, "I will see what I can do."

"Thank you," his father said, his voice back to normal. Michael felt bad for basically lying to his father, but he didn't know what else he could have done. He just hoped that his father would realize it wasn't going to work and let it go. Or perhaps he would forget about it, which made Michael feel even worse thinking about.

***

"I could come with and help out," Gavin said. He and his father were in the car on their way back to the house. After his father told his grandfather that he would think about it, the two of them stayed for another few minutes and then made their exit. At first there was silence in the car and finally it was broken by Gavin. "I have spent a lot of time with him, so I know when he is doing okay or not."

"I appreciate you offering, Gavin," his dad said but there was something with the tone of his voice that Gavin didn't like.

"You said you would think about it and see if it would work. Are you not going to do that?"

"I have already thought about it. It won't work this summer. This request came at a bad time."

"What? Is this about your new job?"

"Gavin, I don't expect you to understand, but I have certain responsibilities that can't just be thrown out because Grandpa feels the need to go on a trip," he said while staring out the windshield.

"How can you say that? It is more than a trip to him. You have not seen him the past month. His memory is fading. He has been having difficulty remembering details of his own life!"

"I know that, Gavin."

"Really? If you really knew that, you would take him. He said next summer would be too late. And I would have to agree," Gavin told his father. This was the longest conversation they had had in a long time.

"Gavin, this is not your thing to worry about."

"Why not? He's my grandfather, and I love him. He wants to do this. He should be able to do this on his own, but he cannot. He needs help."

"Gavin, I'm done having this conversation." Gavin could tell by his father's tone that he was done discussing it, but Gavin was not.

"You said you had responsibilities and that I would not understand. I understand responsibilities just fine. What about the one you have to your father?"

"Damn it, Gavin!" his father shouted and pulled the car over. They were a few blocks from the house, but Gavin's attention was on his father. "I told you I'm done with this. He may be your grandfather, but he is my father. I understand this situation a lot better than you. If you keep on wishing to discuss this, then you might as well get out and walk home."

Gavin unbuckled his seat belt, opened the door and got out. The passenger door was barely shut as his father drove off, leaving him on the side of the street. There were people out that had stopped doing their yard work and were staring at Gavin.

"You okay, son?" an elderly man yelled across the street. He was holding a rake and had a ridiculous wide brim hat on his head.

"Yeah, I am fine," Gavin said but didn't look at the man. He had tears in his eyes and felt embarrassed to be crying in public. How could his father do that to Grandpa? Grandpa's request wasn't a flight of fancy at all.

He realized that he was still standing in the street and started to walk in the direction of his house. Not wanting to see his father again but not knowing where else to go, Gavin moved on in a slow pace.

He hadn't been yelled at by his father like that for a long time. The last time was when he locked his then five-year-old sister in a closet because she was annoying him. Normally it wouldn't have been a big deal, but she had been in there for two hours. His parents had been outside working and occasionally would check on them. His sister escaped notice because his parents took turns checking. Gavin had answered them honestly because they never specifically asked if his sister was locked in a closet.

He passed Mr. Lipkinsky's yard and was glad to see that no one was outside. He didn't feel like explaining why he was walking home. His pace didn't change as he crossed the street, still two blocks away from home. He saw a familiar car coming toward him; it was his mother's black Chevy Impala. She saw him and pulled over.

"Get in," she said. Gavin thought for a moment not complying, but changed his mind. After he got in, his mother asked, "Want to tell me what that was all about?"

"No."

"Okay, let me rephrase that. Tell me what you did to get your father so upset."

"How is this my fault? Dad is the one that won't help Grandpa out. I just asked him why," Gavin said as he looked out the window at the passing house. They passed their house and did not stop. "You passed our house."

"I know. I want to give your father some time to cool down before you go in. I also want to know what happened. All your father would say was that he let you walk the rest of the way home. I was worried that you wouldn't come home at all."

"Where would I go?"

"I don't know, maybe the Mile."

"It is too late to go there."

"Fine, tell me what happened," his mother said, and Gavin knew that his mother wouldn't give in until he told her. So he did, starting at finding his grandfather looking at pictures for the past month. When he was done, he felt he was still in the right to test his father on why he wouldn't take Grandpa.

"I think you owe your father an apology," his mother finally said. "He shouldn't have gotten mad and let you walk, but you shouldn't have pushed him on this. Your father is under a lot of stress this summer. His new job takes a lot of his time."

"He is always under a lot of stress and his job always takes a lot of time," Gavin told her.

"Gavin, I know you and your father don't see eye to eye. It's common in fathers and sons, but please don't push him like that. Don't you think that Dad wants to help his father? And the fact that he can't, makes him even more upset?"

"Why cannot father help him? It should not take that long to go to Colorado, spend a few days, and return."

"Orientation starts in a few weeks and after that there's the professional development. Maybe if your grandfather would have brought this up in June, Dad could have found time," Gavin's mother said, but her voice was doubtful and the way she didn't look at Gavin told him she didn't believe that either. "Grandpa is just going through a rough patch right now. He's living in a good place and things will get back to normal."

"Yeah, but what will normal look like for him? Will it be where he loses his memory more and more every day? It is not like he is going to wake up and everything will be fine again. This is not fair!"

"Almost nothing in life is fair," his mother said, and Gavin fell silent. He had learned that lesson a long time ago. "We are going to go home, eat a now cold dinner, and you will apologize to Dad. I don't care if you mean it or not. Then you are going to drop this. You let your father worry about Grandpa."

"Yes, mother," Gavin said and the rest of the drive was quiet. His mother drove around for another ten minutes and then pulled into their garage. His father's car was on the usual right, and Gavin was reminded about the argument he just had in there. His father was not in the kitchen when Gavin went in, but in the living room watching television. He glanced over at Gavin briefly and then went back to the screen. "I am sorry, Dad. I will not mention it again."

His father was silent, and Gavin thought his father hadn't heard him. Then he said, "Thank you, Gavin. Please understand that there just isn't a way."

"Yes, sir," Gavin said and then walked back to the kitchen to eat his cold dinner. It was spaghetti, usually his favorite, but he hardly tasted it at all.

After dinner, he went downstairs to his room and lay on his bed. He would have read some books, but he couldn't concentrate. At around ten, there was a knock at the door; it was his mother to come say goodnight. He said it back and then went back to the bed.

He lay on it again and could not fall asleep. Coming to a decision, he knew what he was going to do tomorrow after mowing. He was going to go to the library to do some research. It was the kind of research he didn't dare do at home.

Chapter 6

Writing Entry for Friday, March 6

When my grandfather was eight, he broke his arm while hiking at Warren Dunes State Park. The park is located on the western part of the state, along Lake Michigan. The land along the lake is made up of sandy dunes where a person can sink in up to his or her ankles. It is quite a popular place to visit; I have gone a couple of times myself with my family. My grandfather went when he was eight and was having a good time until the accident happened.

The accident had been his fault; he fully admits that. He had wandered off from his parents and siblings to go exploring. He had slipped away unnoticed and started to play explorer like the ones he had learned about in class. He had on what he called his explorer hat which was a genuine raccoon skin cap, complete with a tail. My grandfather said the day was slightly overcast, not that it contributed to his accident. It did not take long for my grandfather to lose sight of his family as he strolled over the dunes. Driftwood was plentiful around, and he stopped to pick up a piece to use as a walking stick.

The sun eventually came out, which encouraged my grandfather to go farther. He had started to come to rockier terrain when he came to a cliff that overlooked Lake Michigan. Anyone that has seen the Great Lakes can attest to how beautiful they are. I could imagine what my then eight-year-old grandfather saw standing on that cliff, looking out at the lake. The only thing he would see was water.

He was starting to get warm, so he took his cap off and held it as he gazed out at the water. Looking straight down the cliff, he saw that there was a scrap of shoreline no wider than three feet. The cliff extended out of sight to the north, and he could see where it rose in the south. He started to move toward the north when his foot got caught on a piece of buried driftwood. Stumbling, he caught himself using his walking stick but letting go of his cap in the process. The cap hit the edge of the cliff and went over before Grandpa could catch it. He lay down on his belly and looked once more over the side. His cap had not fallen all the way down to the ground, some 20 feet below. It had landed on a rock that was sticking out of the side of the cliff.

Grandpa could have played it safe and returned back to receive his lickings for going off on his own, but of course he did not. He wanted his cap, which had been given to him by his grandfather. Looking at the side of the cliff, he saw several other rocks protruding out and figured he could climb down to get the cap.

At first the climb down was going fine, and it was not until he was close to the cap that it all went to hell. His left foot moved onto a rock, which he thought was secure, but ended up not being safe. The rock came out of the side of the cliff, and he started to fall. It was not a clean fall either as his body bounced along the side of the cliff. Amazingly enough, my grandfather had the insight to make a grab at his cap as he passed by mid-fall. He managed to snag it and then a few seconds later made a hard landing on the ground below. His left forearm hit first, absorbing most of the impact. Grandpa said he had never heard his body make that kind of sound, nor felt that kind of pain before. But he got his cap back.

His vacation was cut short as his parents had to take him to the nearest hospital, which back then was not that near. His left arm was put in a cast which he had for the rest of the summer which obviously limited an eight-year-old boy's summer activities.

I asked him why he risked so much for a cap. Had he just gone back to his family, he would not have broken his arm and had a lot better summer. My grandfather told me that there were some things in life that were worth it no matter the risk. At the time, his cap was worth the risk. Would that always be the case with it? No, but then it was. I also asked him why he left his family in the first place. He said he wanted to have an adventure, which he did get. Life is not worth living if one does not go on an adventure every once and in a while.

I must say that was the first advice of my grandfather's that never sat well with me. It's probably not that much of a surprise, but adventure and I do not mix very well. I like my routine; I know that. Routine makes me feel secure. Everything is right when I know what is coming up. Adventure sounds messy to me. On a true adventure, one does not exactly know what to expect. If I could plan out adventures, then maybe I would be more open to them. People throw around that word a lot. A vacation is an adventure, some will say. A vacation can be an adventure as long as you did not plan it out beforehand and then the unexpected happened during it. My grandfather had an adventure when he was eight and was awarded with a broken arm. Give me routine anytime.

End of Entry

+ + +

"Checkmate," Gavin said, moving his bishop into place. He was sitting in the social room at Lake View. His grandfather sat across from him staring at the chessboard. The game had only taken ten moves and even that was a stretch. His grandfather wasn't having an off day, it was just his head wasn't in the game. Gavin had told him about his father not taking him on the trip like it was discussed the day before. At first his grandfather looked disappointed, and then he said he knew it wouldn't happen. His grandfather was sullen for the rest of the time after that. Gavin suggested chess and received a nod. His grandfather didn't even ask him what he did that day, which was the usual mowing along with a trip to the library.

"Hey, Gavin, how's it going?" Howard Grotts said as he approached the table. Gavin's eyes went up and then dropped back down.

"Okay. Grandpa is not too into the game though, sir," Gavin responded.

"That's too bad. Nothing like a game of chess to keep the old mind sharp," Howard said and pulled up a chair. "So, still mowing?"

"Yes, sir," Gavin said. "I did some earlier today."

"That's a good job to have. I can remember mowing lawns when I was a boy. Of course I didn't have one of those new mowers with engines, just a push one."

"Shut up, Howie. There were motorized lawn mowers back then, and I bet you had one," Grandpa said and Howard laughed.

"Never could fool you, Bernie," Howard said and stood up. "Good seeing you again, Gavin. I'll leave you two alone. Play another game. Who knows, Bernie? Maybe you'll win one!"

"Bye, Mr. Grotts," Gavin said, even though Howard had told him numerous times to call him by his first name. Howard stood up, his knees popping in the process and then walked off. "Do you want to play again?"

"Not really. I want to go back to my room," his grandfather said. Gavin picked up the chess pieces and stowed them in their proper place.

"Howard looked better today. His arthritis must not be acting up so bad today," Gavin said as they walked down the hall, mainly to fill the quiet. A few minutes later they arrived at his grandfather's room where Grandpa took his usual position in his easy chair.

His grandfather just nodded. The pictures were by the side of the chair and he picked them up. He was quiet as he shuffled through them, finally stopping on the honeymoon one. It always went back to that one. Gavin wasn't going to make a decision yet, but he felt there was no other way. "Grandpa, do you still want to go to the Rocky Mountains?"

"Yes, but you said that your father didn't have the time to take me." He didn't look at Gavin but remained staring at the picture. Gavin watched him for a moment as he stood next to him, feeling almost like an interloper.

"There is another way," Gavin said slowly. "I will take you."

"What?" his grandfather asked, and this time he looked up.

"Yes, I will take you," Gavin said, this time with more conviction. "I do not know all the details yet, but I promise you, you will see the Rocky Mountains again."

"Gavin, don't get me wrong, you're a great kid, but how do you propose getting there? You don't even drive," Grandpa said and shook his head. "I suppose I could drive, but how safe is that? And we don't even have a car."

"Let me worry about that," Gavin told him. It was a problem to say the least. He had thought about maybe taking a bus there but decided against that. He knew he would be going without his father's permission and had to find a way that was undetectable by him. "Do you want me to take you?"

"Yes, if you can find a way," Grandpa said and smiled. It was the first time Gavin had seen him smile all day. It only added to his resolve of taking his grandfather. "When would we go?"

"I think we could go next week," Gavin told him. Next week Tuesday was the first of August, and Gavin didn't want to wait any longer than that. Summer was slipping away as it usually did. He knew if this was going to get done that it had to get done as soon as possible. "There are still plenty of areas I have to figure out."

"What about money? You know your dad controls my finances," his grandfather said, and Gavin had already thought of that.

"I have 5,000 in my account. If I start taking small amounts out, they will not alert Dad. His name is secondary on my bank account. I should be able to get out at least 2,000 by next week."

"Gavin, I don't want you to use all of your savings for me."

"Grandpa, this is important to you. I have watched you the last few weeks and know just how important this is. You will get to the Rocky Mountains. Do not worry about money," Gavin told him. His grandfather was silent for a moment and then stood up. He wrapped his arms around Gavin and hugged him. Gavin wasn't the best hugger in the world, but this time he tried to return it. It was an awkward return, but at least he tried.

"I think I know where I can get some more money, so you won't have to eat into your account so much. We wouldn't want Mike finding out before we even begin our journey," Grandpa said after the hug ended. Gavin knew he should have felt bad about keeping this from his father, but it was actually kind of exciting. They would be going on a journey if Gavin could find a way there.

* * *

Gavin sat in his swivel chair next to the desk in his room. He was turning the chair one way and then would go the other. He often did that as he thought important matters over. Gavin had gone straight home after he left Lake View. He was quiet at dinner, but that wasn't too out of the ordinary. His sister chatted about what she did with her friend Jane, and Mom talked about her day at work. His father was still at school.

After the meal was over, Gavin went downstairs to his room. He had his papers there from his research at the library. According to Google, it was 1,309 miles to Estes Park, Colorado. Estes Park was the city that was right next to Rocky Mountain National Park. Gavin wasn't sure if that was exactly where his grandfather wanted to go, but it was a start. He would find out the exact spot next time he talked with Grandpa. Google claimed it would take 20 hours to get there, but Gavin knew better. It would take 20 hours if one did 65 miles per hour and went nonstop. They would have to stop for gas, food, and bathrooms. Gavin thought it was lucky that Grandpa didn't have an issue with having to go to the bathroom all the time. So, if he went the most direct route, he was guessing two days.

Should they take the direct route? His father was sure to be upset when he realized his teenage son took his Alzheimic grandfather on a road trip. The authorities would be alerted and the direct route would be searched.

Gavin thought it might be best to avoid the direct route, and take the one that his father would never think of. Going north, west, and then south might work. Gavin had looked at a map and thought about going to the Mackinac Bridge which was about a four hour drive from St. Clair Shores. Gavin had been there once on a family trip. The bridge was five miles long and connected Michigan's upper and lower peninsulas. There was a toll to pay in order to go on it, but it wasn't all that much. It was also the fifth longest suspension bridge in the world. Gavin knew all this because he had looked it up when he found out the family would be traveling on it. It was quite the experience going across a bridge that was five miles long. When in the middle, the coast of either of the peninsulas was just a sliver, if visible at all.

When Gavin had gone there, he was amazed at all the boats that could be seen on the water surrounding the bridge. The view was spectacular to say the least.

From there, Gavin thought they would angle their way west to Minneapolis. Gavin had never been to the city before and would have to do some research on it. They could start heading south then, but Gavin felt it would be too early. He thought about going west from there a little more and going to Bismarck, North Dakota.

He had never visited North Dakota and again more research would be required. It would be at Bismarck where they would start south, going through the Black Hills in South Dakota, another spot he had never been to, but only seen on television. Mount Rushmore was a famous American landmark, and Gavin hoped to catch at least a glimpse of the four presidents. After the Black Hills, they would go through Wyoming and then into Colorado. With the way Gavin was planning on going, it would be a total of 1,881 miles and about 27 hours of traveling. Gavin thought it would take about three days.

What he needed now was a way to get to all those places. Taking a bus was out of the question and so was renting a car. Who would drive it? Gavin finally wished he had gone on to get his license, but it was too late. There was no way he could get a license in less than a week. So, Gavin's options were limited. Of course, he would have to think of any options first.

He stopped his chair, stood up, and went over to his bed. The bed rebounded hard as he threw his body onto it. It always made his dad mad when he did that; apparently bedframes cost money. He lay on his back staring at the ceiling.

Was there anyone he knew that could help? He thought about someone from Lake View. Perhaps his grandfather had a friend that could still drive. Gavin thought a little more on that idea and decided against it. He didn't want to bring in one of Grandpa's friends in fear that he would spill the beans.

That left Gavin. Gavin didn't have many friends, and the few he had would not take on such an undertaking. Being social had its advantages, Gavin guessed. The one good friend he had, he hadn't talked to for quite some time because his father didn't like him.

Gavin's body suddenly shot up to a sitting position. That was it! It was almost too perfect. Now, if only he would agree to Gavin's plan.

Chapter 7

Writing Entry for Friday, March 13

My grandfather said that everyone should have a friend like Bucky Stevens. Grandpa would often talk about Bucky, whose first name actually *was* Bucky. Who names their kid that? Is that not a nickname?

Grandpa did not meet Bucky until he moved to St. Clair Shores when he was five. Bucky lived down the street but might as well have lived at the same house with how much he was over there. Bucky lived with his dad; his mother had either died or left. Grandpa was not sure which one because Bucky never talked about her.

The two of them were inseparable; see one and you saw the other. Knowing someone and being friends with him or her at such a young age basically makes him or her family. That is what my great-grandparents thought about Bucky too.

From all that Grandpa would talk about with Bucky, it sounded like those two got into a lot of trouble together. Of course it was back in the 40s and 50s, so it was not the same kind of trouble as now. They were often the neighborhood pranksters. Old lady Gregory had a huge trough that she would use to catch water from the downspouts. She would use that water for various things. After a big rain, which normally would fill the trough, Bucky and Grandpa would sneak over and empty the trough. On days that were dry, they would sneak over and fill it.

My grandfather said they did stupid pranks like that; ones where no one would get hurt. I asked him if Mrs. Gregory ever found out, and he told me that no, she never did. Sometimes she would ask the neighbors about it, but that was all.

Another time, Bucky brought a goat from a nearby farm. He said he was just borrowing it, but the owners did not know yet. They put the goat inside their teacher's car. That was when they were in the ninth grade. They thought it would be funny when Mrs. Lanster came out and found the goat in her car. The problem was that when she did go out, she found the goat had eaten much of her upholstery and gotten sick all over the interior. Bucky and Grandpa did not fess up over that one either. They thought it was best to remain anonymous. The farmer did get his goat back, though.

Grandpa said everyone should have a friend like Bucky because of the way Grandpa felt when Bucky was around. Grandpa felt like he had someone he could confide in without the fear of judgment. Bucky might not have been the smartest kid around (he by far was not from what Grandpa said), but at least he knew how to listen and keep his mouth shut.

Even when they were teenagers, Bucky was over all the time and often spent the night even though he lived so close.

Grandpa said it was because of Bucky's father. Bucky's father worked at the docks for a small shipping company. Huge cargo ships did not dock at St. Clair Shores, but smaller ships with cargo often did. Bucky's dad's job was to unload those ships. Real exciting work. The job was enough to keep him in booze. Grandpa said Great-grandfather often wondered how Frank (Bucky's dad) was able to pay for the house with how little his job paid and how that little pay went to pay for so much booze.

Frank was drunk just about every night, and by the end, it was every night. So Bucky was welcomed and stayed many a night at his friend's. Bucky would sometimes go on trips with Grandpa (he was not along for the trip to the Dunes) and family. Grandpa thought if his parents could have adopted Bucky, they would have.

Grandpa said the relationship he had with his wife was the best, but the one with Bucky was a close second. He thought that he would have Bucky in his life forever, but as is usually the case, life had other plans.

End of Entry

+ + +

Bernie knew that he shouldn't even be thinking about going to Colorado with his grandson. He had no right to put that kind of pressure on the boy. True, Bernie had not asked Gavin to do it, but that didn't matter. He should have discouraged the idea from the beginning. But he didn't. He didn't because deep down he knew that this was his last opportunity. With how much his mind was deteriorating, waiting until next summer would be out of the question.

Just that morning he woken up and had to really think about where he was. People in pictures were harder to identify. Sure, it was just family members such as distant cousins, aunts, and uncles, but that was enough. He did not look forward to the day where he relied on someone to do the basic necessities like eating, bathing, and helping with going to the bathroom. That was no way to live.

The stories about assisted suicide always sickened Bernie, and he never understood why someone would want to do that. He understood now, not that he would ever go that far. Perhaps life should have a point where a person can bow out when the time is right. Of course, when was the time right? For him, he felt the time was coming.

He wished Michael would be the one to take him but wasn't too surprised that his son wasn't going to do it. The reasons Michael gave were understandable, but there came a point in a person's life when a bigger responsibility came along that dwarfed the others. Bernie felt that this was one of them. The fact that Gavin took over for his father proved just how important this was. Gavin had seen that and took up the mantle.

Just how they were going to get there was a problem. Gavin was right in the fact that they couldn't take a bus. Michael would look into that. Gavin not being able to drive was a problem, although Bernie suspected that he could teach the boy enough to get by. Bernie thought about driving, but he actually was nervous about that. Yes, he had put up a fuss when his license was taken away at Michael's insistence, but the truth was that he was actually relieved. Driving had gotten more difficult for Bernie, and he was lucky that he hadn't killed anyone with his last outing. Besides, where would they get a car for him to drive? They couldn't rent one because that would be like going on the bus, too traceable. Gavin said he would think of something, but Bernie worried the boy took on too much when he promised they would go.

The need to go was growing every day for Bernie. As his memory faded daily, the need to go to the one place where he could clearly remember Belinda didn't. Standing in the same spots that he had stood with his wife over 50 years ago felt like the right thing to do. It felt like a powerful force was calling him there, but he was unable to answer that force himself.

It was strange that he could not just get a ticket on a bus and go by himself. He was 75 years old, not ten. He should be able to go where he wanted to, but that was no longer the case. He should be able to live on his own as well, but there were certain things with growing old that one just could not do any longer. The reasons behind him not being able to do those things were sound, but that still didn't make them any easier to swallow.

So with little choice, he had to put his hopes in Gavin finding a way to get him to the Rockies, where hopefully he would have one last recollection. Perhaps it would be a tidal wave of memories hitting him when he got there.

He tried to think of Belinda, but although he could picture her face in his mind, it was fuzzy. That had to be the most unfair part of all about the disease, the fact that he could not remember the person he loved most in life. She wouldn't become a stranger. No, she would be gone, nonexistent to him. She would cease to exist because she was no longer alive to see every day like Michael and Gavin. Those two would become strangers. Would Gavin keep coming when that time arrived? Would it even matter?

Bernie realized that this trip to Colorado probably would be the last thing in his life he had to look forward to. That was a truly depressing thought.

***

Gavin arrived at the house on Edwards Street at two in the afternoon. He had worked hard to get his mowing done quickly that morning. He was paid by Mr. Lipkinsky and knew he would not be putting the money in the bank. He had already gone to the bank and removed $500, which he believed was the highest amount he could remove before the bank alerted his father. His father would find out soon enough about the withdrawals but by then Gavin and his grandfather would be well down the road.

He hadn't been to the house for quite some time. He had tried calling on his phone, but the number he had was no longer in service. Gavin wasn't too surprised by that. His friend Roadkill Solphis lived in the house. Roadkill obviously wasn't his first name, but a name given to him because of a special talent of his. Roadkill was able to identify any kind of dead animal on the road no matter how mutilated it was. Gavin wasn't sure the usefulness of the talent, but it was true. Gavin had witnessed it himself on the bus on field trips. They had passed some badly mangled animals, but Roadkill quickly identified each one. Some doubted that he was right, but Gavin knew he was.

Roadkill was the closest thing Gavin had to a best friend. When Roadkill was still in school, they would hang out in the commons area during free periods and eat together at lunch. Roadkill was not as judgmental as some of the other students.

Their hanging out at school ended when Roadkill dropped out. After that, Gavin was not allowed to hang out with him outside of school because of his father. His father did not approve of Gavin's friendship with Roadkill, which also wasn't that shocking. Roadkill's interest in school was minimal at best. His grades reflected his interest in classes. When he dropped out, he was passing only one class and that was French. Roadkill told Gavin the only reason he was passing French was that the teacher was hot.

Gavin hadn't seen Roadkill since his last day in school. He was a little nervous going up to his house. How would Roadkill receive him? Would he slam the door in Gavin's face as soon as he saw who it was? Would he laugh at the request and tell Gavin to get out?

Gavin paused at the front door and then finally rang the doorbell. There was no sound, so he knocked. No one answered. Did Roadkill even live there? Or maybe he was at some job. Roadkill had issues with keeping himself employed. In a span of five months, Roadkill had gotten and lost four jobs. That was another reason Gavin's father couldn't stand him.

Gavin walked around to the back, noting how the yard hadn't been kept up. Gavin had been in Roadkill's house one time and that was when they had done a school project together. The project was for eighth grade science and it never even got finished. Gavin had entered the house through the back door. He thought it strange at the time and still did. Who didn't have their guests come in through the front door?

As he walked back, he could hear music playing from inside the house, coming from the basement. At first Gavin thought it was just a bunch of noise, but then his ears finally identified it as music. Heavy metal music, if Gavin recalled correctly. Roadkill preferred that kind of music; the noisier, the better.

The back door was down a small set of stairs and Gavin pounded harder on it. The music continued, so Gavin pounded again. Perhaps Roadkill was not there and had accidently left his music on. Perhaps it wasn't an accident and he left it on to make the neighbors upset. The latter sounded more like Roadkill.

The music suddenly was turned down, and Gavin heard someone coming to the door. The door opened, revealing Roadkill in all his glory. The first thing Gavin noticed about his friend was that he had gotten taller and put on more weight. Roadkill had been taller than Gavin before, but now he towered over him, and Gavin wasn't that short to begin with. Despite the height gain, Roadkill looked like he had put on about 50 pounds, adding to his already bigger frame.

"Son of a bitch! It's Gavy!" Roadkill said, still sounding the same. Gavy was Roadkill's nickname for him, which he tolerated at most. "Damn, it's been like a long time!"

"Yes, it has," Gavin responded. Roadkill pulled him into a friendly hug which felt more like Gavin was going to be crushed.

"Holy shit! Never expected to see you at my house! Hell, after your dad ran me out of school, I thought I might never see you!" Roadkill and his mother blamed Gavin's father for Roadkill leaving school, although his grades and effort hadn't helped much. Despite Roadkill's feelings for Gavin's father, he still liked Gavin. "You look the same, man!"

"I would say you do too, but bigger."

"Yeah, I've packed on the pounds since I last saw you. "Taco John's will do that to you. And McDonald's, Burger King, Sonic, and so on."

"Are all those places you have worked?" Gavin asked, his voice not hiding the amazement.

"All except Sonic. I just eat there, wouldn't work there. Guy's gotta have some standards you know."

"Are you working somewhere now?" Gavin asked and was worried that Roadkill had a job and would not be able to do the favor Gavin was going to ask.

"I am currently in between job opportunities," Roadkill said and sounded like he was proud. His full face looked like it hadn't seen a razor for some time, but that wasn't shocking for Roadkill either. "Come in! It's too nice a day to stay outside!"

"Thanks. I can only stay a little bit," Gavin said, following Roadkill into the house. The room he was led to was the downstairs living room, which also doubled as Roadkill's bedroom. There was a strange, sweet smell that dominated the odors of the place. A flat screen television, currently paused on a game, was in the corner.

"Call of Duty. Best damned game ever," Roadkill said as he noticed Gavin looking at the screen. Gavin didn't play video games himself, but he didn't look down on those that did. "So, Gavy, what brings you to my fair abode?"

"I wanted to ask you about something," Gavin said and was unsure of how to start. He wasn't worried about Roadkill talking to his father, but he was still nervous about divulging what he was planning. "My grandfather has Alzheimer's."

"Yeah, I remember you telling me."

"He wants to go to Colorado one more time. Colorado is where he went on his honeymoon with my grandmother. He thinks that by going there, he will be able to remember better," Gavin said and the more he talked, the better he felt. "It has to be this summer because Grandpa thinks by next summer it will not matter anymore."

"Dude, that's gotta suck the big one," Roadkill said. Gavin knew what 'the big one' was from prior dealings with his friend. "So what do you want from me?"

"I cannot drive and neither can Grandpa."

"What about your father?"

"He said he does not have the time to do it this summer. I think he is just saying that to get out of it completely," Gavin told him.

"That's cold, man," Roadkill said and flopped down on the green, saggy couch. Gavin took a look at it and decided standing would be his best course. The couch was covered with clothing, probably dirty, and the parts of the couch that could be seen through the scattered clothing had unidentifiable stains. Roadkill seemed to sense Gavin's hesitation and said, "Dude, the couch is cool. I jerk off on the bed."

"I am okay. I like to stand," Gavin said and knew it sounded feeble. Looking down at the couch again, he sat on it. It sank further down, and Gavin wondered how it had lasted this long.

"Good! You passed the couch test. I was joking about the jerking off, you know."

"Okay, I do not really need to know about that."

"So, what do you want from me?"

"Do you still have that Ford Taurus?" Gavin asked, still trying to feel comfortable on the couch and realizing that he probably never would.

"No, that crapped out on me a few months ago," Roadkill said, and Gavin nearly let out a cry. "Got a van now. I upgraded!"

"Really, where?" Gavin hadn't seen it outside.

"It's in the garage. Neighbors been griping about it sitting out on the street too long. Put it in there for now. It's a 1989 Dodge Conversion. Beaut."

"That sounds great," Gavin said with some hope. A van would be perfect. Now came the tricky part. "Are you doing anything next week?"

"Man, I don't know my schedule that far off. My mom's been ragging on me about getting another job. You want me to go with, don't you? You still can't drive and now you need good ole Roadkill to bail your ass out. I don't see my so called friend for a year, and now here he is wanting a huge favor."

Gavin never thought it would go like this. He hadn't thought of Roadkill ever being vindictive. He was about to apologize and then take his leave, when Roadkill started laughing and clapped him on the back. "Just pulling your chain, man! You should see your face! It's like someone stepped on your puppy! Now, tell me more about this trip."

Chapter 8

Writing Entry for Friday, March 27

I have mentioned earlier in my writings (that I'm being forced to do) that my grandfather dropped out of high school when he was 17. He is not embarrassed about that by any means. He never went back to complete the few courses he had left, and he never got his GED.

With my father, the fact that my grandfather is a high school dropout 'sticks in his craw' as Grandpa would say. Grandpa would often bring up that fact about high school to Dad just to see his face. I do not know many high school dropouts, but the ones that I do know are not like my grandfather. He turned out to be successful; the ones I know, not so much.

I think my grandfather was able to get along without a high school diploma for a couple of reasons. First was because of his skill and work ethic. Grandpa already knew what he wanted to do and school was not going to help him with it. Another reason I think my grandfather succeeded was because of the time period. There was not all the technology there is now where one would have to go to school to at least grasp some of that knowledge.

Honestly, if I could drop out of school, I would. However, I cannot because my parents would never allow it, even though I am 17. Also, unlike my grandfather, I do not know what I want to do with my life. He already had a job as a mechanic when he dropped out. They just took him on full time. With me, it is different. The only job I have is mowing lawns in the summer. That is not a full time job. It could be in the summer, I mean but not in the winter. Unless I add shoveling driveways and sidewalks.

So here I remain, suffering away at all the indignities that find their way to me. I still have one more year of high school left, but it feels like 50. I am sure you have heard that plenty of times being a teacher.

How can you be a teacher? It is a question that I have often thought about when I was supposed to be paying attention to teachers. What drives a person to become one? Wanting to be a sadist? That was mean. Teachers are valuable resources in the community. Without teachers, people would not be able to learn what buttons to press to order food at McDonalds.

I am getting off topic again. As I said earlier, Grandpa had no regrets about dropping out. It was just what worked for him. My friend Roadkill (you remember him, I bet) dropped out last year and really has not done much. I know of others that just sit around their parents' houses or apartments and do nothing. I do not want a life like that.

There is another factor that led to my grandfather dropping out of school: the death of Bucky Stevens. Cliffhanger!

End of Entry

+ + +

Gavin walked into Lake View Sunday afternoon carrying a duffle bag. In it he had a cheap chessboard and pieces. The items inside were just a ploy because he needed the bag for something else.

Gavin had the transportation all lined up. Once he told Roadkill about his plans and that he would pay for the gas and pretty much everything else, Roadkill signed on.

The following day he had gone to Lake View and told his grandfather that they had a driver and a vehicle. He had been able to get $1,500 out so far, but was starting to worry that any more would cause suspicion. Grandpa nodded and told him that amount would be all he should take out. He also said that he would take care of the rest. Gavin asked how, but Grandpa did not answer.

With the transportation problem solved, Gavin went on to solving how he was going to get his grandfather and the stuff he needed out without raising questions. He had thought for a while on that one, but the answer hit when he was playing his grandfather in chess Friday afternoon. He could bring a chess set in, and if questioned, say that Grandpa wanted to play in his room. Gavin had one at home that he could use. Then on his way out, he would carry the bag, still with the set in it, along with some clothing his grandfather would need. He figured doing it twice would be enough.

He had asked Grandpa about the medications he took and if he had enough of them. His grandfather's medication was given to him daily by the nurses. It was the policy that all the residents' medications were handed out by the nurses and kept in a locked room. His grandfather took Aricept for his Alzheimer's and Lasix for his high blood pressure. Gavin couldn't see a way around that and felt that their plans would become derailed, but again it was his grandfather who thought of a way. He told Gavin that he would palm every other day's dose and save those pills for the trip. Gavin asked if it was safe if he didn't take the pills every day and he assured Gavin that it was.

Gavin hoped he had thought of everything, but remembered what his father said about vacations-that one cannot remember everything and something will be left. Gavin just hoped that the thing left would not be important.

In two days they were planning on going. Gavin had gone over to Roadkill's yesterday and checked out the van. The van was a mix of red and black. On the driver's side there were two larger windows that had been tinted. Several rust spots were scattered across both sides, but they didn't look too bad. Roadkill gave Gavin a ride in it and the engine sounded fine, although Gavin realized that he really didn't know what to listen for with a bad engine. To Gavin's pleasant surprise, the inside of the van didn't smell too bad. It seemed Roadkill had been busy cleaning it before Gavin's inspection. It was Roadkill who suggested Gavin look it over, which made Gavin feel even worse for not having kept in touch.

Roadkill agreed he would be ready to go by Tuesday. They would leave in the morning. Gavin planned on going to Lake View at nine and asking if he could take his grandfather for a walk. It wasn't unheard of; Gavin had done it before. He hoped the weather would be good enough for that excuse.

There had been only one little problem to overcome: what to do about his mowing job. He could have just left and said nothing, but there were several reasons not to do that. First, it was that it was his responsibility to his clients. He had never left them high and dry before. Second, if he just left without getting someone to cover, one of his clients might worry and call his parents. That was not acceptable to Gavin.

He thought about it for a while and then remembered Jordan Crawler. Jordan was in a grade below Gavin, and Gavin would have considered him for a friend if he wasn't so annoying.

Before school ended, Jordan had asked if he could join Gavin on his mowing job, and Gavin had told him he would think about it. Two days ago, Gavin called Jordan and told him that he needed someone to temporarily take over. Gavin told Jordan that if he did a good job, he would consider taking him on. Gavin actually felt a little grown up telling him that.

Jordan agreed and the next day, Gavin went around and introduced Jordan to his customers. He explained that he was taking a partner on for a little bit. Gavin said nothing about his planned trip because he didn't want anyone knowing. He had told Jordan to keep it quiet, and the kid wanted the job so bad that Gavin knew he would. Jordan had his own lawnmower and weed eater, so that wasn't going to be an issue. Gavin's mowing responsibility was taken care of for now.

Gavin found his grandfather in his room, as usual. After knocking, he walked in and didn't see his grandfather right away.

"Grandpa?' Gavin called out. There was no answer. He walked back to the bedroom and found his grandfather standing by his bed in his underwear. His body looked thin in the sunlight. He wasn't what Gavin used to remember when he was small. He remembered his grandfather being strong, lifting Gavin over his head when he was little. "Grandpa, are you okay?"

"Who-?" his grandfather started out saying as he turned to face Gavin. There was a blank stare on his grandfather's face that scared Gavin. "Wait, you're Gavin."

"Yes, it is me, Gavin," Gavin said and walked over to his grandfather. There was clothing on the bed, and Gavin picked out a shirt and pair of pants. He handed them to his grandfather, who took them but didn't put them on. "Go ahead, Grandpa. Put them on."

"Right!" his grandfather said in a loud voice like it was the best idea in the world. "Sorry, I don't know what happened there."

"Did you get breakfast?"

"Yes, I did. Afterwards I came back and started to get some clothes out, I think. Why am I getting clothes out?" Grandpa asked and that worried Gavin. He was having an episode. It had been a while since Gavin had seen his grandfather have one. He waited for a moment to see if his grandfather would remember. "I was getting clothes out for, for a trip."

"That's right. Have you told anyone about the trip?" Gavin asked.

"No, I know better than that," his grandfather said and started to put on his clothes. "Why did I take my clothes off?"

"Maybe you wanted to pack them," Gavin suggested. Grandpa started to laugh, and Gavin had to reach out to steady him before he fell. It seemed his grandfather was coming around, a lot quicker than usual too.

"Thursday, right?"

"Tuesday morning. Do you remember where we are going?" Gavin asked, testing his grandfather.

"Colorado," his grandfather said with some irritation. Then his face changed to a more contemplative look. "The name of the cabins we went to were the Cottages Along the Thompson."

"That is great, Grandpa," Gavin said. It was the first time he heard the name of the place. He would have to look it up to see if the place still existed and where it was.

"I have something for you," his grandfather said and went to his dresser. He opened the top drawer and pulled out a wad of money. "I told you I would get more."

"Wow! There is like $2,000 here!" Gavin said after he counted it out. Along with his, they had about $3,500, which should be enough. "Where did you get this? It was not from your account, was it?"

"No, it was not from my bank account. I can't access that anymore thanks to your father. Let's just say I have my ways, and when we get back, your father will have to pay someone back from my former account."

His father would be furious about what they were doing. Gavin did not want to think about what was going to happen when they returned from their little trip.

Gavin had never been grounded or spanked as a child, but there were other ways his parents punished him. The punishments usually involved taking something they thought he cared about away, but that actually didn't faze him. Sure he didn't like losing whatever was taken, but either he would get it back or he wouldn't. Soon his parents realized that method wasn't working and tried others. It wasn't like Gavin was a bad kid. It's just that punishments didn't deter the behavior like his parents hoped they would.

He had never done anything like what he was planning to do with his grandfather though. This was an entirely different stadium of trouble he was entering.

"Do you have more clothes for me?" Gavin asked, and his grandfather nodded. Gavin told his grandfather to pack for six days. He figured they would spend a few days down there and then head back.

If they ran out of clothes, they could always find a laundromat and wash them, even though Gavin had never washed clothes before. How hard could it be?

Gavin put the pile Grandpa indicated into his duffle bag and zipped it up. He had taken the medication that his grandfather needed on the last visit. There were enough doses to last three days, but his grandfather would take the meds every other day to make them last.

"Okay, let us go over one more time about tomorrow morning. I will come here at nine and then ask the nurses if we can go for a walk. We should probably go for another walk in a little bit so it does not look so strange."

"Okay," his grandfather responded. They had started going for walks on the last two visits so it wouldn't seem out of the blue tomorrow. "Where will your friend be?"

"Down the block waiting. Everything we need will be in the van," Gavin said. Roadkill told Gavin to bring along pillows and sleeping bags. Gavin was going to bring his pillow anyway because he needed it to sleep. He was very particular about the pillows and pillow cases he used when he slept. Gavin hoped they wouldn't have to sleep in the van, but that might have to be a possibility if a hotel wasn't available. "We will head north, to the Mackinac Bridge."

"That seems out of the way," his grandfather said.

"I don't want to take a direct route in case Dad figures out right away what happened to us. He'll alert the authorities and they will look on the most direct route."

"That's so nuts that it might actually work," Grandpa said with a smile. "Plus we get to see some of the country I haven't seen for a while or at all."

"Good, I am glad you agree," Gavin said and then told him the rest of the trip's itinerary. When he told Roadkill about the route, Roadkill had also questioned the indirectness of it. After Gavin explained why, Roadkill just shrugged his shoulders and said that Gavin was the boss.

Was he really in charge of this adventure? That fact actually made him feel proud and nervous at the same time. If anything went wrong, he would be the one to blame. That was what it meant to be the boss. When things went wrong, no matter what, it was the person in charge that got the axe. Gavin accepted that because he was the one that agreed to take his grandfather along.

Gavin then thought about Roadkill. Would Roadkill get in trouble for this? He shouldn't because he was just helping a friend out. If necessary, Gavin would go to bat for him as much as he could, but he knew his father would try to get Roadkill in as much trouble as he could.

Gavin wondered if he should just tell Roadkill it was off and find another way. The problem was, there wasn't another way to Colorado for them. This was it. If this trip failed, there would not be another chance because his father would make sure of that.

Gavin stayed with his grandfather for a little bit longer and then left. It was past five, and he would head home to complete the final preparations for the trip. Gavin was all packed; he had been for days. His bag had been hidden under his bed until last night when his mother came into his room and sat on his bed in a vain attempt to talk about his day. Gavin tried to play it cool, but his eyes kept going to under the bed. He thought for sure his mother would look and then ask why he had a packed bag.

She had stood up, walked to the door and then gave a glance back to the bed but didn't say anything. Perhaps she thought it was just a *Playboy* under there. Gavin didn't want to take any chances, so he moved his bag to the back of his closet.

He doubted that he would be able to sleep that evening with how nervous and excited he was. He felt like a plane in a holding pattern waiting to land in a storm. While the plane was in the holding pattern, everything was in limbo. He did not know if the result would be good or bad. Once the plane started to descend into the storm, then all bets were off. Tomorrow morning Gavin would be descending into his own storm.

There were so many questions swirling around him, and all of them couldn't be answered until the trip got underway. How would his dad respond? What kind of trouble was Gavin going to get into? He had no doubt that he would be in trouble. Would his dad call the police and have him arrested? That was a possibility.

Then there was his grandfather. How many times would Grandpa have his episodes? Gavin didn't lie to himself and think his grandfather would go the entire trip without an episode. Gavin just hoped that he would be able get his grandfather back on track after one of them. He had made a promise to his grandfather, and he intended on keeping it.

***

Bernie was having trouble sleeping as well. Everything seemed to be ready for tomorrow's departure. The money he had received was with the clothes he had gotten ready for the day. He had gone to Howard and told him he needed some money right away. Howard asked why, and Bernie told him it was just a family emergency. Howard had looked like he was going to press the issue, but he didn't. He gave him the money and Bernie promised to pay him back in a week or so. That was when he expected to be back from this little outing.

Bernie planned on there being trouble when he returned. Just what kind of trouble that was the question. How would Michael react when he found out that his son and father had taken off to Colorado? Bernie would do his best to keep the trouble off Gavin, but he knew that the boy would receive some. If that could be avoided, Bernie would try to help make that happen.

Again, he felt he had no choice. He felt that if he didn't go on this trip now, then who he was would be gone much sooner than later. Bernie knew what was going to happen to him. His brain cells were dying off every day, but if he could just keep his memories a little longer. Going on this trip would prove to him that he could remember what was important. If he just held on to a certain number of memories, maybe then he could feel human. The pictures were becoming meaningless to him, probably because he had looked at them so often. He needed more than just those pictures. Going to those actual locations should jar his mind.

Visiting the garage he worked at most of his life was out of the question because the company that bought him out had it torn down and replaced with a different building. The house that he lived with his wife was also gone. As soon as he sold it at Michaels' insistence, the new owners tore that down to put up one that met their needs.

His old life wasn't just fading away in his mind, it was also fading away in St. Clair Shores as well. He was hoping that the cabins were still there, but if not, the mountains would be. It was hard to tear those down. That one particular spot had to be there as well. He just couldn't quite picture the spot, but he knew it had played a big role in his life.

Bernie looked at the clock and saw that it was a quarter after ten. He was in his pajamas and sitting on the edge of his bed. The room was quiet, but his mind was not. His mind would not shut down enough for him to go to sleep. He could call down and get something to help him sleep, but he didn't want to do that. Sleeping pills always made him groggy in the morning. He wanted to try to be functioning enough that he didn't scare Gavin and his friend.

Gavin had told him a little about this Roadkill. Bernie decided to wait to form an opinion until he met this kid. It was an interesting nickname to say the least.

Bernie leaned back and tried to go to sleep. Shutting down his mind was nearly impossible. All he could see when he closed his eyes were mountains.

Chapter 9

Writing Entry for Friday, April 3

I left off on a cliffhanger. I wanted to see if you were really reading these entries or just assigned them. You did not ask me about it, so I am assuming it is the latter. I am going ahead and write about the death of Bucky Stevens and how it affected my grandfather.

They both were juniors in high school. I already wrote that they were inseparable and that Bucky spent a lot of time at my grandfather's house. I also alluded to Bucky's father being an alcoholic.

The year they were juniors, Bucky's father lost his job at the docks. You would think that would make a person reevaluate his or her life, but for Bucky's dad, all it did was make him drink even more. Where he got the money for booze, I do not know.

Bucky soon had to get his own job, so Grandpa did not see him as much. When my grandfather was able to hang out with him, Bucky appeared with more and more bruises. He told my grandfather exactly where they came from. My grandfather told his parents.

My great-grandfather went over to their house and confronted Bucky's father. From what my grandfather said it did not go well. I can imagine that many conversations like that would not go well. When my great-grandfather returned, he told Bucky that he was staying with them from now on. I asked Grandpa why the authorities were not called and he responded that it was the fifties and parents pretty much could do whatever they wanted to discipline their children.

So Bucky started living with Grandpa until Bucky had to return home to get some belongings after about a week. He had been wearing Grandpa's clothes for the time being but decided he wanted his own. I could understand that. I have never been too keen on wearing other people's clothing. Bucky went back for other items as well. He had had no contact with his father since the discussion with my great-grandfather.

Bucky went in the middle of the day because his father usually was a bar then. Bucky never told Grandpa's parents that he was going to go, or else they would have told him not to or they would have gone with him. He did not even want Grandpa to go with him, even though he offered. It was a spur of the moment decision, one that cost him his life.

Bucky never came back. Grandpa waited two hours and was going to call his parents when he heard fire trucks coming down the street. He looked out the window and saw smoke coming from the direction of the house that Bucky had shared with his father. Grandpa rushed out and ran over, but the house was completely engulfed, so he could not get close. He yelled out his friend's name over and over again. When the firemen arrived, all they could do was to make sure the surrounding houses would not burn down. The fire was so intense that they just had to wait it out.

It took six hours for the fire to die down enough to be put out. There was nothing left of the house. Two bodies were found. One was Bucky's of course, and the other was his father. It seems his father had not gone to the bar that afternoon. The bodies were badly burnt, but the police were still able to find a bullet hole in each of the skulls. They deduced that when Bucky arrived home, he was shot by his father and then his father poured gasoline around the house, lit a match, and then shot himself. Had my grandfather gone with Bucky, he probably would have been shot too.

Bucky's funeral was separate from his father's. My great-grandparents paid for Bucky's, not his father's. After Bucky's death, my grandfather went into a depression. His grades, which were not all that great anyway, got worse. The only thing he kept doing was tinkering with fixing cars. That was when he got a job at Al's Garage. He then put all his effort into that.

Grandpa says that Al's Garage saved his life. He said if he had not had that job there, he would have let the depression take complete control.

Grandpa did not finish his junior year. His parents did not agree with that move, but they did not try to stop him. School was not giving him what he needed like working on cars did. It might have been different if Grandpa did not have the skill he had, but he was very good at what he did. His parents understood that and did not stand in his way.

Grandpa had lost a good friend when Bucky was killed. That kind of relationship is hard to find, and he told me he never found it again. His relationship with my grandmother was of a different nature. Sure, Bucky and Grandpa were friends but there was obviously something more.

As I listen to my Grandpa talk about his relationship with Bucky, I feel a little jealous. I do not have a relationship like that and never have. I know I am socially awkward. I cannot help it. I do not know what to say to people. I want to talk about sailboats, but I am sure that most people are not all too interested in that subject. I see a person standing next to me, and I feel like I should say something. Usually nothing comes out or if some words do, I sound like a

complete idiot. As for finding a female to share my life with, well I am not even going to go there.

End of Entry

The morning arrived early for Gavin. He had managed to get some sleep, not his usual amount but enough. He lay in bed, hearing his parents move around upstairs. His father would get going early to work and his mother would follow shortly after. His sister was still be sleeping, which would benefit him. It took his parents half an hour more to finally leave. By that time, Gavin was dressed and sitting on the edge of his bed waiting.

The night before, Gavin risked looking up Cottages Along the Thompson on the home computer. He needed to know if the place was still there and get directions. At first Gavin was disappointed when he found out that there was no longer such a place, but his search did reveal that there was a resort in the cottages location. He felt that it would still work. Gavin knew he couldn't book any rooms, not without a credit card, but he thought he would think of something when they arrived. The name of the resort was Whispering Pines, and they did have cabins as well.

When he heard his mother leave, he got up, took the two duffle bags, and started upstairs. Upon opening the door to the kitchen, he found his sister sitting at the table having a bowl of Fruit Loops.

"What's that?" his sister immediately asked as she spied the bags.

"You are up early," Gavin said, choosing to ignore her question. "Why are you up early?"

"I'm going over to Jenny's to swim at her pool. What's in the bags?"

"Jenny does not have a pool," Gavin said. He mowed the lawn that was right next to Jenny Upland's house. "You are going to the lake!"

"Am not!" Pauline shouted.

His father didn't want them going to the lake to even swim, much less go on a boat. Gavin felt his father's fear was irrational but oddly justified after knowing the story. Pauline did not know the story, and Gavin wondered if he should tell her. He decided against it, mostly because it would take too much time to explain. They stared at each other for a moment and then Pauline said, "You're going to tell Mom and Dad, aren't you?"

"Tell you what," Gavin started out saying. Normally he would rat on his little sister. After all, she would do the same to him. "I will not say anything about the lake. But you do not say you saw me this morning, either. Deal?"

"That sounds too easy," Pauline said. She knew if she got caught in a lie about where she was going, she would be on house lockdown for a while. "What's in the bags?"

"Something for my job, that is all." It wasn't a lie. He considered it his job to get Grandpa to Colorado.

"Then why don't you want Mom and Dad to know I saw you with the bags this morning?" His sister wasn't a stupid girl by any means. The fact that her brother was going to give her a free pass at deception usually didn't come without a price. This price seemed too cheap to her. Gavin had to think of something that would placate her, but deception wasn't his specialty.

"Look, I was just trying to let you off without looking like a weenie. I thought by making this compromise, I could give you an out. If you do not want to take it, then fine. Let us call Mom or Dad right now."

Gavin hoped that it sounded sincere. There was no way he was calling either of his parents. He acted like he was going for the phone, and his sister stopped him.

"Fine, I'll take the deal," she said, in a sullen voice that always annoyed Gavin. "You won't tell Mom and Dad about my going to swim in the lake, and I won't say I saw you this morning."

"Agreed then. Each of us will not talk about the respective subjects."

"You sound like Dictionary.com," Pauline said, but the fight seemed to be out of her as she sat back at the table. "Maybe you should try using words people understand."

"I am sorry I do not speak chimpanzee for you," Gavin said and started to go out the door. He had intended on having breakfast, but now that Pauline was there, he wanted to make his exit as soon as possible. Before he took his final leave, he hesitated. "Just be careful."

"You sound like Dad. It's just a lake after all," she said.

Gavin left and walked out of the garage to the yard. The bus stop was three blocks away, and by the time he got there, the duffle bags felt like they weighed 100 pounds each. The driver gave his bags a funny look but didn't say anything to him as he carried them onto the bus.

The ride to the stop closest to Roadkill's house took 15 minutes, and by the time Gavin arrived, it was a quarter past eight. He had told his grandfather nine and worried he was running behind. Hopefully Roadkill was up and ready.

***

Sleep had not come easy to Bernie, but it did come. Morning came a lot harder, but it usually does to a person that had slept poorly. He had set his alarm for seven because he didn't want to miss breakfast. Everything had to look normal to the nurses at the home.

When he awoke, he knew where he was, which he took for a positive sign. After getting dressed, he headed down the dining area. Breakfast had started at six-thirty, so it was busy at the moment.

"Look at the early bird!" Howard shouted out when he caught sight of Bernie. "You rarely come down at this time!"

"If I had known your ugly face was here, I would have waited," Bernie said back, getting a laugh out of Howard and Carl.

"Hurry, get your food. I don't think we can keep all these old farts from taking your spot," Carl said, and Bernie went to get his meal.

It wasn't a big surprise that his spot was still there when he got back and sat down. Howard and Carl were deep in conversation about North Korea, and Bernie just ate. As he ate, he found his eyes constantly going to the clock. It was seven-thirty, and Gavin wasn't coming until around nine.

"Expecting a hot date?" Howard asked, surprising Bernie. He saw Bernie's confused look, so he said, "You keep watching the clock. So who is it?"

"I bet it is Frida from the third floor. She's been a little sweet on Bernie," Carl said with a smile. "Course, most of them are. He still has his hair."

"My grandson is coming over this morning. I think we are going to go for a walk," Bernie said, and it was the mostly the truth.

As he walked to the dining hall, he had looked out the window and saw the sun shining. It looked hot, but at least it wasn't raining.

"Little early for Gavin to be coming," Carl said. Leave it to Carl to take note of that. He was a retired detective after all.

"Yeah, he wanted to go for a walk in the morning because it would be cooler. Said he doesn't mind mowing in the heat," Bernie said, thinking quickly. "Someday he will mind, but he's young."

"Mayhap, I'll go with you. Could use a good walk myself," Howard said, alarming Bernie so much that it must have showed in his eyes. "Don't want company?"

"No, I'm fine with it. Gavin may not be. You know how he is."

"Thought he was fine with me, but I won't budge in on your walk. I can always take my own. Carl you interested?"

"Shut up, you old coot. You damn well know that I ain't interested in a walk. You would have to push me anyway, and we wouldn't even get down the block before you'd have a heart attack."

"Solo then," Howard said but was smiling. "Think I'll stay in and watch *The Price is Right*."

"Show ain't the same since Bob Barker left," Carl said.

"Still got pretty girls showing off all that crap, though," Howard said and all three nodded. "You want to join me, Carl?"

"What the hell else do I have to do?" Carl said. As the two were laughing, Bernie glanced at the clock again. It was seven-forty. Time was crawling by.

***

Roadkill did not answer the door when Gavin knocked. Gavin had skipped the front door and went right to the back door. He knocked again, this time louder and longer. The van was in the driveway, so Gavin was guessing Roadkill was sleeping.

"Shit!" Gavin heard come from inside. "I'm up! I'm up!"

Gavin waited outside for another five minutes and then the door opened, revealing a hurried Roadkill. He was dressed, but his hair was a mess. Actually it usually was anyway. He grabbed a trash bag and then came out.

"Crap, I'm not used to getting up this early!"

Gavin noted it was eight-forty. Roadkill jogged upstairs and Gavin thought he was going to put the trash bag in the garbage, but instead, he threw it in the back of the van. "All right, bag's in. Let's hit the road!"

"That was your clothes?" Gavin said, staring at the bag.

"Hell, yeah. Who needs fancy luggage? *Glad* works for me all the time!"

Gavin shrugged and loaded his two duffle bags which looked almost alien next to the plastic trash bag. Roadkill climbed into the driver's seat, and Gavin took the passenger seat next to him. He couldn't believe this was actually happening. They were going to pick up his grandfather and then start for Colorado. The van fired to life and they were off.

As they drove down the street, Roadkill pointed to something on the road. It looked like a squashed animal of some sort.

"Squirrel," Roadkill said, and Gavin nodded. He wasn't too impressed because even in its condition, the animal had to be a squirrel. What other animal was that size and found on a city street? "Right away, man. That's gotta be good luck!"

Gavin didn't think it was all that lucky for the poor squirrel.

***

It was past nine o'clock. Granted, it was only five minutes past but still no Gavin. Bernie was back in his room, sitting in his easy chair. *The Price is Right* was on the television, but it wasn't being watched.

Gavin was always on time. He could set a watch by that kid. So why was he late on this, of all days? Bernie didn't think his grandson changed his mind, but something else might have happened. Had Michael found out about their plans? If that happened, then Bernie could expect to see his son at the door soon.

A knock came, and Bernie held his breath.

"It's open," Bernie managed to say. The door opened, revealing his grandson.

"Sorry, I am late, Grandpa. Roadkill slept in," Gavin whispered. Bernie nodded and stood up. "Are you ready for our walk?"

"You bet I am," Bernie said. He realized that he was crossing the point of no return, but that did not make a difference. "Let's go."

The two of them walked toward the front door together and stopped at the receptionist's desk.

"What a nice surprise to have your grandson come in the morning!" the receptionist, a Kerry Willows this time, said. "He tells me you two are going to go and enjoy the morning!"

"Yes, we are," Bernie said and smiled. He could feel himself shaking a little, but if Kerry noticed, she didn't say anything.

"How far are you going to go?"

"Just down the street, maybe look at the lake a little," Gavin said. The boy sounded nervous. Bernie knew then that the two of them would never be robbing a bank together. "We should be back in half an hour."

"Okay, just be careful and have fun," Kerry said with the same smile on her face.

She looked back down at some paperwork, which was an indication that Gavin and Bernie could leave. Gavin opened the door for Bernie, and he walked outside. He realized it had been over a week since he had been outside. He couldn't believe that was true, but it was. There really wasn't a reason to go outside much around here.

"Well, step one is done," Bernie said as they started walking away from Lake View. It was a nice morning out, but there was a feeling in the air that said the day was going to get hot.

"Step one? More like step twelve," Gavin said, and Bernie knew his grandson was not telling a joke. Gavin probably had gone through eleven steps before getting his grandfather out. "Roadkill is parked down the street some. Did not want him too close. Do not want people linked to Lake View to see us get in."

"Smart idea," Bernie said and looked down the street. He saw a van parked there and immediately recognized it as a Dodge Conversion. He couldn't tell what year it was, though from this distance. From the outside, the van looked like it had seen better days, but Bernie knew what mattered was what was under the hood. He found himself longing to take a look at the van's engine. It was a feeling he hadn't had for quite some time. He took it as a good sign about his mental health.

"That is the van," Gavin said even though Bernie had already figured it out. When they got close to the van, someone got out of the driver's side and waited by it. Bernie assumed that the person was the aforementioned Roadkill. The young man was dressed in a black shirt that had 'Megadeth' written on it. He was also wearing black shorts with black shoes. Bernie guessed there was a theme there.

Bernie knew if Roadkill were to walk into Lake View, most of the residents would have judged him already. He tried not to be like that, but it was hard at times. Roadkill's face was covered with a beard which made him look older than 18, which Gavin said he was. His hair looked as if it hadn't seen a comb in about three years.

"Grandpa this is Roadkill."

"Please to meet you, Roadkill," Bernie said and held out his hand. "I want to thank you right now for helping me out."

"Pleasure's all mine," Roadkill said and shook Bernie's hand. The grip was firm but not too firm, and Bernie liked that. "Young Gavin here has told me about your predicament. You can consider me your chauffeur."

"I would help you out if I could, but my driving skills lately have been severely questioned," Bernie said, but Roadkill just waved his left hand in the air like the subject didn't matter.

"We probably should get going. I do not want anyone from Lake View seeing us," Gavin said, and he was looking around as he spoke.

Roadkill opened the door that led to the back of the van. It opened with a loud squeak, as if it wasn't used very often.

"Do you need help in, sir?" Roadkill asked, and Bernie shook his head, no. He wondered if Roadkill was always this polite or if it was just a show.

Bernie climbed in and saw that there were cushioned benches in the back, along with some bucket chairs. Between the benches were two duffle bags and a plastic trash bag. Bernie recognized the duffle bags as the ones he had when he returned home from Vietnam. He had given them to Gavin to use a long time ago. Gavin had also used one to smuggle his clothing out from Lake View. There was a distinct aroma to the inside, one he recalled smelling before, but couldn't quite place what it was or when he had smelled it before.

Bernie selected the chair behind the passenger seat and settled in. It had been a long time since he had gone on a trip or even sat in a vehicle other than the Lake View shuttle bus. Roadkill and Gavin got in, and the van started up. Bernie was glad to hear that the engine was running well. His ears picked up some issues with it, but they were minor.

"And, here we go!" Roadkill said, putting the van into drive. They had truly passed the point of no return.

* * *

It was one day away from August, and Michael wished it was still the middle of June. He had accomplished a lot over the summer, but there was still a lot left to get finished before school started.

It was ten o'clock in the morning and he had just gotten out of a meeting with the administration staff at the school. All of them had been holdovers from the last principal, so they were comfortable with each other. Michael saw the pros and cons of having them return, and he thought it was probably better for him that they were still at school.

As he was walking to his office, Patty, who was on the phone, saw him and waved him over. He heard her tell the caller that Michael had just walked in. Putting her hand over the receiver, she said, "It's Lake View. They have a concern about your father."

Michael's forehead crinkled in confusion and worry as he took the phone.

"This is Michael Pierce."

"Mr. Pierce, this is Kerry from Lake View, and we are worried about your father. Your son Gavin came this morning and took Bernie for a walk. That was right after nine. They have not come back yet," the voice said on the phone. Michael had seen and heard Kerry many times, and she always sounded cheery. She didn't sound that way currently. "They told us the walk would only be half an hour."

"Did you send someone out to look for them?" Michael asked, while Patty looked on with concern.

"Of course, we did. James Parsons, an orderly here, went to look. He just came back and said there is no sign of either of them."

Michael tried to think if there were any businesses around Lake View that Gavin would have taken his grandfather to but came up empty. Where the hell were they?

"Could they have just gone to a nearby business? A restaurant perhaps?" Michael asked, hoping that was just the case, though it would be unlike Gavin to do that because he knew the workers at the home would worry.

"There isn't any place like that around here, not in decent walking distance."

"Let me make some calls, and I will call you back," Michael said and then hung up.

"What happened?" Patty asked as he hung up the receiver.

"Nothing, hopefully. My son took my father on a walk and hasn't returned. They're half an hour overdue. Probably lost track of time."

"Do you need to go and see to this?" That was a good question. Michael felt conflicted at the moment. It could be nothing but a misunderstanding and if that was the case, he would lose some valuable time at work. It also could be something big, and if he didn't take the time to figure it out, it could end badly. "It's quite understandable if you did."

"I'm going to make a few phone calls and go from there," Michael responded and walked to his office. He took out his cell phone and brought up his wife's number. He wished that Gavin had a cell phone, but the boy had no interest and Michael hadn't pushed the issue. Nancy answered on the third ring, sounding surprised that Michael had called.

"Have you heard anything from Gavin?" Michael said after saying his hellos.

"No, should I have?" his wife said over the phone. Concern had crept in her voice. "What's going on?"

"Lake View called and said that Gavin came by around nine and took my dad for a walk. They haven't come back yet."

"That's not like Gavin."

"What? Not coming back or going over there in the morning?" Michael asked. He had just realized the fact that Gavin had gone over there in the morning and not the afternoon. What was that about?

"Both. Have you called the house?"

"Not yet. Was going to do that next. Can you call Pauline on her phone to see if she knows anything about this?"

"Sure. I'll do it right after we hang up," Nancy said and then the conversation was over. Michael dialed the house number next and listened as the rings kept coming. Either no one was home, or if they were, they weren't answering.

Michael wanted to get rid of the phone at home, but with Gavin not having one, couldn't. He waited a few minutes and was about to call Nancy when she beat him to the punch.

"Hello," Michael said into the phone.

"Pauline says she hasn't seen Gavin all day."

"Damn it," Michael said quietly into the phone. "Where is that kid?"

"What are you going to do? Go over to Lake View?"

"I'm going to call them back first. I don't know if I'll go over there now. I might just give it some time to see if they wander back in."

"Don't give it too much time, Michael," Nancy said and then they said their goodbyes.

Michael called Lake View and Kerry answered the phone. He asked if there was any new news and was told there wasn't. Michael told her that he had come up empty with trying to locate Gavin. Looking at the time, he saw that it was ten-thirty. It was a little early for lunch, but he thought he'd go anyway. Telling Kerry he would be there within the half hour, he ended the call. He would use his lunch hour and hopefully find out what happened to his son and father.

Chapter 10

Writing Entry for Friday, April 10

My grandfather is surprisingly religious. I know that sounds like a strange thing to write, but one would not know that about my grandfather unless you really got to know him. I do not mean that he is one of those extremists that blow themselves up for their faith, or that he stands on a corner pounding a Bible and preaching to all the sinners. No, I just mean that he hides the fact that he has a spiritual side quite well.

He used to go to church every Sunday. Quite a feat for a Lutheran, I'm told. I know of some Lutherans that only go on Christmas and Easter. My grandfather said that he knew one guy that went so little that the pastor had changed since the last time he attended. The next time the guy went to church, he thought he was in the wrong one!

It was my grandmother that made my grandfather so religious. She did not force him to attend church and believe in all that stuff, but it was the fact he had met here and married her that did it. I have told you that my grandfather has had two special relationships in his life–Bucky and my grandmother. I also said that those two relationships were different. My grandmother was a churchgoer when Grandpa met her. At that time, my Grandpa was Methodist, but he converted after returning from Vietnam. His parents were not too disappointed since they were not every week goers with their own religion.

After my grandmother died, Grandpa still attended church on a weekly basis. My family went to the same church, so we would often go with him. I did not mind going to church then, not like now. My beliefs have changed since that time, but that is understandable since most young children's beliefs are forced on them by their parents. My grandfather stopped going to church on a weekly basis when he was put into Lake View. He started to miss a week, then two, and sometimes whole months. Soon he was one of those Christmas and Easter attenders.

I asked him why he stopped going, and he told me he really did not know. He said it was like he forgot that it was important or something. How can one do that? To forget something that is supposed to be as important as religion? Was it the Alzheimer's kicking in? Grandpa did not seem quite affected by not going. At least he never said anything about missing church.

I found that strange because it had been a big part of his life. He even was a volunteer there. It was not like he could not get there on Sundays. Lake View had a shuttle that would take its residents to whatever church they were a part of, within reason of distance of course. It just seemed that the part of his brain that enjoyed being spiritual had died away.

Oh, it would flare up every once and a while, but then die down again.

That was when I stopped going to church as well. That was when I started to question if there was a great powerful deity too. If there is a God, how can he (or she) allow that to happen to someone like my grandfather? How can God take away the part of Grandpa's mind that worshipped him? How can God take away a person's memories of his or her loved ones? Is that fair? Is it right?

End of Entry

+ + +

The landscape flew by at 70 miles per hour. So far all Gavin had done was look out the window. He had brought books, but they were in the back in one of the duffle bags. They were three and a half hours into their trip and only 60 miles from the Mackinac Bridge. All in all, Gavin thought they were making decent time. They had stopped three times, one time to get gas and for all three of them to use the bathroom. Lunch had been some food they bought at the gas station. His grandfather actually slept a good portion of the trip, and Gavin wondered if he hadn't slept well last night either.

Gavin was feeling pretty good about the trip all in all. By now, he knew that his grandfather would have been reported missing at Lake View and his father would have been notified.

What Gavin wasn't sure about was whether they would think they had left the city or not. Gavin wanted to listen to the radio to find out if there was a report on their disappearance, but the problem was, the van's radio didn't work. Grandpa had volunteered to look at it, but Gavin didn't want to take the time to do so. Perhaps when they stopped for the night. Gavin wasn't sure if him kidnapping his own grandfather would make the news or not, but there were stranger stories on the air. He thought kidnapping was a harsh term, but what else would it be called in the eyes of the law?

As they drove on Interstate 75 towards the bridge, Roadkill seemed to be having a good time driving; he hadn't complained once yet. He seemed to be keeping a tally of animals they have seen so far on the highway. So far the strangest animal they had seen dead was a Holstein cow. It wasn't like Roadkill kept a physical account, which would have been strange. He just kept a count in his head.

"Should we stop at Mackinaw City?" Roadkill asked. Mackinaw City was the town that was right before the five mile long bridge. It was a good idea. Gavin felt he needed to stretch his legs, and he knew they needed to stop frequently for his grandfather.

"That sounds good," Gavin replied. It was two-thirty and so far the sun was still holding strong. The van did have air conditioning, but they used it sparingly because Roadkill had said it could give out at any moment. The windows were halfway down and the wind felt good on Gavin's face. He was excited to see the bridge again; the last time he saw it was when he was nine. He remembered how awed he was going over it. Five miles of bridge was an amazing human accomplishment. It saved a lot of time by connecting the two parts of Michigan.

"Woodchuck," Roadkill said, and Gavin's eyes went to the road. There indeed was a brown, furry lump coming up.

"Could be a beaver," Gavin said.

"No, it's a woodchuck. No flat tail," Roadkill responded. Gavin wanted to protest that the tail was underneath, but knew it was futile. "Besides, I know beavers." That was followed by a wink, which Gavin caught.

"Do you like beavers?"

"You bet I do. Nothing better than a fine beaver." Roadkill laughed after he said it. "Been awhile since I've seen one though."

"They have them at the zoo," Gavin said. He liked the zoo when he was little. His mom would take him there every other week, and he would walk around looking at all the animals. It was quite relaxing. He realized that he hadn't been to the zoo in years. "You could see some there."

"If only that was possible!" Roadkill said and laughed again. Gavin was going to point out that it was possible but decided against it. There was something he was missing. Perhaps Roadkill had been banned from the zoo for some reason or another. Gavin didn't want to embarrass Roadkill by prying into the matter. They passed by the aforementioned roadkill, but Gavin didn't get a good look at it to prove Roadkill wrong.

"So, Gavy, things seem to be going well," Roadkill said. "I know it's early yet, but so far so good."

"Yeah," Gavin responded. It was early in the trip. The first day of a long journey usually went well with everyone in high spirits of anticipation. The true test would come in the morning when they resumed their trip. Gavin didn't even know where they would stay tonight. They would drive until evening and then see where they were. He didn't want to tire Roadkill out too much. He knew of the stories of overtired drivers and what could happen.

When they had gotten ten miles out of Mackinaw City, Gavin moved to the seat next to his sleeping grandfather. He gently shook his grandfather to wake him up. His grandfather's eyes opened, and Gavin did not see any recognition in there.

"Grandpa, we are going to be stopping soon," Gavin said in a low voice.

"What? Where am I?" his grandfather asked, his voice sounding disoriented. He looked around, and his face got worried. "Whose car is this?"

"We are coming to the Mackinac Bridge. We are in Roadkill's van. We left this morning," Gavin told him. We are on our way to Colorado."

"Oh, yeah," Grandpa said and seemed to settle down. He looked around again and then nodded his head. "That's right. We're taking the scenic route."

"Yeah, the scenic route," Roadkill said from up front. "That's a way to say it."

"What time is it?" Grandpa asked and Gavin told him. "What city are we stopping in?"

"Mackinaw City. It's the one right before we get on the bridge."

"That's right. I took your grandmother there a few times. Your dad, aunt, and uncle too. There's a nice park right before the bridge. I believe they have some kind of fort there."

"Did you want to go there, Grandpa?" Gavin asked. Gavin had been there himself when he had gone with his family. It was the Colonial Michilimackinac Park. A replica fur trading post had been constructed there, using a map of the original one.

"No, that's okay. I imagine time is against us, and we can't stop at every little memory we come to."

"If you really want to, Mr. Pierce, we could swing it," Roadkill said. "My dad took me there once. It's one of the few good memories I have from my father."

"What happened to your father?" Gavin asked. He had never heard Roadkill talk about his father before.

"Beat the shit out of my mom and then left when I was 11. He was a good man until he started drinking," Roadkill said and then was silent.

"I'm sorry to hear that. I had a friend whose father was a heavy drinker," Grandpa said. "Would you like to stop?"

"No, actually maybe it would be better if we continue on," Roadkill said, not looking back. His voice sounded strange to Gavin.

"That's fine then," Grandpa told Roadkill. "And please call me Bernie."

"Okay, Mr. Pierce, I mean Bernie."

"What is your real name? Surely, it's not Roadkill." Grandpa asked. Gavin had always known Roadkill to be *Roadkill*.

"It's Clarence Jr.," Roadkill said. "I don't use that name anymore. It was my father's."

"Okay, I'll keep calling you Roadkill then."

They drove into Mackinaw City and stopped at a McDonalds. Since it was a nice day, they decided to go to the nearest park to eat their food. Since they were between two Great Lakes, the air smelled of lake water. Gavin didn't mind. After all he was used to it.

The park had a playground in it with a few small children playing. There were some parents with them. They looked at Roadkill first, looked wary and then saw Gavin's grandfather and the worry dissipated. It seemed that since there was an elderly man that looked harmless with the two rowdy teenage boys, it was okay.

The park wasn't next to one of the lakes, which disappointed Gavin somewhat. He have would liked to have seen the boats on the lake, but he knew he would see some when they went over the bridge.

"Well, I think it's time to hit the road again," Roadkill said after throwing the garbage away. "We have a long bridge to cross."

"Make sure you have the right change to pay the toll at the end," Gavin's grandfather said. "That way we can sail through."

"Aw, man! They have cameras," Roadkill said and his words alarmed Gavin. He hadn't thought of that.

"It is too late to switch routes," Gavin said.

"I wouldn't worry about that," said Grandpa. "By the time they would see the van on the cameras, we'll be long gone. I bet they don't even think we left the city yet. When they come across the bridge's surveillance system, we'll probably be in Colorado." Gavin calmed down some because his grandfather made sense.

The three of them got into the van again and soon were underway. They arrived at the bridge a few minutes later and started to cross. The speed limit was 45 miles per hour, and Roadkill made certain he obeyed it.

Gavin watched out the window and looked at the water. There were several boats on the water, many of which were sailboats. All of the sailboats were personal craft, and a few of them were of the bigger variety. He looked behind him and saw his grandfather staring out at the water as well.

Was he thinking about the sailboat he had been in when it capsized, killing his youngest daughter? Was he thinking about what he could have done differently? Gavin wondered if that was one memory his grandfather would gladly get rid of.

Soon they came to the first of what Gavin had called a fake island when he was nine. It was a spot in the bridge that extended out some and had emergency supplies for cars that broke down. Gavin knew that on the other end was another 'fake island.'

As they rode along, Gavin found it hard to believe that the Mackinac Bridge was only the fifth longest bridge in the world. It felt like it should have been the first. It truly was a magnificent piece of engineering.

"I've forgotten how great this bridge is," his grandfather said, seemingly mirroring Gavin's thoughts.

"This is cool," Roadkill agreed. They traveled the remaining time on the bridge in silence, just taking in everything. The other side came way too soon for Gavin, and soon the toll booth was coming up. There was only one side that had the toll because it covered both lanes. One could not do a U-turn to try to skip out on the toll because there was a police force present.

The line going north wasn't too long and soon it was their turn to pay. Gavin gave Roadkill the four dollars, and he gave it to the attendant. That was it. They were on the north peninsula of Michigan.

Gavin got out his notebook that had the travel plans in it.

"We should be coming up to Highway 2 in a few miles. Go west on there," he said.

It wasn't an interstate, but it was the closest roadway that went west. Gavin had hopes they could maybe make it to Shawano, but that was five hours away. Marinette was closer, but Gavin wanted to get as far as they could on day one.

"How are you doing, Grandpa?"

"I haven't felt this good in a long time," Grandpa said. "Boys, I can never thank you enough for doing this for me."

"It has been a good day so far," Gavin said and smiled. He hoped every day of the journey would go this well, but he knew that probably wasn't going to happen.

***

Michael had a headache. His head was currently in his hands, and he was staring at the floor of the St. Clair Shores police station. He was in the office of Detective George Wellington. Detective Wellington was typing away on his computer at the moment. The detective was a big man and his hulk wasn't diminished by sitting behind the desk. The man looked like he would have been more comfortable playing defensive end for the Detroit Lions. Michael wondered where such a man found suits.

"So you think the two of them are together," Detective Wellington said in his deep voice after a moment. Michael had gone through this already with the patrol officer earlier but managed to keep his impatience in check.

"Yes, I do. Gavin went to pick up my father this morning and they went for a walk," Michael said. His years in high school administration were paying off as he held onto his patience. He had gone to the police department at four in the afternoon. It was currently five-thirty. When he had gone to Lake View, he talked with the administrator who told him that the morning had been normal. The only thing that was out of the ordinary was that Gavin had come in the morning and not the afternoon. Michael checked out his father's room and didn't see anything different. That was until he opened the drawers to the dresser. The drawers seemed emptier than they should have been. He thought his father had more clothing than that. He decided to keep a mental note on that and went back to see the administrator.

Michael did not make it back to work that afternoon. He drove to the Nautical Mile on the off chance Gavin had taken his father there. He hadn't been to the Mile in a long time, but wasn't surprised to see a lot of people there. There was no sign of either his son or his father.

He went home and looked around his son's bedroom. His son's drawers were not as empty as his fathers, but Michael couldn't recall if Gavin had more clothes than that or not.

After the house, he went to the police station. At first they were not all that helpful. His father and son had only been missing since nine that morning and the rule of thumb was 24 hours. Michael felt he couldn't wait that long. He persisted on getting the matter checked out, and after explaining his father had Alzheimer's, the situation changed. That was when he was sent to Detective Wellington.

"So, where do you think they could have gone?" the detective asked.

"First I thought the Nautical Mile, and I did check that out, to no avail."

"Why the Mile?"

"My son likes to go there a lot. He likes to watch the sailboats," Michael said and hated how that made Gavin sound like a little boy. "He's 17, but has slight autism."

"Autism?"

"A social disorder. With Gavin it's not too bad. He just has some small quirks, like liking sailboats."

"I know what autism is, Mr. Pierce. So your autistic son and Alzheimic father are missing together," Detective Wellington said with a raised eyebrow. "How much trouble can they get into?"

"I'm more worried about what might happen to them. My father's Alzheimer's is in the middle stage where he forgets minor things from time to time. My son doesn't always see certain situations like other people do. In fact a week ago, we had an argument about my father…" Michael stopped. He was thinking back to that disagreement he had with Gavin about taking his father to Colorado. "No, it can't be."

"What can't be, Mr. Pierce?" Michael thought for a moment and then decided it would be best to tell Wellington what happened. As he was talking, Detective Wellington kept silent and listened. When Michael was finished, the detective said, "Is it possible that your son and father went off to Colorado together?"

"My first answer would be, no way. But the more I think of it, it actually makes sense."

"Why would your son and father do this?"

"My dad wanted me to take him there this summer, but I just got my first job as a principal and don't have time. My son argued with me about it and could have decided to take it upon himself to take his grandfather to Colorado." Michael couldn't believe that it was possible, but now that he thought more about it, it was. "Gavin was upset with the fact that I couldn't do it. I never thought *he* would."

"Couple of questions, Mr. Pierce. Does your son have a cell phone?" Michael shook his head no. "Can your son drive?"

"*No*, to that as well. He had his permit but never took the test for his license. My father hasn't driven for five years and doesn't have a car anymore," Michael said. He knew without a valid driver's license, there was no way to rent a car.

"Okay, so they could have taken a bus or a plane. That's easy enough to check into. The next question is that of money. Did the two have access to any?"

"My father's account is under my name now. My family thought it was for the best with his illness and all. My son does have a bank account, but I am listed on it as well and would be notified if a large amount was taken out."

"How large?"

"Over $500," Michael said and then thought for a moment. "May I use your computer for a moment?"

"Looking up his account?"

"Yes," Michael said and Detective Wellington led him around to use the computer that was on his desk. Michael logged into his bank's site and then brought up Gavin's account. He quickly discovered that $1,500 had been taken out over a course of three days. "Damn, their system of letting me know has a flaw. Gavin removed $1,500 over three days."

"That's not enough for two plane tickets. Must be by bus then," Wellington said as Michael logged out of the bank's website. He felt a vibrating in his pocket and took his phone out. Nancy was calling him.

"Can I take this?" Michael asked and the detective waved him on. He answered the call and asked if there had been any word from Gavin. His wife said there hadn't but that she called because she had just talked with Pauline and their daughter fessed up. She had seen Gavin that morning carrying two full duffle bags. Michael thanked her for calling and said he would be home after he was done at the police station. He then filled Wellington in on the call.

"Top that off with your father's light drawers, and I think part of the mystery is solved," Wellington said as he took control of his chair again. "I'll look into the bus idea. They'll give me the list easier than they would you."

"Thank you, Detective," Michael said and wrote his number down on a piece of paper. "Please call me anytime with news. What should I be doing?"

"Not much, I'm afraid. Let me know if you think of any more ideas about how the two of them might be traveling. That reminds me, does Gavin have any friends that can drive?" Wellington asked and Michael thought for a moment.

"None that I can think of," Michael answered.

Chapter 11

Writing Entry for Friday, April 23

I have written about my grandfather's time in Vietnam before and mentioned how lucky he was to be stationed where he was at. Saigon was out of the action for most of the war, up until the end when the United States left and North Vietnam overran the south. His time in the motor pool kept him busy, but he did find some time to himself. I mentioned he stayed away from houses of ill repute and did not do drugs. He drank a little, but nothing that would get him in trouble. Grandpa just wanted to serve his time and be done. There was, however, a time over there that he did get in some trouble.

I stated early on in my writings that my grandfather could fix anything. It was his gift and skill. One day while he was off duty, he was walking around Saigon and came across a 1945 Harley Davidson Knucklehead. The motorcycle was not a part of the military, but a privately owned one.

It was in great disrepair. The Knucklehead had been black at one time, but the color had faded away to a dull gray. Both tires were flat, and Grandpa thought he noticed it missing some parts, but could not be sure until getting a closer look.

The motorcycle was tucked away behind a restaurant in the back alley. From the looks of it, it had been there for quite some time. Grandpa was actually shocked to stumble across it in Vietnam of all places. Harley Davidson Knucklehead motorcycles looked bulky, but they had power. Older ones were worth some money if they are in good condition.

After finding that gem of a ride, Grandpa went into the restaurant to see who owned the bike. Once he found someone that spoke passable English, since Grandpa only knew a few words in Vietnamese, he found out that the bike had been left there years ago. The kids that lived around the area would sit on it and play.

Grandpa asked if he could take it, but the owner frowned and said the kids would be disappointed. Grandpa asked if ten bucks would curb their disappointment. The man said it would and that he would give the money to them. Grandpa knew that the man would not, but still forked over the money.

The next problem he had was how to get the motorcycle back to base. With the flat tires, pushing it would be next to useless. As he was pondering the dilemma, he saw a military transport coming down the street. It was empty and if they would give him and the bike a ride, it was perfect. It took only minor convincing, namely cartons of cigarettes that my grandfather did not smoke anyway, and soon the bike was loaded.

Grandpa had the bike dropped off at the motor pool, where he hoisted it to the back and threw some canvas over it. It would be two days later when he could first assess it. Even though he told me most of the details, I'll spare you most of them because when Grandpa talks about his fixing days, he mentions every part and every fine tune he put in. Let us just say that it took my grandfather four months to even get the engine running. He got the spare parts from around the motor pool and by finding them at other installations. Some parts were not meant for a Knucklehead, but Grandpa got them to work anyway.

The last thing left to do to the bike was to give it a new paint job. Basically, the only color they had was olive green, and Grandpa was not too keen on that color. He had to do a lot of wheeling and dealing to get the black he desired. All together it took him seven months to get that Knucklehead to where he wanted it.

Grandpa was over at Vietnam for a total of eleven months and found the bike two months into his tour. Grandpa said that working on restoring that bike was what kept him from going crazy. He missed my grandmother badly and wrote to her every chance he got. The bike was a surrogate, one that would not get him a disease or make him feel guilty.

Grandpa said he only rode that bike two times after getting it completely restored. I bet he was quite the sight riding down the crowded streets of Saigon. Grandpa said the majority of the traffic on the streets were military vehicles or bicycles. That Knucklehead must have made quite the noise as well. I bet it scared the heck out of the South Vietnamese that were within hearing range. Probably thought the Viet Cong were marching down the street, which they would during the Tet Offensive in 1968. Thankfully Grandpa was long gone by then.

Eventually, Grandpa's bike caught the eye of a certain four-star general who had just been stationed in Vietnam. Through a series of underlings, it was made quite clear that Grandpa's restoration project was wanted by this general. Grandpa could have put up a fuss, but knew it would not do any good. The Army would just say that he should not have the bike in the first place and take it away.

So Grandpa made it a gift for this general. What happened to this bike, Grandpa never knew. The general was later recalled back to the states after the debacle that was the Tet Offensive. If the bike went with him, that was unknown to Grandpa.

When Grandpa's service came up, he was a little worried that it would be extended because of the war going on. It wasn't. Grandpa liked to think that his motorcycle was the reason he was able to go home. He wanted to think that the general had a hand in his tour not being extended.

Grandpa left Vietnam and a few years later, it really went to hell.

When he returned back to St. Clair Shores, Grandpa was able to start his life again with the woman he loved. Many young men who went to Vietnam were not so lucky.

End of Entry

+ + +

The bed felt different to Bernie as his body started to wake up for the day. The room felt strange as well. He opened his eyes, and found that there was someone in bed with him. He tried to get up, but got tangled in the sheets and fell out, his head hitting the wall.

This wasn't his room at Lake View. Where was he? Who was in the bed with him? Another form was on the floor with blankets on him. Who was that?

"Grandpa, are you okay?" the person in the bed asked. Bernie thought he recognized that voice, but the pain in his head was making him foggy.

"Who? Where?" Bernie said and knew his words were jumbled, nearly incoherent.

"Grandpa, it is okay," the voice said again.

Gavin! It was Gavin, his grandson. He calmed down a little. "Are you okay?

"I, I don't know," Bernie said. He felt his head and didn't find any blood on it. There wasn't a lump either. He felt lucky about that. When one is 75, falling could be deadly serious. "What is going on?"

"We are in a motel room at Shawano. It is the start of our second day's journey to Colorado. Roadkill is the one on the floor," Gavin said as he got out of bed. Bernie saw that Gavin was wearing pajama tops and bottoms. He seemed to recall that the one Gavin called Roadkill laughed good-naturedly the night before when he saw his grandson wearing them. "Are you remembering?"

"Yeah, I think so. Your jammies are helping me recall," Bernie said, and saw Gavin relax. Bernie also took note of the pillow Gavin was using; it was his personal one. Roadkill made mention of that too. "Just got a little disoriented there."

"Okay, that is understandable," Gavin said and went over to Roadkill's still sleeping form. "Hey, Roadkill! Time to wake up!"

Bernie tried to remember Roadkill's real name. He thought he heard it yesterday. It had something to do with the young man's father. Clarence Jr.-that was it. His father was a deadbeat. The situation reminded him of his childhood friend, Bucky Stevens. Yesterday was the first day in years that he had thought about his old friend. It was funny how things would strike a memory like a match.

Now that he thought about Bucky, some memories were coming back to him. Bernie knew that all his lost memories would not return. It was not the nature of Alzheimer's. The memories he was recalling were stored somewhere in his mind that had just lay dormant for whatever reason. Yesterday he thought he was doing better, but after this morning, he realized he was not. The mornings seemed to be bad for him. That was when his disorientation would really hit him.

"Roadkill! Get up!" Gavin said and shook the sleeping form again.

"What! What time is it?" a voice said from under the blankets.

"It is seven-thirty," Gavin responded.

"Really? Hell, it's early then. Let me sleep till ten," Roadkill said. Gavin shook him again. "All right, all right! I'm getting up."

It seemed Bernie wasn't the only person that had issues in the morning.

"I want to get on the road by eight. We have a lot of road to cover today. It would be great to make it to Fargo before stopping for the day," Gavin said. "Grandpa, do you want to use the bathroom first?"

"That would be nice," Bernie said, glad that his grandson had given him the opportunity. He had gotten up during the night to go, and strangely enough, didn't have any issues about where he was at. Of course, the bathroom was in the similar place to where his was in his room at Lake View. That might have made the difference last night.

He turned on the light and immediately saw himself in the mirror. He looked younger than he last looked. Perhaps it was just a trick of the eyes, but he swore that he did. Could it be the journey he was on? Was that even possible? It didn't matter. Bernie knew he couldn't keep having mornings like this one. He had to think before doing what he did. He needed to find a way that would help him remember where he was when he was on this trip. Not for him, but for his grandson.

***

"So, where are we stopping for lunch?" Roadkill asked as they were 20 miles out of St. Paul, Minnesota.

The sky was finally clearing from a morning shower, but the roads were still wet from the downpour they had driven through. They had been on the road for three hours and had to stop once because the rain had been coming down so hard.

Gavin looked back at his grandfather and got a smile from the elderly man in return. The feeling of the trip wasn't like yesterday. There seemed to be more of a resignation of the long road ahead today.

"Where do you think we should stop?" Gavin asked. This was his first trip to Minnesota, but he found it looked much like Michigan and Wisconsin. There were a lot of trees.

"Getting sick of McDonald's," Roadkill said. They had eaten at the Golden Arches once yesterday and then again for breakfast.

"I did not know your palate was so refined," Gavin said and that got a laugh from Roadkill. "Burger King then?"

"How the hell is Burger King more refined than McDonalds?" Roadkill asked.

"Burger King does not have a clown," Gavin said. This got another laugh from Roadkill and also one from the back of the van.

They passed some billboards and one seemed to catch Roadkill's eye as his head turned with it as they passed.

"The Mall of America," Roadkill said, and sounded like it was the second coming. "I have never been there, but I have heard stories."

"Is not that the biggest mall in America?" Gavin asked.

"Would be in the northern hemisphere if it wasn't for that one in Canada. Stupid Canucks. I would have gone there for choir if I hadn't dropped out."

"Did you want to go there now?" Gavin asked. He guessed they could stop there for lunch and spend an hour looking around. "They must have places to eat there."

"You bet they do! How about it, Mr. Pierce? Would it be okay if we stopped?"

"Told you to call me Bernie. And yes, it would be fine. If you boys want to have a look around there, why not?" Grandpa said. Gavin figured it would not set them back on their schedule too much. Fargo was only four hours away.

"Then it's a go!" Roadkill said. The excitement in his voice was hard to ignore.

"So how do we get there?" Gavin asked.

Getting there actually wasn't that hard. They followed Interstate 94 until they turned on to Interstate 494, which took them right to it. The Mall of America seemed to be in the heart of Minneapolis and was located next to the airport.

"Look at the size of that thing," Grandpa said as the Mall of America came into view. Gavin couldn't fathom just how many stores the tremendous building could hold. It even had an amusement park inside.

"Modern consumerism at its finest," Roadkill said and turned into the ramp that would take them up to parking.

The parking ramp was separated by levels, and each one had the name of a state. Being eleven on a Wednesday, the lot didn't look all that busy. There were plenty of cars but also plenty of empty spots. Gavin could only imagine what the lot looked like around the holidays. Though there were plenty of empty spots right next to each other, Roadkill selected a spot next to a brand new Buick Enclave. "Bet the owners shit a brick when they see my van parked next to theirs."

Even though he said that, Roadkill was careful not to hit the car with his door. Gavin did the same and then opened the back door for his grandfather. The door only opened from the outside. Grandpa said he would take a look at it, but Roadkill said it gave the vehicle character. Earlier, his grandfather had taken a look at the radio, but he said without taking it completely out and apart, there was nothing he could do.

"All right, remember we're parked in Indiana," Roadkill said as they walked to the entrance.

As they walked in, all three stopped and took in the enormity of it. Gavin couldn't believe the size of the place. He never would have thought something could be so big. In front of them was a directory, so that was the first place they headed.

"There is a food court on the third floor," Gavin told the other two.

"There's a café called the Rainforest on the first floor," Grandpa said. "Let's treat ourselves."

They went further into the mall and saw that it branched off in many directions. In the middle of each wing, they could see all the way down to the first floor. As they made their way down, Gavin thought his neck would get sore from all the turning and looking he was doing. There were a lot of other people that were walking around. Some were not speaking English as they passed by.

"Airport is right across the street. A lot of people must come here between flights," Roadkill mentioned.

Gavin wished he would have known they were coming here so he could have looked up the mall's history. He felt so lost not knowing anything about the place.

They arrived at the Rainforest Café and found it closed. "Well, that makes it hard to eat there," Grandpa said.

Ten minutes later they ended up at the food court on the third floor. "This is even better! More choices!" Roadkill said. Gavin gave him a 20 dollar bill, and Roadkill made his way off to some place that served Asian food.

Gavin and his grandfather settled for a place called the Great Steak and Potato Company. The three met at an empty table to eat their meals. Gavin was starting to feel better about stopping at the mall. He wasn't one for large crowds, but this wasn't too bad.

"Was not this place targeted by some terrorist group?" Gavin asked as they ate. He remembered seeing something last fall on the news.

"What place isn't?" Roadkill said. "Yeah, they mentioned this place, plus a lot of others. Nothing came of it. Bunch of religious blowhards."

"You watch the news?" Gavin said. He knew it probably sounded rude, but he was genuinely surprised.

"Always pays to know if the world is going to end," Roadkill said and didn't sound offended at all. "I'm not all video games and babes."

"That's good. Those two things rarely go together," Grandpa said and both Roadkill and Gavin just stared at him. Had he just made a joke? And at Roadkill's expense?

"Good one, Mr. P.," Roadkill said.

After finishing their lunch, they cleaned the table and left the food court area.

"So, should we get going?" Gavin asked.

"What's the hurry? Let's look around some more!" Roadkill said. Gavin looked at his grandfather, who just shrugged his shoulders. Roadkill took that as a gesture of affirmation. "Let's check on this floor first. I saw a game store that I want to look into."

They headed over and found the store Roadkill wanted to visit. He went in, and Gavin and his grandfather sat on a bench that was just outside the store.

"Never understood video games," his grandfather said.

"I guess they are a way for people to escape their lives for a while," Gavin responded. He didn't play video games much himself but could see the attraction for some people.

"People like Roadkill?" his grandfather said, and Gavin nodded. There was a lot that Gavin didn't know or understand about Roadkill, but one thing he did know was that Roadkill was there for him when it mattered.

Roadkill came out of the store and said that it was kind of a disappointment. There wasn't anything that he hadn't seen back in St. Clair Shores. Gavin asked him if he expected the Mall of America to have completely different games than other stores. Roadkill said that he actually did.

They walked around some more and went into the stores that interested them. By the time they made it to the first floor, 40 minutes had passed since lunch.

"Damn, look at that Lego Store," Roadkill said and Gavin nodded.

Gavin turned around and looked behind him, but he didn't see his grandfather.

"Grandpa?" Gavin called out. Fear crept in, and he tried to keep it down. He tried to think about the last time he saw his grandfather. "Roadkill, when is the last time you saw my grandfather?"

"Man, now that I think about it, it's been some time. Second floor maybe?" Roadkill said. "Maybe he's back at Victoria's Secret. If I got lost at the Mall of America, that's where I would be."

"I cannot believe this," Gavin said, looking around frantically. There were many people milling around them, but none of them was his grandfather. It seemed that their trip was endangered before it barely got going. "I lost my Alzheimic grandfather at the Mall of America."

***

Bernie was doing fine until about the second floor and then he started to get tired. He hadn't done this much walking in a long time. They passed store after store, and Bernie couldn't believe the size of the place. Gavin and Roadkill's wonderment seemed to have settled down, but Bernie's had not. He was keeping up fine until he passed a store that was selling home décor.

There were pictures on display at the front of the store. One caught his eye enough that it stopped him in his tracks. It was a painting of a sailboat on a lake. The boat was trying to navigate during a storm. The water around it looked rough.

The sailboat was a small yawl, much like the one that he had last ridden in, the one that the accident happened with. In the picture there was no land visible, just rough water, clouds and that poor little boat. Bernie couldn't make out how many people were aboard the small boat in the picture with how it was positioned in the water, but it didn't matter.

Bernie wanted to take his eyes off the painting, but he couldn't pry them off of it. He hadn't thought of the accident for a long time. In fact, until now the memory could have been one of those that he'd lost. But after seeing the picture, it was back and more vivid than ever. He staggered back and ran into someone who shouted for him to watch where he was going. Bernie gave a quiet apology and managed to make it to a bench, where he sank to a sitting position.

The memory of that day kept replaying in his mind. The way the storm moved in so fast, the sailboat tipping over, him scrambling to get a hold of his children. Michael screaming over and over again how he had her but she just slipped away.

Michael hadn't slept well for a long while after that. The dreams he had were the memory of his little sister escaping his grasp.

Bernie himself didn't sleep well after that either. Bernie realized that he still blamed himself for the accident. He shouldn't have taken his youngest daughter on that sailing trip.

How could he have forgotten such a powerful memory? What else lurked in his subconscious, ready to spring up at the mere sight or smell of something? A small part of him said if Alzheimer's was going to make him lose this memory, then so be it. However, that meant losing the other memories as well. The whole point of this trip was to see if he still had some of his memories buried and it appeared he had.

"Sir, are you okay?" a voice said, and Bernie looked up. A woman in her forties stood there with a look of concern on her face. She was wearing a nice dress with a name tag that said her name was Janice and she worked for Abercrombie and Fitch. Bernie thought it might have been a clothing store somewhere in the mall.

"I, I just had a moment," Bernie said and realized that she probably wouldn't understand what that meant. "I mean, I felt a little faint there."

"Well, just rest until it passes. Are you here alone?" It was an innocent enough question, but Bernie wondered how he should answer it. He didn't want to tell her he had lost track of his grandson because that would bring in security.

"My daughter is shopping in the store next door. I told her I would wait out here," Bernie lied and felt bad. Janice was just trying to help. "She should be out any time now."

"Well, okay. Just take it easy, sir," Janice said and smiled. Bernie thanked her and she went about her business. Bernie waited until she was out of sight and stood up. He looked around and saw no sign of either Gavin or Roadkill. For a moment, Bernie had to think about what section he was on and then remembered. He was on level two, and they had been heading to level one. That was a place to start at least.

An escalator took him down and he patiently rode it. He could remember his children riding an escalator for the first time. All had been wary at first and a couple he had to carry down. Once the fear subsided, that's all they wanted to do. It was another memory that he had forgotten that came back.

He was so lost in the memory that the bottom came, and he stumbled when the last step did not move. Bernie managed to stay standing, but it was close. Again his memories were getting the best of it. Several people looked at him, but this time no one asked if he was okay.

The first level was similar to the others, and Bernie could have sworn he had been on this level before. He walked away from the escalator and moved to the side to get out of the way.

What would happen if he didn't find Gavin and Roadkill? He would have to get help then. He could go back to the van, but he couldn't remember where it was parked. Some *state* he thought. Wandering around the parking lot would not be wise because sooner or later security would notice him. He tried to think about what stores Gavin and Roadkill would go to but couldn't. He tried to keep the panic down because he knew that his mind would just get worse if he didn't do that. He had to keep his wits about him if he was going to find the two.

Bernie looked down the section he was in and saw some bright colors. He headed that way and found that he had been looking at an amusement park in the mall. It was called Nickelodeon Universe.

Bernie was vaguely familiar with Nickelodeon. He believed that it was a television station for children. He had grandchildren that would watch some show on there about some square, yellow creature that had an annoying laugh.

He arrived and then saw a huge statue of the creature he had been thinking about. He wondered whatever happened to the good cartoons like *Bugs Bunny*. There were a lot of young children with parents, but he didn't see Gavin or Roadkill anywhere. Surely by now they had to notice he was missing. Roadkill might be in his own little world, but Gavin would have noticed.

Bernie then remembered what was told to hikers when they were lost in the woods. The best thing to do was to sit and wait in one spot. By moving around, one he was just making it more difficult to locate. That was what Bernie decided to do. He picked a spot by the roller-coaster and sat down. Gavin and Roadkill were bound to be by soon enough.

***

"Okay, let's think this out rationally," Roadkill said. Gavin knew he was getting visibly upset, but who wouldn't in his place? "We last saw your grandfather on level two, so let's start there. We'll split up and make our way round the level and meet back. Damn, this is where having cell phones would be great."

"Yeah, well, wish in one hand, poop in the other, as my grandfather would say," Gavin said.

Roadkill's idea was a good one, though. They went back up and then split up. Gavin went in and out of each store he came to looking for any sign of Grandpa. After a while, he had attracted attention of the clerks, so he stopped. He didn't want them to think he was casing the joints and call security.

Half an hour later, he was back at the spot he had left Roadkill. He sat down and waited. Twenty minutes later, Roadkill showed up, holding a soft drink and a soft pretzel. Gavin gave him a 'what the heck' stare.

"What? I got hungry. It was my own money," Roadkill said in defense. "No luck, either?"

"No. Now what? Do we do the same on level three?"

"Let's try one. Maybe he remembered we were heading there and went down."

"This time do not stop for food," Gavin said as they headed down an escalator.

They split up again and repeated the process. Gavin realized that if their searching of the levels came up empty, they would have to go and alert security. He didn't want to, but knew that it would be better for his grandfather if they did. He couldn't have a man in his seventies with mild dementia wandering around the mall, lost. They could check the parking lot, and Gavin thought that might be their next step after level three. He hoped Grandpa didn't go out there because the chance of getting hit was always there.

Gavin came to Nickelodeon Universe and almost skipped it because he thought it would be the last place Grandpa would be. Then he thought that he'd better leave no stone unturned. He entered it and was turned off by the sheer tackiness of it. Gavin never was one for rides and always skipped out on the carnival when it came to town.

He walked past a statue of that annoying SpongeBob when he saw his grandfather calmly sitting on a bench.

"Grandpa!" Gavin shouted out and ran over to him. He felt like a small child that had lost and found his parents in a big store. His grandfather stood up as Gavin rushed over. "Are you okay?"

"I'm fine," Grandpa said and looked relieved that Gavin had found him. "Just got a little mixed up, that's all."

"I am so glad to have found you! Thought we were going to have to get security involved," Gavin said. "Let us go and find Roadkill. We split up to find you."

"Looks like all he found was some popcorn," Grandpa said and pointed to a spot behind Gavin. Gavin turned and saw Roadkill walking and looking at all the rides. He apparently did not see the two of them. In his hands he had a fountain drink and a bag of popcorn. As he walked, his head would dip down and he would take some popcorn with his mouth. The process reminded Gavin of a bird eating some seed.

"Roadkill!" Gavin shouted, and his friend looked up so quickly that popcorn fell from his mouth onto the floor.

"Hey, you found him! Cool!" Roadkill said. "Want some popcorn?"

"After seeing you eat it like a dog, I will pass," Gavin told him. "I cannot believe you stopped to get food again."

"Hey, I was hungry and thought it would help me in the search. Besides, we found him, didn't we?" Gavin was going to say more, but his grandfather's hand came to rest on his arm, stopping him.

"All ends well," Grandpa said. "Should we get going?"

"Yeah, that is a good idea," Gavin said. All told they had just lost an hour looking for Grandpa, which actually wasn't that bad. "We should stop at a bathroom first, though."

"Good idea, I do have to pee," Roadkill said. Again, Gavin wasn't surprised Roadkill had to urinate with how much he had to drink.

After finding a bathroom, they started their way back to the second level where the parking ramp was. Roadkill led the way, while Gavin took the rear. Whenever they passed a security guard, Gavin became nervous and tried not to look back as they passed.

The parking ramp came up and they walked into it. "Does anyone remember where we parked?" Roadkill asked.

"Indiana," Gavin responded.

"All the way *there*!" Roadkill said and Gavin was going to say not the actual state but realized it was a joke. They found the van (the Buick was gone) and got in it. The inside was hot, and they rolled the windows down right away.

Roadkill drove out of the parking garage and got back on the interstate. It felt like hours since they had last been in the van, but the time was two. Gavin figured they would get to Fargo around six and then maybe they could go on to Bismarck. He thought they would reach the Rocky Mountains in a couple of days at their current pace.

He knew they had gotten off lucky with what happened at the mall. It could have been a lot worse. His grandfather was tight-lipped about why he had gotten lost. He just said he was slow and lost track of where they were. Gavin hoped that was what really happened and that his grandfather didn't have one of his fugues.

"So, onward to North Dakota?" Roadkill asked and Gavin nodded. "Never been to North Dakota before. Never had reason to."

"Not many people do," Grandpa said and Roadkill laughed.

"I heard they don't even have working toilets there," Roadkill said with a smile.

"Sure, they do. That is a silly concept," Gavin said.

"I was joking. North Dakota sounds like a fine state," Roadkill said, but still had that smile on his face. He then turned his head and in all seriousness and asked, "Do we have anything to eat back there?"

Chapter 12

My father was born nine months after my grandfather returned from Vietnam. I guess my grandfather and grandmother did not waste any time when he got back. Grandpa was 25 when he had his first child. He was the one that helped deliver my dad as well.

My father was born in the back of a 1959 Chevy Impala. The car belonged to Al Davis (not the Raiders team owner), the owner of the garage where my grandfather worked. Grandpa had been at work that day when Grandma called to say that her water broke, and she needed to go to the hospital. Grandpa had walked to work that day, so his boss threw him the keys and said, "Get going!" My grandfather always talked highly of his boss, said he never worked for a better person. Of course, not including the Army, Al was the only boss my grandfather ever had.

Grandpa drove as if his butt was on fire and picked up my grandmother, whose contractions were already close together. My grandfather said it was going to be a photo finish, not that I would really want a picture of that. They would have made it, too, if it was not for the accident that involved a truck that was carrying ducks of all things. They were about a mile from the hospital when they turned a corner and came across the accident. The truck must have been transporting over a hundred ducks. Who has that many ducks, and why did they feel the need to drive them around?

Grandpa had to slam on the brakes to avoid hitting a car that was stopped in front of them. He was about to put it in reverse, when his wife told him that the baby was coming. My grandfather thought for a quick second, and then pulled the car over to the side, running over some already dead ducks. There were dead and living ducks all over the place. Dark smoke was coming from the truck, which was over on its side. From what Grandpa said, it was quite the sight.

He opened the door and the smell hit him right away. Ducks do not smell good anyway, but imagine a hundred ducks, some of them dead, and you get the picture. The air was also filled with quacking, but Grandpa put that out of his mind. He had other matters to attend to. He gently moved Grandma to the back seat where there was more room, and then tried to think about what to do next. That was when Tricia Yates came up to my grandparents. As it turned out, Tricia was a nurse who was heading for the hospital herself to start her shift. She also was a nurse with 15 years' experience assisting with births. Fate might have sent a tipped-over duck truck, but it also sent my grandparents Tricia Yates.

Tricia took over and Grandpa assisted. Using some blankets she had in her car, Tricia put them under my grandmother and kept one for the baby. When my father came out, he added to the noise with his wailing. The cord was cut with my grandfather's pocketknife, and the baby was handed to Grandma.

By then the police had arrived, and there was quite the gathering around the Impala. The back of the Impala was a mess, though. Al did not mind; he was that kind of guy.

Some people asked if they were going to name my father Donald or Daffy. That got a few laughs. Every once and a while when the back door was opened, a duck would waddle by, look in, and then move on as if it had already seen the scene before. Grandpa said it was quite surreal with how quick it all happened, especially with it being Grandma's first child.

Two ambulances came, one for the driver of the truck and the other for my father and his parents. No ambulances came for the ducks. All told, 37 ducks had died, 53 recovered, 10 went AWOL, and one baby, my father, was born. My father never told me that story, even though it was the kind of story a kid would be quite interested in. Grandpa told me about it, and I never looked at ducks the same way. There would be times when I was tempted to call my dad *Donald* and see what would happen.

End of Entry

+ + +

Michael closed his cell phone and sat back in his chair. He was at his office at school, but his mind was elsewhere. He had just gotten off the line with Detective Wellington who told him that all the bus services in the area did not have Gavin or his father as passengers. Wellington also checked the airlines just to be sure and came up empty. Michael was quite sure that his son had taken his grandfather to Colorado.

Last night he'd looked back on the browser history and found that someone had searched for Cottages Along the Thompson, the place where his parents had stayed during their honeymoon. Michael knew the place no longer existed, but had been bought out and the name changed to Whispering Pines.

Michael called the resort and they had no knowledge of any Pierce reservations. He told that to Wellington over the phone as well. Wellington said he would start getting the word out to the highway patrol but without having an idea on what vehicle they were in, it would be hard. Then that was it for the conversation, so Michael really didn't know more than he knew before the call.

He had spent the morning at home, trying to figure things out. Would $1,500 be enough to get them to Colorado and back? Did the two of them even plan for the return trip?

Michael was confident that at least Gavin did. Gavin was a planner; he hated surprises. That was what made this all the more shocking. Michael would never have thought Gavin would have done this. Perhaps his oldest son but not Gavin.

Michael had also gone over to Lake View to see if there was anything new on their side. There wasn't. After Lake View, he went to work but found it hard to concentrate. Patty told him to just go home, but he couldn't. What was he going to do at home?

Michael was angry, but he really wasn't sure who to be angry at. At times he was angry with his father for allowing

Gavin to take him. Other times he was angry with Gavin for taking his grandfather. Then there were times Michael was angry with himself for not seeing that this was going to happen and for not taking his father. Michael knew he shared a portion of blame for this, and if anything happened to his son or father, he would never forgive himself. Much like Naomi. Even after all these years, he still blamed himself for not saving her. After all, he was the one that had a grip on her lifejacket.

That day would forever be ingrained in his mind, no matter how hard he tried to forget about it: the boat capsizing, the waves crashing against him while he was in the water, and the lifejacket being pulled up empty. Those memories were what haunted him still. That was why he would not set foot on a boat or let his children do the same. Sure there were other ways for his children to get hurt, but he himself had directly experienced one way.

Michael looked at the time and saw it was nearly four. He wondered where his son and father were at that moment. This would be the second day they were on the road, and they surely had to be getting close to Colorado by now. He looked up the mileage and saw that at a direct path, it was around 1,300 miles. If they weren't there by tonight, they surely would arrive tomorrow.

Michael planned on calling Whispering Pines again tomorrow afternoon. If they hadn't seen them, he would ask that they be on the lookout and give them his number. He thought about calling the Estes Park Police, but didn't know what good that would do if the two were not there yet.

Michael had talked to several of Gavin's lawn mowing customers and found out that a friend had taken over for a while. After hearing that, it pretty much sealed it that Gavin and his grandfather were on their way to Whispering Pines.

The hour dragged by and Michael still found it hard to work. At five, he stood up and prepared to leave for the day.

Patty had already left, but before she went, she told Michael to just go home. He waited 15 minutes to do so.

When he arrived home, he found his wife and daughter there. Michael had wanted to yell at his daughter for not telling the truth right away, but his wife convinced him that Pauline felt bad enough already. She was worried about her brother and grandfather too.

"No word?" Nancy asked, after hugging Michael. He shook his head no. He told her about the call from Wellington and his call to Whispering Pines. "Do you think they will go directly there?"

"Why wouldn't they?" Michael asked.

"Because it's Gavin," Pauline said. Michael hadn't noticed her in the room. He looked at her and gave her a quizzical glance. "When has Gavin *ever* done anything that made sense to us? It makes sense to him. Maybe he decided to go an indirect route to Colorado."

"Why would he do that?" asked Michael.

"Because he probably guessed that you knew where he was going and didn't want anyone stopping him before he got there," Pauline answered.

Michael was silent. It actually did make sense, and it sounded like something Gavin would think of. If it was true, then there were numerous ways he could have gone, and it would be hard to trace. It also meant that they probably wouldn't arrive at Colorado today or tomorrow.

"You're thinking of something," his wife said as she looked at him. "You have that look on your face. What is it?"

"I think Pauline is right. Gavin wouldn't take a direct route. That means it will take them longer to get there, but I still wish I knew exactly how they were getting there."

"Son of a bitch!" his wife shouted, surprising Michael. His wife rarely swore. Pauline giggled.

"What, honey?"

"Last night we were talking about who Gavin might know with a car and ruled out a lot of people that would not do this crazy stunt. We forgot about *one* person. I didn't even think Gavin was still in contact with him."

"Solphis," was all Michael said. He had forgotten about Clarence Jr. Solphis! The kid had been a pain in his side at St. Clair Shores High School, at least on the days Solphis decided to show up for class. Michael also remembered that Solphis liked to go by the disgusting name of Roadkill. Michael refused to call him that and that made Solphis upset. For some reason he did not like the name Clarence Jr. and insisted on Roadkill. Why would a person rather have that name than their true one? "Could it be?"

"Who else does he know?" Nancy responded.

"Is that the guy who goes by the name Roadkill?" Pauline asked. "Didn't you kick him out of school?"

"He did that to himself, Pauline," Michael said. He then gently took a hold of Pauline's shoulders and steered her out of the room. "You've been a great help, now scram."

"Thanks, Dad," she said and floundered upstairs in her usual teenage way. He waited until she was all the way upstairs before returning to the conversation.

"Why would Gavin turn to Solphis?" Nancy asked.

"Because he had no choice," Michael answered and sat down in his easy chair. "It didn't end well with his mother. She blamed me for Clarence leaving school. Truth is that she is probably right in a way. I didn't exactly work hard to keep him in. He was such a bad influence on Gavin."

"Does he hold a grudge against you? Would he do something to Gavin or your dad to get back at you?"

"I don't think so. His mother, maybe, but not Clarence. Of course, we don't even know if that is who is driving them," Michael said and stood up. He went over to the computer and turned it on.

"What are you doing?" Nancy asked as she followed him over.

"I'm going to look up Solphis's information. I should still have access to it," Michael said. It took him a while to login into the St. Clair Shore's Public Schools system. Thankfully he did still have access and went through the proper channels in finding the information he wanted. When it came up, he jotted it down.

"What are you going to do with it?" Nancy asked.

The truth was that Michael was conflicted. He knew he should call Wellington with the information, but that would take some time. He would call Harriet Solphis and ask her himself, but she probably would not tell him anything. It was worth a shot, he guessed. He decided to do both.

"Can you get dinner started? I'm going to run a quick errand and be back by six."

"You're going over there, aren't you? Is that wise?"

"Probably not, but I need to do something," Michael said and headed for the garage. "I'll be back soon."

On his way to the Solphis house, he called Detective Wellington and got his answering service. He told him about their idea and gave the address and phone number for Solphis. Michael did not tell the detective that he was going over there at that moment.

The lawn in front of the Solphis house looked like it hadn't been mowed in quite some time. Michael wasn't too surprised. He parked along the street and got out. It didn't look like anyone was home, but he trudged up to the house anyway. He was not looking forward to this but knew it was something he had to do.

After ringing the bell and getting no response, Michael knocked on the door. It took a while for someone to open the door. It was Harriet Solphis and she had gained some weight since the last time he saw her.

"What the *hell* do you want?' were the first words out of her mouth. Judging from her last conversation, her using *hell* was mild in comparison.

"Mrs. Solphis, I need to ask a few questions about your son, Clarence," Michael said, trying to use his most pleasant voice. "Do you know where he is?"

"Why? What do you want to do to him now? You've already taken his education from him. Going to plant drugs in his room now?"

This was not going well. A small baggie of marijuana had been found in Clarence's locker two weeks before he officially dropped out. The school decided not to press charges since Clarence had already dropped out.

"My son is missing, and I believe that he might be with your son," Michael said in the same voice. "I was just wondering if Clarence Jr. was here. It would clear up things."

"Drop dead!" Harriet screamed and slammed the door. Michael stood there for a moment and then started back to his car. The visit pretty much went as he thought it would. Hopefully Detective Wellington would get something out of Harriet Solphis.

"She gets meaner every day, that one," a voice said to his right. Michael looked up and saw an elderly man on his knees in the next yard. There was a pile of weeds next to him. Michael hadn't noticed him when he arrived because he had been thinking about how his conversation was going to go with Harriet.

"Yeah, she's a pleasant person," Michael responded. "Say, you wouldn't know if her son, Clarence Jr. has been around lately?"

"Roadkill? Na, I haven't seen him for a few days. But that isn't too surprising because there are times where I go for weeks without seeing him. He spends a lot of time inside."

"When's the last time you saw him?"

"About two days ago. It kind of surprised me because it was about eight in the morning. A young man carrying two duffle bags came over. They loaded them in that van of Roadkill's and took off. Haven't seen Roadkill up at that time in a long while," the elderly man said, rising from his knees. Michael dug out his wallet, found a picture of his son and showed it to the man. "Yep, that's the one that came over. Surprised Roadkill had a friend that looked so clean-cut. Don't see many kids like that anymore."

"Thank you, sir. You have been very helpful," Michael said and shook the man's hand.

"That was your son with Roadkill, wasn't it?"

"Yes, it was," Michael answered. He said his goodbyes to the man and got into his car. He called Wellington, and again, had to leave a message. Michael told him what he had discovered and then started his car. As he pulled away, he wondered just how Clarence Jr. got the name 'Roadkill.'

***

"Fawn," Roadkill announced as they were coming up to a form lying in the middle of the interstate. "About four months old."

"Okay, it is a fawn, I will give you that. But how could you know its age? You cannot tell the age by looking at it," Gavin said.

They were 20 miles out of Bismarck, but it was Thursday morning. They had lost a lot of time in Fargo. They stopped for dinner there at a restaurant called Buffalo Wild Wings, and when they went back to the van, it wouldn't start.

Roadkill cursed and Gavin just sat looking at the thing. It was Grandpa that jumped into action. He popped the hood, looked under it for a moment, and then noticed that it needed a new belt of some kind. He used a technical automotive term that Gavin couldn't recall.

Roadkill went back into the restaurant and returned saying that there was an automotive part store a couple of miles away. However, Gavin was the one that ended up going, with the part's name written on a piece of paper. Roadkill had volunteered, but Gavin said he needed the exercise. The truth was that he didn't trust Roadkill to return promptly.

By the time he came back, an hour had expired and it took another hour for Grandpa to fix the van. They ended up staying in Fargo for the night.

The only thing Gavin could remember about Fargo was that a serial killer had been caught there over the winter. Otherwise, he knew next to nothing about the city.

This was only the second day of their journey, and they had stopped at two locations that were not planned. Gavin wondered how many other stops would be unscheduled as well.

"So what can you tell us about Bismarck, you walking history dictionary?" Roadkill asked. This was a question Gavin could answer. He had read up on some history of the city because he knew they would be at least passing through.

"Well, it is the capitol of North Dakota. Its capital building is the only skyscraper in the state. It originally was named Edwinton, but later the name was changed in honor of Otto Van Bismarck, a famous German leader," Gavin said and thought about some more that he knew. "The Missouri River runs next to the city, once a great source of trade and transportation. Across the river is the city of Mandan, where one would find Fort Lincoln. Fort Lincoln was established to protect settlers from Native American attacks. It was from Fort Lincoln where General Custer started off to the Battle of the Little Bighorn. That was where he was killed by the Sioux."

"Custer was a moron," Grandpa said, making Roadkill laugh. "That egotistical maniac should never have been made a general."

Three motorcycles passed them in the passing lanes. Gavin normally wouldn't have given motorcycles much notice, but he had been seeing them all day. Most of them were passing the van and heading west.

"Know some history too, Mr. Pierce?" Roadkill asked.

"Some. That part of history always interested me for some reason. I can remember playing cowboys and Indians when I was little. I was the cowboy and Bucky was the Indian," Grandpa said and then grew silent for a moment. A smile came across his face.

"I think the correct term now is Native Americans, Grandpa," Gavin said gently. "They were first called Indians because of Christopher Columbus and the name stuck."

"Damn! Where were you in history class! I might have actually passed that one!" Roadkill said with a laugh. "So, Mr. Pierce, Gavin tells me you dropped out of high school too."

"Call me Bernie. Yes, I did. I dropped out when I was a junior."

"What does your son have to say about that?"

"He doesn't like me talking about it. So, what are your plans now?" Grandpa asked, and Gavin didn't like the direction of where the conversation was going.

"Plans? I just take the days as they come to me," Roadkill said.

"Do you have a job?"

"Currently I am between employment opportunities."

"Meaning you don't have one," Grandpa said. "What are you going to do with your life?"

"Shit, now you sound like your son." This was the first time Gavin felt there was tension in the van on the trip. He tried to think of a way to diffuse the situation, but couldn't. "Weren't you a success even though you dropped out? Gavin said you owned several successful car repair shops."

"That's right, I did. The difference is that I had a skill. I already had a job when I quit that I was good at. Today, an education is very important. Roadkill, I got really lucky when I quit school. I have been lucky for most of my life, but I *really* was at that time," Grandpa said, his voice sounding gentle. "You seem like a good-hearted young man, but you seemed to have lost your way."

"I don't need a lecture, Mr. Pierce," Roadkill said and Gavin could tell that Roadkill was holding his temper back. "I get those enough."

"Did you know that New Salem has a huge statue of a Holstein cow?" Gavin said, hoping to change the topic. "They call it Salem Sue."

"How do you know that?" Roadkill asked. Gavin's ploy seemed to have worked. Two more motorcycles passed them. This time, both drivers had their helmets on. The bikes looked loaded down with camping supplies, much like the other ones.

"When I was looking for routes, I came across it. There is a way south from Mandan and one from New Salem."

"Oh, dude, we have to go see that! We already saw the world's largest buffalo!" Roadkill said and the situation seemed diffused. They had passed the statue of the bison in Jamestown, which also boasted two live albino bison. Gavin didn't bother to correct Roadkill's use of 'buffalo' though. "Not to mention that large crane-thing in Steele!"

"It seems North Dakota has more oversized statues than trees," Grandpa said.

"Wow, what's your beef with North Dakota! That's your second slam on this state," Roadkill said but he was laughing.

"Nothing, it seems like a fine state."

"Number one in oil production," Gavin said. "In the western part of the state there is what is called the Bakken Formation that has a lot of oil in it. It was not until recently when new drilling techniques were perfected, making the oil accessible."

"Is there any way to shutting him off?" Roadkill asked, but sounded like it was in good nature. "Even Han Solo could do that with C-3PO."

"I am just giving you the history lesson you never got in high school," Gavin said, trying to be funny. It fell flat because of their previous conversation. Worrying that the argument would start up again, Gavin tried to think of more knowledge he could expel. "Did you know that Bismarck's first state capitol burnt down and then the current one was built? There are some people who believe that the fire was intentionally set to get rid of it?"

"Enough, Gavin. Please," Roadkill said. They drove the rest of the way to Bismarck in silence.

***

"I have to go to the bathroom," Gavin said. They were on Highway 49, traveling south. New Salem was 30 minutes behind them. Salem Sue was seen, appreciated, and passed by. About eight miles later, they turned onto the two lane highway and headed south.

"Wow, man! We stopped in Bismarck for lunch and pee break! You're bladder is worse than Mr. Pierce's back there and he's 80!"

"Seventy-five," Grandpa said.

"Seventy-five! But I'll pull over."

"What do you mean? I just told you so we could stop at the next town," Gavin explained.

"Dude, just piss alongside the road. You're a guy. It's your privilege!" Roadkill exclaimed. "Have you never peed on the side of a road before?"

"No, I have not. That is disgusting," Gavin said. He had never gone to the bathroom other than in a toilet, except when he was really little but that didn't count.

"Holy crap, man! You're not a true guy unless you've gone outside. That's like what separates us from the ladies!" Roadkill started to slow down to pull over to the side.

"What are you doing? I am not going on the side of the road! What if someone comes by?"

"We haven't seen anyone for a while. Besides, if you're worried about that, just walk down into the ravine a little. It's not cold outside. Your winky will be just fine."

"My *winky*? You mean my penis? It is not the weather I am worried about. Grandpa, help me out with this," Gavin said turning to his grandfather.

"Sorry, Gavin. I'm with Roadkill. Pee on the side of the road," his grandfather said. "I've peed in stranger places, trust me."

By now Roadkill had come to a complete stop. Gavin wished he didn't have that feeling anymore, but it was actually stronger. He looked at Roadkill and then at his grandfather. No help in either of their faces.

"Fine, I willl go in the tall grass like some animal," Gavin said and got out. The wind hit him right away, and it felt warm yet uncomfortable. At least it was a west wind and not an easterly one.

Gavin was about to walk down into the tall grass when he remembered about ticks. That was probably the last place he wanted a tick to cozy on in, so he stayed out of the tall grass. He unzipped, took out his 'winky' as Roadkill called it, and waited for the urine to flow.

It took a while, but when it came it felt good. He spotted a ladybug crawling up one of the grass leaves and turned his stream. The ladybug was washed away, making Gavin laugh. He finished his business, zipped up, and started to return to the van. He realized he had no way to wash his hands. He told himself that he didn't get anything on them, but it would be the first time he didn't wash his hands after going to the bathroom.

As he was getting back in the van, two motorcycles went flying by, heading south. Gavin had gotten done just in time.

"So how was it?" Roadkill asked with a smile.

"It was fine. And that is just *creepy* to ask a guy how his urination process went."

"Just wondering. Saw you laughing there and couldn't figure out what was so funny. Then I remembered your pants were partly down."

"Shut up and drive," Gavin said.

The van drove off with Roadkill laughing and Gavin's grandfather in the back having a few chuckles as well. Five minutes later they passed through the small town of Elgin. Roadkill laughed ever harder at that.

Chapter 13

My great-grandfather Frank Pierce died when he was 68. My grandfather was 38 at that time. Both men were much too young for such a tragic death.

Great-grandfather died from testicular cancer that had gone undetected for too long. If there is a greater argument for there being no god, I would like to know what it is. Why can a man even get cancer in that spot?

After his father died, my grandmother made Grandpa go in to get checked. He said it was not pleasant, but came out clean (no pun intended).

His father's death hit Grandpa hard. I have already written about another death that hit him hard, Bucky Steven's. With his father, Grandpa lost a father and a friend.

Grandpa said he always looked up to his father for many reasons. It was his father who started him on the path to automotive repair. Frank saw the skill in my grandfather right away and made sure to nurture it. It was Frank that was so supportive of Bucky and his issues, and when Bucky died, it was Frank that made sure my grandfather did not do anything stupid. When my grandfather told his parents he wanted to drop out of school, Frank did not fly off the handle and shout. He talked calmly with my grandfather and listened to the reasons. Ultimately, my great-grandfather saw that it was the right choice for his son.

I often look at my grandfather and think back to the stories he tells of his father, and I wonder about my own father. I love my father, I do. I do not have the same relationship with my father as Grandpa had with his. Perhaps part of it is my fault and my 'social issue.' I guess I could be more open with my father, but it is hard to share my feelings. Whenever I want to share them, I stop because they suddenly seem like they are unimportant.

Then there's the fact that my dad works a lot. You've seen him around, Mr. Kubach, he's always here. He goes to nearly all the extracurricular activities too. When he is home, he always seems so short with me, so it can be hard to talk to him.

He probably would not want me writing about this subject, and I do feel like I have gotten off track. I think I have written this already, but I have a better relationship with my grandfather than my father. My father does not talk about his relationship with his father, so I really do not know how it is. Grandpa does not say much about it either. There seems to be some block that is between them, and my guess is the block's name is Naomi.

Well, back to my grandfather and the death of his father. When Frank died, his wife was still alive. It was my grandfather who took over looking out for her, much like my father does for Grandpa. He told me that he promised his father right before he died in the hospital that he would look after his mother. My grandfather made good on that promise too.

My grandfather took the death of his father hard, but not nearly as badly as that of Bucky Stevens. Perhaps it was because he was more mature, or perhaps it was because he had Grandma at that time. He told me that death is death no matter who or how, but it is how one deals with it that really matters. I think I am starting to understand that.

End of Entry

+ + +

Four motorcycles sped past the van and swung back into the southbound lane, nearly in unison. Grandpa identified all of them as Harley Davidson bikes.

"Can't mistake a Harley engine sound," he said as they went by. He had just woken up from a nap, and Gavin wondered if the bikes were what woke him. It was an hour after they had stopped to let him urinate.

"Tabby cat," Roadkill said. Gavin's eyes went to the road and indeed he saw, tabby cat there. It had a collar around its neck, so Gavin thought it wasn't just some farm cat but someone's pet. The cat was on the other side of the highway, and it looked like it had just about made it across when it was hit.

A few minutes later they passed a handmade sign that read- "Fresh Corn for Sale, Next Left!" Roadkill perked up when they passed that sign and then started to slow down.

"What are you doing?" Gavin asked. "Do you have to go to the bathroom?"

"Didn't you see that sign? Fresh corn on the cob! We have to get some!" Roadkill exclaimed. "There's nothing finer than fresh corn on the cob!"

"How are we going to cook it?" Gavin asked slowly.

"Oh, something will come along. We can actually grill it if we get tinfoil. I have small Weber Grill in the back. Thought it might come in handy if we had to camp out."

The turn came up, and Roadkill turned the van onto road. It was a dirt road and the ruggedness was immediately felt as the van was jostled up and down. "Hang on! It's going to be a bumpy ride!"

A neatly kept farm house appeared after a few minutes and Roadkill pulled into the dirty driveway. A barn with the doors slightly open was across from the yellow house. Inside the barn, piles of corn were visible. The barnyard seemed deserted. The van came to a halt, and the three just stayed put.

"Don't think anyone is home," Grandpa said.

As he finished saying that, the house's door opened and a woman came to the doorway. Her hair was gray, and she was wearing a long flowered print dress. She looked like she was in her late fifties.

Roadkill opened the car door and Gavin followed suit. Roadkill put on his biggest smile in order to show he wasn't dangerous.

"Hello! We saw your sign about the corn," Roadkill called out and started to walk toward the woman, who remained in the doorway.

The screen door was still closed, and Gavin bet it was locked. Before going over there himself, Gavin pulled open the back door of the van to let his grandfather out. Upon seeing Grandpa, the woman seemed to relax, and then she came out.

"Oh, I have corn all right," she said. "That I have a plenty."

"How much?" Roadkill asked.

"You can have ten ears for two dollars."

"Cool! I'll take 30!" Roadkill said. The excitement in his voice was hard to miss. Gavin wondered what he was going to do with all of the corn because he doubted it would even make it back to St. Clair Shores. It got hot in the van.

"Follow me to the barn," the woman said as she stepped off the porch. "I'm Georgia Jansen, by the way."

"Nice to meet you," Grandpa said. "I'm Bernie Pierce, the thin one is my grandson, Gavin, and the other is his friend, Clarence. Is your husband out in the fields?"

"My husband has been dead for three years. I have help getting the corn in. Most of the acres I rent out to others," Georgia said.

Gavin wondered why Grandpa introduced Roadkill with his real name.

"Sorry to hear about your loss," Grandpa said. Gavin had never really seen him in the presence of a woman his age other than at the home. "Live here by yourself then?"

"Well, yes, and no," she said and hesitated. "This is going to sound stupid, but I do have a cat. I haven't seen Rascal for a day or so, though."

"What color cat is it?" Roadkill asked.

"Orange and white. A tabby cat."

"Oh, he's dead on the road a ways back," Roadkill said nonchalantly.

"Roadkill!" Gavin shouted out, appalled. Then he realized what Georgia must have thought about what he shouted. "Sorry, ma'am, but his nickname is Roadkill."

Georgia burst into tears and Grandpa went over to her. He surprised Gavin by putting his arm around her and then started to quietly tell her something. Roadkill had walked over to the van and hopped in.

"I'll be back in a few," he said and started the van up. He tore off before Gavin could ask where he was going. Gavin was worried for a moment that he wasn't going to come back, but that was a ridiculous thought. Roadkill was impulsive, but he was loyal too.

Grandpa still had his arm around Georgia and was leading her to the house. She seemed to have calmed down some. Gavin was surprised that she responded so emotionally over the death of a cat. Couldn't she get those things anywhere?

"Gavin, will you please get the door for us? Georgia was nice enough to invite us in for some lemonade," his grandfather said while Gavin walked ahead to get the door.

"I know it must seem stupid to cry that way over a cat," Georgia said as she went to the refrigerator. Gavin and his grandfather went to the kitchen table that was in the room and sat down.

"Don't you fret over that," Grandpa said. "You have nothing to be ashamed of."

"My husband got me that cat four years ago, two before Randal died. He also got me the cat before that one and the one before that."

"You must like cats," Gavin said and his grandfather gave him that 'keep your yap shut' look.

"I don't know why I'm telling you this, but it feels good to talk."

"Talking about memories sometimes does that," Grandpa said.

"Randal and I always wanted a child of our own. When it was determined that I couldn't have children, we both were devastated. Oh, we could have adopted, and even looked into it, but it wouldn't be the same for us. That was when Randal brought me the first cat. I never thought much of cats, but I fell in love with this one. Randal said if we couldn't have children, then we could give out love to some little critter," Georgia said blushing as she put the lemonade on the table. "Listen to me going on to a bunch of strangers.

"Well, when the first cat died, Randal got me another and then another. Now Rascal is gone, and my Randal isn't around to get me another," she said breaking down in tears again.

Grandpa struggled to his feet and shuffled over to comfort her. Gavin wanted to ask why she just didn't go and get another cat, but remembered his grandfather's gaze the last time his spoke.

"I'm sorry we're causing you to remember those memories," Grandpa told her.

"No, no, it's okay. My memories of Randal are good ones. I just wish he was still here."

Roadkill finally came back. They were still inside drinking lemonade when the van came roaring back, kicking up a giant dust cloud. They watched Roadkill get out of the van, go around to the back, and then reappear holding a white bag with something in it.

"Hey, anyone home?" he called out. The three of them went outside to see what Roadkill wanted. He held the bag up, and Gavin got a closer look at it.

"Hey! That is my pillow case!" Gavin exclaimed.

"Yeah, I needed something to put Rascal in," Roadkill said. "Do you have a shovel, ma'am?"

"Yes, yes I do," she said, all the while staring at the bag. "Is he really in there?"

"I think so. This was around his neck," Roadkill said and took the blue collar from his pocket.

"That's his collar," Georgia said and Gavin was afraid she was going to cry again. "I do have a shovel in the barn."

"Can I borrow it? Also, where would you like him buried?"

"Over behind the house. That's where the other cats are buried. Rascal might as well join them too," Georgia said.

The group walked behind the house, where she pointed to a spot. When the hole was big enough to hold a cat's body, Roadkill stopped and then lowered Rascal's body into the grave, still in the pillowcase.

Gavin stared at the pillowcase and sighed. There were plenty more pillowcases out in the world.

"We gather here today, to pay reverence to Rascal the cat," Roadkill started out saying as he finished filling in the dirt in the grave. "He was a cat, but also a companion to Mrs. Jansen here. He was loved and will be missed. He might be gone, but Mrs. Jansen can always be comforted by the memories he left behind."

"That was lovely, young man," Georgia said. Gavin was actually surprised that the words came out of Roadkill. "Thank you for that."

They stood around the fresh grave for a few more minutes and then walked back to the front of the house.

"I suppose you boys will be on your way then," Georgia said. "It's been nice to have company."

"We thank you for the lemonade," Grandpa said. "You be careful out here by yourself."

"The corn!" Roadkill exclaimed. "Cripes, we nearly forgot what we stopped for!"

"Please, take all you want. I probably won't be able to sell all of it anyway," Georgia said, making Roadkill's eyes get big.

He ran to the barn, opened the door, and went in. He came carrying an armful of corn on the cob. He must have been carrying 40 ears of corn.

"Open the back door!" Roadkill yelled. "I have an empty trash bag back there to put them in!"

"You had an empty trash bag back there?' Gavin said. He was in the process of opening the back of the van and stopped. "And you used my pillowcase?"

"Well, duh! Can't put a beloved pet in a trash bag!" Roadkill said like it was something everyone should know. Gavin sighed and opened the door. Rummaging through the back, he found the bag and opened it up. Roadkill dropped his armful of corn in the bag, and then put it back in the back of the van. "Can't wait to have some of that corn!"

"Well, ma'am, thank you for the corn and everything else," Grandpa said.

"If you're ever back in this area, please stop by," Georgia returned. The three of them got into the van. They waved goodbye, and then drove off down the dirt road.

"How did you know to say those things you said after you buried the cat?" Grandpa asked as they arrived at the highway.

"I don't know. It just seemed like the right thing to say. I figured she loved the cat because of how she reacted when she got the news. I went from there."

"That was a good insight you had there, Roadkill," Grandpa said. "Having people skills can make it so you get along in life a lot easier."

"Hasn't helped me yet," Roadkill said.

The van's interior smelled of fresh corn, and Gavin found the aroma better than the one it replaced. He found that he, too, was looking forward to having some.

***

Friday afternoon found Michael at home, packing. He tried to go into work, but the office staff had gotten together, discussed the matter and then sat him down. Howard Davis, the assistant principal that had been there the longest, was the one that talked to Michael. Howard told Michael that he needed to take some days off to deal with what was going on with his son and father. Michael protested, said that the new school year was starting soon, but was told that they could handle it for a few days. Howard said that they were actually a little ahead of the planning process.

Michael felt they were just saying that, but deep down he did appreciate it. He felt torn between two worlds. Of course, now that he didn't have work to worry about, he was at home with nothing to do but think about where the two were.

Detective Wellington had called once and shared with him his latest news. He had gone to Lake View and talked with the staff and two of the residents that were good friends of Michael's father. Wellington said that one of the men had loaned his father $2,000. Michael was surprised, but said that the man would be reimbursed the amount from his father's account.

Wellington also had gone to the Solphis house and talked to Clarence Jr.'s mother. Wellington said he didn't get much information from that woman and that she really had some interesting things to say about Michael. She told the detective that she hadn't seen Clarence for a while. She also gave the make and license number of the van her son drove.

An APB had been put out on the van. Every highway patrol and other law enforcement agency would get it. That was all Wellington had to report.

Michael felt completely useless staying at home and pacing around. He went on the computer a few times to look up sites on Colorado but really didn't know what he was looking for.

His wife came home for lunch and saw the worried look on his face. She wasn't surprised when he told her he was going to Colorado. She asked him if it was a wise idea. She said that something could happen and he would be needed at home. Michael told her that he would drive back if need be. He said he just couldn't sit at home doing nothing.

Michael didn't know how long to pack for, so he packed for four days. He decided he would drive the most direct route to the Rockies. He felt Gavin and his father's destination would be Whispering Pines, even if they hadn't made a reservation there. Michael had made some calls, one to Detective Wellington. The detective had advised not going, but Michael said that wasn't an option anymore. Wellington said he understood and that he would be in contact. Michael should do the same.

Another call he made was to Whispering Pines. He asked if they had any cabins open this weekend. He hadn't expected one would be open, but thought he would at least try. It was not a surprise to find out that they were all booked up. He asked them to call if an opening came up, but he wasn't very hopeful. Michael wanted to call other possible places to stay, but didn't want to take the time. He would have to hope to find something open when he got there.

"How far are you planning on driving today? You're not going to drive all night are you?" Nancy said. She still wasn't too happy about him doing this, but at least she stopped trying to talk him out of it. "Pauline and I could come with you."

"I know, honey, but someone has to stay here like you said earlier. I don't plan on driving all night. I'll stop sometime around nine, depending on where I am. I have to do this."

"You keep saying that. Why?" Nancy asked. He looked at her and realized how lucky he was. His father often said that about his wife too.

"Because, if something happens to either one of them, I don't know what I'll do. Gavin shouldn't have done this. He's in over his head and doesn't realize it."

"He has help," Nancy said.

"Clarence? I don't know how much help that kid can be. He's a washout. I'm worried that he's driving high all the way there."

"Gavin wouldn't allow that. You know he doesn't have anything to do with drugs."

"I thought that, but things change," Michael said, zipping his bag. He was all set.

"If you do find them, what are you going to do?"

"Drag their asses back here," Michael told her. "This comedy of errors has to end."

"Michael, be careful. And if you do find them, don't go too hard on Gavin," Nancy said and took Michael by the shoulders. "He's your son. He loves his grandfather and meant well. You have to admit, it was a pretty gutsy thing to do."

"And stupid," Michael said and his wife gave him that look that husbands know they have gone too far. "All right, I'll keep my temper in check. Realistically, if I do find them, I'll probably be too relieved to yell."

"You call me often. If you get tired, pull over. Take a nap. Drive carefully," she told him and then kissed and embraced him. He hugged her back and then the embrace ended.

"I'll call you tonight when I get to wherever I am staying," Michael said. He looked at his wife for a moment and turned away. "Give Pauline a hug for me."

"You know she is not going to be happy you left without saying goodbye."

"Yeah, well I can't wait around forever," Michael said.

When he first heard about her lying that she didn't see Gavin, he wanted to ground her, but Nancy talked him out of it. Pauline seemed truly sorry when she heard what her brother had done.

Michael then left. The urge to stay and say some more goodbyes was strong, but he fought against it. Goodbyes are never easy, and one could hang around forever doing so. He got into his car and drove out of the garage. He gave his house one last look and then went on his own adventure.

Chapter 14

Writing Entry for Friday, May 14

When Al Davis decided to retire, the question came up regarding what he was going to do with the shop. Grandpa wanted to buy it but the funds just were not there. A few months earlier his wife had given birth to their first child, and she was no longer working. Grandpa said they were not living pay check to pay check, but it was close. Since Grandpa could not afford to buy the shop, the question concerning who would buy it and be Grandpa's boss arose. My grandfather even talked to Grandma about having to find a different place to work if the new boss turned out to be a dink.

Grandpa liked Al, and they worked well together. I already wrote about Al loaning his car to Grandpa when Grandma went into labor. Al was not even upset about the mess in the back.

Grandpa found out a week earlier that the shop had been sold, but Al would not say who he sold it to. Grandpa took that as a bad sign. Al was always open with him, and if he kept his mouth shut about this, then it had to be bad. Al told Grandpa that he would find out who the new owner was during his retirement party.

Seriously, by this time in the story, I thought there was something fishy about Al not telling Grandpa, but kept my mouth shut. I liked listening to my grandfather's stories and knew when to stay silent.

My grandmother got an earful that night about the whole situation as she rocked baby Michael. My grandfather told her that the new owner and boss had to be a complete jackass if Al would not talk about him. Grandpa said there was no way he was going to work for a jackass and would have to find a new shop to work. Grandma just nodded and said 'yes dear' throughout the entire tirade.

The next day Grandpa just took up where he left off. That day at the shop, Al refused to say anything about the deal no matter how many times Grandpa pestered him. The more Al was tight lipped, the more Grandpa worried and ranted at home. Grandma just nodded and said, 'yes dear.'

Finally Al's last day came. He didn't want a retirement party because he had no immediate family to celebrate with anyway. Al sent Grandpa out to get lunch. Al said that was all he wanted, one more lunch from his favorite spot in town, Fish 'N' Chips, which you can find along the Nautical Mile.

When Grandpa returned with the food, Al was outside the shop waiting for him. Al told Grandpa that the new owner was inside waiting to meet him. Grandpa stood there, holding the bags of food and looking at the building. He then said, 'Let's go meet this guy. He better not be an asshole.'

Sorry about the language, but you will see why I had to keep the exact language he used.

They walked into the shop and there was Grandma with baby Michael. My father was in the carriage, and they had to push him around. He was sucking on a monkey wrench and making cooing noises. Grandpa asked what Grandma was doing there and Al said that she was the new owner.

By now I am sure you saw that coming. All the days my grandfather was complaining about the new owner, calling him a jackass and so on, he never realized that the new owner would be his wife. It seemed that my grandmother had some money saved up that Grandpa did not know about. She was going to put some of it away for Michael's college education but thought this might be a better investment. She was correct in that aspect. Grandpa turned that one shop into three by the time he was ready to retire himself many years later.

Of course, my grandmother was also able to buy the shop because Al gave it to her at a great discounted price. For Al, my grandparents were his family. He would continue being friends with them until he died in 1982.

Grandpa was wrong about his new boss being a jackass, Grandma was tough on him at times, but even after only a year of marriage, he was used to her management style. Just like in their married life, they made a great team in their business life as well.

End of Entry

+ + +

"What is up with all the motorcycles?" Gavin said as another group of Harleys passed them.

They had just left Lemmon, South Dakota after filling up the gas tank and visiting the Petrified Wood Museum there at the insistence of Gavin. Roadkill and Grandpa were just getting tired of his petrified wood facts and agreed to go to shut him up. After looking at the trees that resembled rocks, they piled back in the van and were off.

"Dude, what's the date?" Roadkill asked as another two bikes charged past them. They were the same ones that had been at the filling station in Lemmon.

"Friday, August second," Gavin answered.

As he answered, he looked in the back and saw that his grandfather had fallen asleep. It had been a busy day today. Gavin hoped to make it to Rapid City before stopping for the day. Then tomorrow, they should get to Estes Park. It was strange to think that half their journey would be over soon.

"Holy shit! Sturgis!" Roadkill exclaimed.

"Sturgis? Yeah, that town is coming up in a little over an hour."

"No, no! Not just the town! I'm talking about the annual Sturgis Motorcycle Rally. They have it around this time. That's gotta be where all these bikes are going to! And we're going through there!"

"What? You are kidding me!" Gavin said. He did not share the excitement that his friend had over the rally. Sturgis was on the way to Rapid City. Perhaps there was another route that would take them around the town. "No, we cannot go through there then."

"What do you mean? That is the biggest motorcycling event in the world! We have to go through there. Think of the experience!"

"Roadkill, we are not here to gawk at Sturgis. I do not think it would be wise to drive through there. Thousands of people are supposed to be there. I read about it on the Internet but did not pay attention to the date. If I had, I would have had us take a different route," Gavin said and Roadkill looked at him in disbelief.

"Let's ask Mr. Pierce back there what he wants to do. I bet he'll say Sturgis."

"Grandpa is asleep, and I do not want to wake him for this. We will go around Sturgis," Gavin said. He started to look for the map of South Dakota they had picked up along the way.

"This is bullshit, man! We have an opportunity of a lifetime!" Roadkill said, not letting it go.

"Roadkill, there is too much that can happen. Think of all the people!"

"I am! That's what makes it so inviting!"

Gavin had a feeling that this argument was going to go on for a while, but he was going to be emphatic that they skirt around Sturgis. He was about to say something to Roadkill, when they went down a hill and came across some motorcycles on the side of the road. Roadkill immediately started to slow down.

"What are you doing? Just go around them," Gavin said. There were four motorcycles total, and Gavin tried to recall if he remembered them passing the van. The riders were wearing leather jackets, jeans and some had on red or black bandanas.

"Looks like one of them is in trouble," Roadkill said as he pulled in behind the bikes.

"For crying out loud, one of them must have a cell phone to call for help," Gavin said. He couldn't believe that Roadkill had just pulled over.

"We don't," Roadkill said and stopped the engine.

One of the riders started to walk back to the van. He was a big man with a beard that went halfway down to his neck. Gavin saw that, altogether, there were three men and one woman. Visions of the three of them getting killed in various ways went through his mind. What if these people were part of a motorcycle gang? He had heard that Texas was having issues with biker gangs.

Roadkill rolled the window all the way down to talk to the rider. "Afternoon. Everything okay?"

"My friend's bike broke down. We were about to call for a tow truck," the biker said and Gavin smacked Roadkill's arm as an 'I told you so.'

"Perhaps I can help," Grandpa said from the back. Gavin didn't even know his grandfather had woken up. He had moved up a little so his head was in between the front seats. The biker who looked like he could break all three of them in half, looked at my grandfather and doubt filled his eyes, or so Gavin thought. "I used to be known to fix a bike or two."

"Not to insult you, sir but this is a Harley we're talking about. I wouldn't want someone who didn't know what he was doing, to just make it worse."

"Actually, my grandfather knows exactly what he is doing," Gavin said. He felt he had to stick up for his grandfather, even though he was doubtful himself. Grandpa had fixed the van, but this was a motorcycle. Sure, Grandpa worked on them and even restored one in Vietnam, but it had been a while.

"Doesn't hurt to look," Roadkill said, and the biker shrugged, then stepped back as Roadkill opened the door to get out.

Gavin reluctantly got out himself, just wondering when the bikers would pounce. He opened the back door to let his grandfather out. Gavin said, "I'm assuming you're heading to Sturgis?'

"Is there any other place? Where you folks heading to?"

"Colorado," Gavin said quickly before Roadkill could say anything. "We're going to go around Sturgis."

"That's too bad. It's quite the sight. This is my wife's and my tenth time at the Rally. That's the little woman over there. Say, Kathy, come and meet these people," the biker said. He called his wife *the little woman*, but Gavin thought the biker needed to get his eyes checked. There was nothing little about Kathy as she ambled over. She looked like she just weighed slightly less than her husband. "Name's Ralph, by the way. Come from Butte, Montana."

"We're from St. Clair Shores, Michigan," Roadkill said and stuck his hand out. Ralph shook it and then moved to Gavin, who finally put his hand out. He thought his hand was going to be crushed in Ralph's meaty one. Ralph seemed gentler with Grandpa's hand, thankfully.

"Kathy, this old guy thinks he can fix Scoot's bike," Ralph said as his wife approached them. She had on a matching bandana to her husband's, making Gavin wonder if that was customary. She looked to be in her upper forties, but it was hard to tell with the sunglasses she had on.

"Told that idiot to get a checkup on that thing. We're already late as it is. It's bad enough we had to go to Glen Ullin to pick his dumb ass up. Moron has to work the oil fields! Rally started days ago! Should just leave his ass here," Kathy said. "I swear if we miss any more drinking time, I'm going to smack the piss out of him."

"Kathy says hi," Ralph said.

They made their way over to the bike in question and more introductions were made. The other two were Tony 'Scoot' Saunders and Alex Henderson. All four were from Butte, although Scoot pronounced it 'butt.'

Grandpa didn't waste time as he squatted down to take a look at the bike. Gavin watched as his grandfather's hands moved around the engine with expert knowledge. Every once and in a while, he would nod and then move on. He paused in one place and then fiddled with the engine.

It took 20 minutes, and then he stood up. He went over to Scoot and started to talk in a voice Gavin could not hear. Grandpa looked quite small next to the big man, but if he was intimidated, he never gave any inclination. All the while Grandpa was talking, Scoot was nodding his head and looking over at his bike. Once their conversation was done, Scoot went over to his bike, got on and started it. It fired right up, and Scoot's smile was huge.

"Son of a bitch! He got it!" Scoot yelled. Ralph walked over to Grandpa and clapped him on the back, gently.

"Sorry, old timer. I doubted you and you proved me wrong," Ralph said.

"Wasn't too hard. He'll need to get a new part if he's going to ride it back to Butte. Probably could get the part in Sturgis," Grandpa said.

"You know your way around Harleys, don't you?" Kathy said. She sounded more enjoyable now that Scoot's bike was fixed.

"Know my way around most engines," Grandpa responded. Gavin knew Grandpa's statement coming from most people would sound egotistical, but coming from Grandpa it was the truth. Gavin felt proud of his grandfather. He still had it in him to surprise people.

"How can we thank you?" Ralph asked. Scoot had gotten off his bike to come over.

"Don't worry about it," Grandpa said.

"You guys said you were going to go around Sturgis. How about going there it and stay the evening in our campsite. It's seven now and will be about eight-thirty when we roll in. We have a campsite reserved. Some friends are already there waiting for us. They'll have a nice spread for us when we arrive."

"That would be nice," Grandpa said before Gavin could answer. They were supposed to stay overnight at Rapid City, but it was only half an hour away.

"Are there no hotel rooms available?" Gavin asked. All four bikers looked at him and then started laughing.

"There's no rooms anywhere or campsites for at least a hundred miles!" Ralph said. "You boys really do need to stay with us."

"Cool! It's arranged then!" Roadkill said, obviously excited since this was what he wanted.

Gavin sighed. It was just one night, he thought. He could suffer for one night. They would still make it to Colorado the next day.

"Just follow us," Ralph said and walked back to his bike. "Hope you boys like steak. That's what we're having!"

"I got the corn!" Roadkill shouted back. Soon they were all off and heading to Sturgis.

***

Michael pulled into a Motel 8 on the outskirts of Iowa City at nine that evening. The urge to go farther was there, but he was tired and didn't want to press his luck. It had been a while since he had gone on a long road trip, even longer since going on one by himself. He went to the office and rented a room. He had already stopped for dinner, breaking a personal rule of not eating in his car. The second thing he did after flopping down on the bed was to call his wife. She answered even before the first ring finished.

"Hey, honey. I'm at a Motel 8 at Iowa City."

"Good, you stopped for the night," his wife returned. "I was afraid you would try and push through."

"No, maybe if I was younger, but I know better now. I am pretty tired. After I get done talking with you, I'm going to take a shower and go to bed. I want to be on the road by seven," Michael said. "Everything okay at home?"

"It's fine. Pauline said she would have gone with you if you waited," Nancy said. Michael wondered if it was just his daughter saying that or if she meant it.

"Tell her I didn't know what time she would get home after gallivanting with her friends." Michael knew his daughter hated it when he used the word 'gallivanting.' She would roll her eyes and say *no one uses that word any longer*. Besides, Michael was glad his daughter wasn't along. It would have been just another added stress he didn't need.

"I'll make sure to use that exact word," Nancy said and Michael thought he could hear a smile on her face. "You drive careful tomorrow."

"I will sweetheart," Michael said. "I love you."

"I love you too," his wife said back. The conversation ended, and Michael lay back in his bed. His eyes felt so heavy he thought he would just fall asleep right then and there. That was when his phone buzzed. He had a different ringtone for his wife, so he knew it wasn't her calling back. He looked at the number and saw that it was Detective Wellington.

"Hello, Detective," Michael said.

"Hey, I hope I didn't catch you driving," Wellington said over the phone.

"No, I'm at a Motel 8 in Iowa City."

"Sounds fun."

"No, it's Iowa," Michael said back and both men laughed. "You must have something if you're calling this late."

"I do. I just got word back from a buddy of mine. He works security for the Mackinaw Bridge. I called him this morning on a chance that they went up that way. And they did. My buddy looked at the security footage and saw a van that matched the description. The plate was the same. It's Clarence's," Wellington said and Michael sat up. Why would they go all the way up there? That made no sense whatsoever. Then Michael shook his head. That was why Gavin did it. "Sent me the footage, too. There were two people in the front of the van. Couldn't exactly tell their faces, but they looked like adolescent males. I think it's them."

"Yes, so do I. That is really out of the way," Michael said.

"Yeah, it is. I suppose your son thought we wouldn't think of looking at the bridge's security footage."

"Probably didn't realize it had cameras until it was too late," Michael responded.

"Michael, I need to ask this. Do you want your son charged for kidnapping your father?"

"What? No!" Michael said alarmed. He never thought about what would happen to Gavin over this.

"Okay, I thought that would be the case. Right now, no law has been broken then. I will keep the APB out on them because they can be considered vulnerable adults. Other than that, though, that's about all I can do," Wellington said.

"Thank you, Detective," Michael said. Gavin had no idea what he had done. They ended the conversation, and Michael lay back in bed. He was not as tired as he was earlier. The phone call from Wellington took care of that.

***

Bernie was excited to go to Sturgis. He had never seen the bike rally before, but knew of it. He had many customers that talked about it. He even thought about taking Belinda to it, but that didn't happen.

They passed Bear Butte, and Gavin started giving the history of it. Bear Butte was just outside of Sturgis. It was a lone butte, surrounded by prairie. Gavin informed Grandpa and Roadkill that it was established as a state park in 1961 and that Native American tribes held the butte, which actually wasn't a butte but an intrusive body of igneous rock, in reverence. Gavin said that artifacts had been found on the butte that dated back 10,000 years.

Bernie was amazed at Gavin's mind and how he could remember bits of history. Sometimes Bernie had to admit that it got a little tiring, but this time he found the information on Bear Butte to be interesting. It was strange to see a lone butte, or an intrusive body of rock rising out of nowhere. They went past it, and Bernie continued to look at it, even when it was behind them.

"Holy shit!" Roadkill said from the driver's seat.

Bernie turned to see what Roadkill was so excited over and saw it right away. They were coming up on Sturgis, but even before they got to the town, it was an amazing sight. Motorcycles were everywhere. Their vehicle was in the minority by far. They started to pass biker bars that were all enjoying booming business.

The motorcycles they had been following turned and headed toward what they believe was a campground. It was really hard to tell for sure because it was teeming with people and motorcycles.

The majority of the people in the campground were wearing some form of biker apparel. He saw some women that were wearing clothing that he doubted they would wear outside of Sturgis. Bernie wondered what his grandson thought of those women.

There were tents, motorhomes, and campers all over. Their speed was greatly reduced. They were barely going 10 miles per hour. There was a lot of foot traffic crossing the road. Roadkill did his best to stay with the bikes, but was getting farther behind.

"This is crazy," Gavin said and Bernie had to agree. He had never seen anything like it. It was getting overwhelming.

They saw the bikes turn down a dirt road and then into a campsite. Roadkill followed and soon they were parked. The campsite had three new bikes besides the ones they had followed. The Butte bunch got off their bikes and were hugging the riders that were already there. The three of them got out of the van and went over to the riders.

"That old guy there is a mechanical genius!" Scoot yelled. He already had a beer in his hand. "We would still be on the side of the road if it wasn't for him!"

"*You* would still be," Kathy amended. She not only had a beer in her left hand but one in her right as well. "That gentleman that helped us out is Bernie Pierce. The skinny one is his grandson, Gavin, and the other has the wonderful name of Roadkill."

"Hell, with a name like that, you should be a biker!" one of the new riders yelled out. "Since that Kathy ain't gonna introduce us, I'm Red Franklin, the extremely fat one over there is Harvey Upton, and the grotesquely fat one is Pipes McDonald."

Bernie thought Red was being rude, but then he got a look at the two others and thought his description was spot on. Handshakes were shared and then everyone settled around the fire.

"Steaks should be ready in about 20 minutes!" Red said. It seemed like everything he said was yelled.

"Hey, does anyone have any tinfoil, and better yet, bacon?" Roadkill asked.

"Got some bacon in the cooler," Harvey said. "Was for breakfast though."

"I have some corn in the back of the van. Got it fresh earlier today. Mind if I borrow some bacon to wrap the corn in?"

"Well, I'll be a dog in heat! Never had corn like that. Sure! What the hell!"

"Told you bacon goes best with everything!" the one called Pipes shouted.

Roadkill went back to the van and came back with 12 ears of corn. Harvey handed Roadkill some bacon and the young man got to work.

"How did you come by the name of Pipes?" Gavin asked the overweight man wearing just a leather vest for a top and huge jeans on the bottom. Bernie didn't know they made them that size.

"Because I used to play the bagpipes. Used to because ain't no one wants to hear those things around here!" Pipes said. Many around yelled their agreement.

"I have never heard bagpipes actually played before," Gavin said. "Did you bring them?"

"Hell no. Too much to carry on the hog," Pipes said and sounded disappointed.

Bernie was given a chair with a back and he leaned back into it. The short nap he had gotten had been enough. Soon he knew he would need to go to bed but thought about just falling asleep right there and then. He wondered if they should have come to Sturgis. He knew Gavin hadn't wanted to, but Roadkill did. Bernie thought it would be a good experience for both of the young men.

***

They hadn't even gotten into the town of Sturgis and Gavin was blown away. He had never seen so many people in his life before. A majority of the people were wearing leather jackets. Some of the women either had no shame or had forgotten some clothing at home. Gavin swore he saw one woman walking around without a top on, but it was from a distance and hard to tell.

There was a sign outside the campground that had said people were not to wear colors. Gavin had no idea what that meant. His shirt had colors on it, should he change? Most of the bikers had on black leather, so they seemed to be in accordance.

Roadkill was busy preparing the corn. Gavin had his doubts about the bacon and corn idea and didn't think he would try it.

The campground was noisy, and it wasn't just the sound of motorcycles running. There were people yelling, laughing, and someone screaming. Gavin wondered if the screaming would be looked into.

People passed by their site and seemed friendly enough as they waved. Gavin saw a lot of girls of various ages in bikini tops. He tried not to stare, but it was hard not to do so. Gavin liked girls, and enjoyed looking at pretty ones, but it made him uncomfortable when he started to get hard below. He thought everyone would notice and start to point. Judging how some of the women were scantily dressed, this wasn't a family event.

"So, Gavin, what grade are you in?" Pipes asked as he lowered his huge frame into the empty lawn chair next to him. The chair creaked and looked like it was going to explode from Pipe's weight.

"I will be a senior next year," Gavin said, looking at the ground.

"Shit! A senior! Had you pegged for a sophomore at most!"

"I look young," Gavin said quietly.

"Nothing wrong with that. Really will like it when you are a lot older. Want a drink?" Pipes asked.

"Do you have any Sprite?" Gavin asked. It was past eight and he didn't dare have a Mountain Dew or else he would be up all night.

"No, but you want a beer?"

"I'm only 17, sir," Gavin said.

"Man, you're funny! I'll find you a Sprite!" Pipes struggled to his feet, and the chair seemed to sigh in relief after he got out of it. Pipes wandered off in the direction of the tents. "Hey, who has a Sprite?"

"Why the hell do you want one of those?" someone yelled.

"It ain't for me, but for one of the newcomers!"

Gavin lost sight of Pipes after that. The smell of cooking bacon hit him, and he realized that he was hungry. Roadkill had the grate that covered the fire pit wrapped in tinfoil and was cooking the corn cobs on top. Most of the ears were wrapped in bacon. Sizzling shared the air along with the aroma of bacon. Many of the bikers had stopped their conversations and were looking at what Roadkill was doing.

"Say, damn! I think I'm about to be proven wrong twice today!" Ralph said after a moment. "I doubted your corn idea, Roadkill. But that smells mighty fine!"

"Should be ready in about ten," Roadkill said as he turned around. Gavin was surprised to see his friend holding a can of beer. He couldn't make out the brand, but knew it was a beer. He was about to say something, but he felt a hand on his arm. It was his grandfather of course.

"Let Roadkill have this one," Grandpa said. "He earned it."

"He is not old enough to drink," Gavin protested.

"It will be okay," Grandpa said, and Gavin let the matter drop. Pipes came back and handed Gavin a cold can of Sierra Mist.

"Closest I could find," Pipes said and plunked down in the chair again. Gavin thanked him and popped the top. He wasn't particularly fond of Sierra Mist but kept his mouth shut.

"So where are you from, Pipes?" Grandpa asked.

"From Owensboro, Kentucky. Same as Red and Harvey. Met Ralph's group about six years ago here. Came fast friends after that. Meet here ever since. This Rally is about more than motorcycles."

"What kind of bike do you have?" Gavin asked, trying to make conversation.

"A Fat Bob," Pipes said and laughed. "Ironic, isn't it?"

Gavin wanted to tell him that it would be more ironic if his name would have been Bob, but didn't. Instead he said, "My grandfather here once restored a Harley Knucklehead when he was stationed in Vietnam."

"Jumping cripes! You're kidding me!" Pipes said.

"No, no I am not. Tell him, Grandpa."

"It's true. Found an abandoned one at Saigon and restored it. A general wanted it, so I let him have it," Grandpa said.

"I would told that general to go bite my sack," Pipes said. Then he yelled, "Hey, everyone! Get this! Bernie here once restored a Knucklehead during the freaking Vietnam War!"

The conversation that had started up, stopped and everyone looked at Gavin's grandfather. Grandpa then went into the story of how he found the bike, restored the bike, and then had to give the bike up. The entire time it took his grandfather to tell the story, everyone was quiet and focused on him. By the end of the story, Grandpa had a beer of his own, and Gavin couldn't even remember if his grandfather asked for one.

"That is utterly amazing," Ralph said and his wife nodded. 'Shit, that's a story that should be on the History Channel."

"Corn's ready!" Roadkill shouted and started to pass out the cooked ears.

Paper plates had been provided, and soon everyone dug in. Steak was brought a few minutes later from an area Gavin didn't even know about, and silence fell on the group again as they ate.

Gavin ended up trying the corn and found it tasted good. It was the best corn he had ever had. He wasn't sure if it was the bacon or the fact that it was fresh from a farm. It felt like ages ago that they had stopped at Georgia's farm for it. The steak was excellent too, although Gavin had a hard time cutting it on the paper plate that was provided.

"So, where are we sleeping?" Gavin asked after the meal was over.

More beers were passed around and opened. Gavin wasn't happy that Roadkill was consuming another one, but kept quiet about it.

"Back of the van," Roadkill said and belched.

"Back of the van?" Gavin said, incredulously.

"I'll sleep in the front," Roadkill said. "There's blankets in the back there and you brought your pillow. Missing a pillowcase though."

"I think I'll call it a night," Grandpa said and stood up. "If someone would point out the nearest bathroom?"

"To the right and go down a few campsites," Pipes said. "I'll go with you."

"Mighty fine of you," Grandpa said and stood up. He looked up at the clear, now dark sky and smiled. "Forgotten how nice a night's sky can look."

As his grandfather was going to the bathroom, Gavin decided to get the back of the van ready for when his grandfather returned. It was a mess, and he wasn't sure exactly how that happened. Sure they had been traveling in it for a few days, but they hadn't been that messy. Gavin pushed their belongings to the side and started to create a makeshift bed. When he was done, there was a tight spot that would work fine for the night.

His grandfather returned ten minutes later and Gavin heard him say goodnight to everyone. Gavin found it strange at how quickly this group had welcomed them into it. He knew it was because Grandpa had been able to fix Scoot's bike, but it was still strange. He always thought of bikers as a rowdy, violence-loving group. These people were loud, but they sure didn't seem violent. That might change if they kept consuming their beers, though.

Gavin helped his grandfather into the back of the van and get settled for bed. Then Gavin asked, "You okay, Grandpa?"

"Never been better. Don't you be going to bed early. I'm old and you aren't. Go, mingle, make some memories," Grandpa said and then rolled over to his side. After a few seconds, he heard his grandfather softly snoring. He was tired.

Gavin decided to do what his grandfather said to do and got out of the van. Campfires were roaring all over the campground along with the sounds of a lot of people talking. Gavin walked back to the campfire and didn't see Roadkill anywhere.

"Where's Roadkill?' Gavin asked Pipes, who was back sitting in the same chair.

"Found himself a pretty young girl to talk to. Went with her about 15 minutes ago. You should find one yourself."

"Yeah, okay," Gavin said and looked down.

He hoped Roadkill would be okay and come back. Gavin walked over to the fire to see if there were any marshmallows to roast. What was a campfire without marshmallows? There were none, but he did find a young woman he hadn't seen before. She was standing right by the fire, facing him. She took a step closer to him, and Gavin thought she must have been lost.

"Are you the grandson of the man that refurbished that Knucklehead in Vietnam?" the young woman asked. Her voice sounded very nice. At first his eyes went to her face, which was very attractive. She had long, dark hair that was tied in a ponytail. She was smiling at him and his eyes immediately dropped. They didn't go completely down because they landed on her breasts which were bare. She had on a leather vest, but it wasn't tied in the front and she was open for all the world to see. His eyes went up to her face, then down to her breasts. Finally they turned completely away from her. It felt like he was watching a tennis match vertically. "So, are you?"

"Yeah, I, I am," Gavin said, fumbling for words. It was the first time he had ever seen bare breasts in the flesh before this close. They looked amazing with how round and full they were. And then there were her nipples! He wanted to look at them again but thought that would be rude.

"I think that's just wonderful! I'm Courtney."

"I am Gavin," Gavin managed to say. He thought he should say more, but his mind didn't seem to want to function.

"So, Gavin, are you as good with your hands as your grandfather?" Courtney asked.

"No, I just mow lawns," Gavin told her. Again his eyes wanted to stray back to her chest and a part of him wanted let them. Surely, since she was parading around without a top on, she wanted people to look.

"Well, that's too bad, cutie." Did she just call him cutie? Again Gavin felt he should say something, but the words were lost.

"Well, I have to get back. My campsite is three down from the left, if you want to talk some more, sweetie," Courtney said and then gave Gavin a kiss on the cheek.

She walked off and his eyes didn't leave her. She had on tight denim shorts that Gavin thought were called Daisy Dukes. Did she actually kiss him? What did she mean about talking some more? He could barely talk to her then.

Gavin watched her until the dark swallowed her up and then stood in the same spot. He had an erection and did not want to move until it went down. How old was she? In her early twenties maybe? He thought about Courtney's breasts again and realized he would be standing in the same spot for quite some time.

Chapter 15

Writing Entry for Friday, May 21

As you well know, St. Clair Shores has had a few famous people either born here or who have resided here. There's Dave Coulier, better known as Joey from *Full House*, and then there is Marshal Mathers. Die-hard fans would know Mathers better as Eminem, that white rapper guy.

It has been said that Mathers worked at a restaurant here in St. Clair Shores in the 90s for a while. I believe the place is called Gilbert's Lodge. The place was gutted by fire a few years back but has since reopened.

Now Mr. Kubach, you are probably wondering why I am bringing up Eminem, seeing the fact that I do not listen to rap music. Also, since my writings have had something to do with my grandfather, how does Eminem fit in?

Easy, I believe he once came to one of my grandfather's shops to get his car fixed. It was not his car per say, but his mother's. Back then Eminem was just Marshal and was probably in high school. Did you know that Eminem dropped out of high school? He liked English class but hated math and science.

His mother's car was an old Oldsmobile that looked like it was running on a prayer. Grandpa said there was a lot of rust on that baby. One good hit and the car probably would have disintegrated. Well, Marshall brought it in because his mother, who was a nurse, had to get to work. Grandpa looked it over and found the main problem was that of the carburetor. He fixed that and a few more issues that were related.

When it came time to pay, Grandpa said he did not have the heart to charge the full amount. The car was beat up, and the young man that had brought it in looked tired. Grandpa charged considerably less, namely because the parts he had used had come from wrecks that were sitting out back.

Grandpa said that the young man stayed the few hours that it took for the repairs. He just sat in the waiting room, writing something in a notebook. Grandpa said he offered Marshal some pop and snacks, which he did take. There were times when Marshal would suddenly say something in rhyme out loud.

Obviously, Grandpa had no idea who he had in the waiting room because it was well before Marshal was even Eminem. Even after he became famous, Grandpa had forgotten all about him. Then one time I was at Grandpa's main shop and was looking at some old receipts. Grandpa kept a copy of every receipt he ever created for his customers. Filed away.

I was going through the receipts because I was bored and waiting for my grandfather to get done with work. This was about a year before Grandpa retired and sold his three shops. I was seven at the time and had been interested in the history of St. Clair Shores. I had come across Eminem's name as someone who had resided in the community. He was not as big at that time in the world like he is now, but his name was still known around Detroit. I knew that his real name was Marshal Mathers. I came across a receipt that had that name scrawled on the bottom, and I just stopped.

I pulled it out and went to search for my grandfather. He was in the shop talking with one of his employees. I waited until he was done and then showed Grandpa the receipt. He asked me what he was supposed to be looking at. I told him the name on the bottom and said that it is the same name the rapper Eminem goes by. Grandpa said who and why would someone name themselves after little chocolate candies? I love my grandfather, but he was never hip. I explained about the name and then asked if it could be the same person. Grandpa took the receipt and shrugged. After looking it over, he said that the person that brought the Oldsmobile in had been a skinny white kid, not an African-American. I told him that Eminem was white.

Grandpa laughed and said the kid would never make it as a rapper. I do not know if that is racist. It sounds that way, but if it is, that is the only racist remark I have ever heard my grandfather make.

I wanted to show him a picture of Eminem but did not have one. It was 1998 and the Internet was around, but it was not as it is today. My grandfather had dial up service at the shop and it was very slow. I ended up dropping the subject. So I guess it could have been the same Marshall Mathers or just someone that shared the same name.

End of Entry

+ + +

Gavin awoke stiff from sleeping in the back of the van. The smell of fresh corn invaded his senses as he tried to stretch the stiffness out. His grandfather was still next to him, sleeping. Grandpa had gotten up a couple of times to use the bathroom and Gavin had gone with him. Each time they had gotten up, Roadkill was still not back. Also, each time they walked to the bathroom there were still a lot of people milling around. Gavin wondered when any of them would go to sleep.

He looked at the front of the van and did not see Roadkill up there. Had he not come home or had he gotten up early? It had to be the former because early and Roadkill did not go together.

Gavin quietly opened the back door to let himself out. The morning was warm, indicating that the day would be hot. The sun was just on the horizon, and Gavin guessed the time to be around seven. There were only a handful of other people up as well. Gavin didn't recognize any of them. Gavin made his way to the bathroom and found he was the only one there.

When he was done, he walked back and thought about how quiet the campground was. He knew it would not remain that way. He thought back to the night before with Courtney and wondered just where her campsite was. The mere thought of her started his engine running, and he tried to put the thought of her out of his mind. He did not need that this morning.

As he walked back to the van, he heard some shouting coming from the same direction. The shouting sounded like it was coming from his grandfather.

Gavin broke into a run and arrived a few minutes later. The campsite was no longer empty or quiet when he arrived. Pipes was there, along with Ralph and his wife. There were a few others that Gavin did not recognize. The back of the van was open and Ralph was there.

"Hey, Bernie! It's okay," Gavin heard Ralph say. Ralph looked over to where Gavin was approaching and said, "Here's your grandson now. Everything is okay."

"Grandpa, it is me, Gavin," Gavin said after getting to the van. His grandfather was inside and was shouting something that Gavin couldn't understand.

"Where? Who are these people?" his grandfather shouted. He was finally starting to make sense. "Where am I?"

"Dude's flipping out. He drop acid last night?" one of the bikers said from behind Gavin. It was one of the bikers he didn't know.

"Grandpa, we are at Sturgis. We are on our way to Colorado and stopped for the day," Gavin said. He looked around but still didn't see Roadkill. Where was that guy? Gavin could have used his help at that moment. "It is okay. We met Ralph last night. You fixed Scoot's bike, remember?"

"I, I don't," Grandpa said and the look in his eyes hurt Gavin. His grandfather was having one of his episodes, but this time it didn't seem like he was going to come out of it right away. Had he been taking his medication? Gavin couldn't remember if he had seen his grandfather take any while they had been on the trip. "Where's my room? Where are my pictures?"

"They are back at Lake View. We are on our way to Colorado to see the place where you had your honeymoon with Grandma."

"Belinda? Is she here?" Grandpa asked.

"No, Grandpa. She died 13 years ago." The fact that his grandfather asked for his dead wife really worried Gavin.

"Is he okay?" Ralph asked and sounded concerned. "Do we need to call a doctor or something?"

"He has Alzheimer's. I do not think he has been taking his medicine. He will come around after a bit," Gavin said. He hoped his grandfather would come back around anyway.

"Shit, my grandmother had that," Pipes said. He put his hand on Gavin's shoulder, whose first response was to shake it off but he didn't. "Tough luck, kiddo."

"Let's get breakfast started and leave Gavin to help Bernie," Kathy said. Gavin was thankful for that as the group broke up. Pipes was the only one that stayed behind.

"Gavin, is your father here?" Grandpa asked.

"No, he does not know we came. He could not take you, so I did. Remember?" Gavin asked hopefully. "We are traveling with my friend, Roadkill."

"Roadkill! What a, wait, is he a big guy that doesn't seem to like his father?"

"Yes! That is him!" Gavin said. There seemed to be some glimmer of remembrance in his grandfather. Gavin turned to Pipes and said, "Have you seen Roadkill yet? I do not think he came back to the van last night."

"Haven't seen him this morning yet. Last I saw he was chatting up Janice from the other side of the campground," Pipes told him. "Janice is kind of the camp whore."

"Camp whore?" Gavin said.

"Let's just say she's not too picky on who she spends her nights with," Pipes said and winked at him. So that was why Roadkill did not return. Gavin hoped his friend would wake up soon and find his way back.

"How old is this Janice?" Gavin asked.

"Late twenties or so. Thought she was too old for your buddy, but he didn't seem to mind. She ain't much to look at, but her body ain't bad. If a man has had too much to drink, she's probably pretty," Pipes said and laughed. What had Roadkill gotten himself into now?

"Gavin, I have to go the bathroom," his grandfather said. Gavin nodded and helped him out of the back of the van. His grandfather was still wearing the same clothing he had on yesterday, not that it mattered. Gavin thought most of the people here were doing the same thing.

"Need some help?" Pipes asked. Gavin told the biker that he could handle it and then led his grandfather to the bathroom.

"Where in Colorado are we going?"

"Estes Park. The cabins you stayed with Grandma closed some years back, but there is a new one there now."

"Whispering Pines!" his grandfather said and Gavin nodded. "The Bike Rally is going on, isn't it?"

"You bet it is," Gavin answered him. "Quite the spectacle, isn't it?"

"Yes, it is. What's with all the corn in the back of the van?"

***

Two hours after leaving the motel, Michael found himself going through Des Moines. He had woken up at six thirty and was on the road by seven. According to the GPS on his phone, he was now nine hours away from Estes Park. Michael was thinking about biting the bullet and just going all the way there today. He probably wouldn't get there until after ten.

His car started to feel smaller than yesterday, which was not unusual when he traveled long distances. He realized if he found them, the car would feel really tiny on the return trip.

Michael hadn't given too much thought about what he would do if he did find them. He knew that this was a shot in the dark but still felt it was the right thing to do under the circumstances. His first urge would probably be to yell at both of them- his father because he let Gavin take him on this insane trip, and Gavin because he was the one that took his grandfather. Michael didn't have any idea what he would say to Clarence Solphis.

After finding out that they had gone north, Michael evaluated when the three of them would get to Estes Park, providing that they got there at all. He figured they would get there either today or tomorrow. That was another reason he thought he would just continue on driving today. He didn't want to miss them if they did show up at Whispering Pines.

Michael had his phone number programmed into his car so he could receive calls and also make them. As he was driving he called work to see how it was going.

"Good morning, Fraser High School, this is Peggy. How may I help you?" Peggy's voice came over the speaker.

"Hey, Patty. This is Michael."

"Oh, hey, Michael. Everything going okay?" Patty asked, her voice changed from business to a little more casual.

"Haven't found them yet. I'm just calling to see how everything is going."

"Going just fine. We haven't fallen apart yet without you," Patty said. "Howard's holding down the reigns. Don't you worry about us."

"Thanks, Patty." This was a new feeling for Michael.

It was the first time he had left work for something like this. When his mother had died 13 years ago, it was during the summer and Michael had been teaching at that time. There had been no work to miss. That summer he had taken off to take some classes to work toward his doctorate.

Michael had his doctorate, but never went by the title doctor. He didn't feel comfortable using that term because he wasn't in the medical field. It was silly, but he felt more at ease when people just referred to him as Mr. Pierce.

"You go find your son and father," Patty said and then they said their goodbyes.

Michael wished that he had let Nancy come along like she initially wanted. However, he also knew someone had to stay at home in case something happened or they came home.

One thing about driving so long and by oneself, there was a lot of time for thinking. He had the radio on, turned to some classic 80s station but was barely hearing the music.

He thought about his mother and father's relationship and his with his own wife. He had fallen in love with Nancy almost immediately after they met. They met at college;

Michael had been a junior and Nancy a freshman. It was actually in a botany class. Michael needed a science class for credit and so did Nancy. They ended up working together on several projects in the class. He asked her out the second week of class and was pleasantly surprised when she said yes.

It had been a textbook romance, an almost too perfect one.

There had been fights over the years but nothing major. A lot of their fights were about Gavin and what to do about him. Nancy was not a pusher by nature, and she thought that that was the best approach on how to handle Gavin. Michael told her that Gavin needed to be pushed or else nothing would get accomplished.

During one fight, Michael brought up that he worked with adolescents, which made him more of an expert. That remark did not go over well. She reminded him that she gave birth to the boy, so that made her more the expert.

What to do about Gavin was still an issue, but they no longer fought over it. Gavin was Gavin. It was hard to get the kid motivated one way or another. College was looking less likely for his youngest son, but Michael was still holding out hope. Gavin's grades were not the best, but he did pass everything last year. It was close, though.

Michael thought about his parent's relationship as well. They had a good marriage, probably one of the best Michael had ever seen. Like Michael and Nancy, there were fights but not many. Michael had been 37 when his mother passed away. She had been in her sixties, still quite young. He was heartbroken but remembered that his father was that way as well. By then Michael had his wife to lean on, but who did his father have? His mother had been his father's whole life up to her death. It was his Mother who had helped him get his first shop. It was also his Mother that got him through Vietnam. His father had been lucky on the Vietnam tour because he saw no fighting.

Michael didn't want to imagine life without his wife. How hard it had to have been for his father to lose his lover and friend? Now, his father was losing his memories. What he had left of his wife was slowly slipping away.

When they first received the news of the diagnosis, Michael knew it would be a rough road. What he hadn't realized was how long it would take his father's mind to degenerate. At times it seemed his father was just fine- a little forgetful but nothing too bad. Then, there were days when his father had a hard time remembering people he had known all his life. Those days hadn't been many, but they were starting to become more and more frequent. How frustrating it had to be for his father to be in that condition. He was forgetting everything that made him Bernie Pierce.

Michael knew he shared some of the blame for what happened with the trip. His father had asked him to take him. Michael now realized that his father was asking for more than a buddy to go along on the trip. He was asking his oldest son to help him remember his life. Soon his father's memories would be gone and there would be no chance at recovering them.

Michael knew he should have taken him to Colorado. Hell, he could have taken Gavin along too. It might have helped their relationship. If anything happened to either one of them, Michael didn't know what he would do. Losing Naomi had been hard for him to swallow. Granted he was only seven at the time, but it was still difficult. This was his fault. He should have been the one to take his father. He had traded one responsibility for another.

"What have I done?"

***

Roadkill finally returned to the van at 10:15. He was of course wearing the same clothes as yesterday. There was a smile on his face as he approached the van, oblivious to the fact that he was so late.

"It is about time!" We could be well on our way by now!" Gavin shouted when he saw Roadkill. "What took you so long?"

"Well, if you really want to know," Roadkill said and opened the side of the van. He rummaged through some bags and pulled out an individual size bag of Rice Krispys. He opened it and poured the entire contents into his mouth. Through chewing he said, "Woke up around nine, but Janice couldn't just let me go."

"Did you not tell her that you had to get going?"

"She was very convincing on why I should stay," Roadkill said and swallowed the last mouthful of cereal. "Besides, what's our hurry? It's not like the mountains are going anywhere. I want to stay another night."

"What! No!" Gavin said in disbelief. "We could still get there today if we leave right now."

"Yeah, well, I want to stay. You're free to go if you like."

"You know I cannot drive!" Gavin said, and Roadkill just shrugged.

"One more day ain't gonna kill you," Roadkill said. "Besides, don't you want to go to Mount Rushmore? We could do that this afternoon. It's one day, Gavin."

"I am not sure," Gavin said. "Let me talk it over with Grandpa."

"Fine by me."

Gavin went to the van where his grandfather was sitting in on one of the back chairs, his eyes closed.

"Grandpa," Gavin said gently. His grandfather had gotten better as the morning passed. Gavin made sure he took both of his medications and his earlier fear had been affirmed when he saw the full supplement of pills still in the pill bottle.

"I'm awake," Grandpa said and opened his eyes. Gavin explained what Roadkill wanted and then waited for his grandfather's response. "Well, I guess we stay another night. It is after all, his van."

"Okay, but we have to get going tomorrow," Gavin said.

He went back out and told Roadkill the news. He thought his friend would be happy, but he just shrugged his shoulders again.

That morning they went into the town of Sturgis to truly behold the wonder that was the Bike Rally. Everywhere they looked, there were motorcycles. There were even two rows of parked bikes right in the middle of the main street. People crowded the streets, and one could only drive at a snail's pace.

Gavin quietly kept a lookout for Courtney but doubted he would see her in the streets with that many people. He did see a lot of other women with bikinis on, though.

"Wow! What a sight!" Roadkill said, and Gavin wondered if he meant all the bikes or the women. "And you wanted to miss all this!"

That afternoon they went to Rapid City, which was also teeming with motorcycles. They intended on going to Mount Rushmore which wasn't too far away. Pipes and Roadkill's girl from the night before, Janice, joined them. Janice was sitting in the spot in the van that was usually occupied by Gavin. Gavin had been relegated to the back in the spot next to his grandfather. Pipes sat on the floor behind them.

"Of all the times I've gone to the rally, I've only seen the faces once," Pipes had said when he heard where they were going. Roadkill then offered him a ride, which he gladly took.

Janice talked nonstop, and her train of conversation was hard to follow as she would jump from one topic to another. She talked about her friends back in Meridian, Idaho. Gavin thought the state she was from was actually fitting to what she really was. Janice would then go on a tirade about her job at the Piggly Wiggly, some grocery store, Gavin guessed.

Looking at her, it was hard to tell what Roadkill found so attractive. Her face was covered in acne scars, and her eyes didn't seem to be level. She wasn't overweight, nor was she skinny. The way she had been constantly pawing Roadkill, she seemed to be interested in him. Gavin wondered why she couldn't find someone who was more in her age range. She had to be 10 years older than him.

"It sure is beautiful here," Gavin said to his grandfather.

They were fully in the Black Hills. Gavin knew they were called the Black Hills because, from a distance, the mountains looked black with all the evergreen trees covering them. Gavin had shared that fact earlier with the company in the van and received a lukewarm reception.

Janice laughed and started calling him professor after that. Gavin would find out later that Janice had passed high school but did not go beyond that. Gavin guessed that one did not need a college degree to work at the Piggly Wiggly.

"Wait until you see the Rockies," Grandpa said.

They came up to the town that was right before Mount Rushmore, Keystone. It was a complete tourist trap with numerous stores that lined the street. They could have avoided Keystone, but Janice insisted they go through it. She also insisted they stop because they had the best gold necklaces there. Gavin didn't want to stop, but Roadkill did anyway.

"We might as well get out and look around," Pipes said.

Janice and Roadkill were already out, and she was dragging him by the hand to the nearest tourist trap. Motorcycles were everywhere and so were bikers. Gavin noticed a lot of security personnel as well, especially by the stores. He had already lost sight of Roadkill and Janice.

They walked down the sidewalk, which was barely passable with all the people. Most of the people had biker gear on, and Gavin wondered if they had brought any normal clothes or if they even owned any. There were a few families milling about but not many.

"This must be the busiest time for this area," Gavin said as he looked into a window of a store. There were displays of necklaces that claimed to be made of Black Hill gold. Gavin wondered how that was different from any other kind of gold. The fronts of some of the buildings that were along the street were made up to look like Old West structures with the large panel on top. To Gavin, it was all too much. Perhaps it was all the people that were overloading his senses, but he wanted to leave.

"This area is busy all the time. Not like this but still a lot of people," Pipes said. "I've never been here other than the Rally, but I heard that this is a big destination for vacationers."

"I read that the Sioux Native American people have been trying to get the Black Hills back from the government," Gavin said. "They said that they were tricked and taken advantage of when they lost the Black Hills."

"Who hasn't been?" Pipes said. "That won't happen. This place is too much of a moneymaker, and besides there is Rushmore to consider.

"Native Americans hold the Black Hills as sacred."

"Then this must really piss them off," Pipes said and shook his head. "History is full of unfairness and loss. Sadly, it's the way of human nature. One believes he is strong, so why not take advantage of the weak?"

"What do you do back in Owensboro?" Grandpa asked Pipes.

"I'm a philosophy professor at a university," Pipes said.

"No way!" Gavin said, and covered his mouth. Grandpa looked at him with a smile.

"What? What's hard to believe about that? Can't a professor be a biker? Or is it because I'm fat?" Pipes asked with a lightness in his voice. "It's okay, Gavin. I get that a lot. I like to have fun with it."

"I never would have imagined. I thought you were just a biker," Gavin told him.

"Not much money in that. You would be surprised at how many professionals are here. Ralph is a financial planner in Butte. His wife works at a high school as a secretary. Scoot is only Scoot here. Back in Butte, he's Dr. Saunders, an ophthalmologist. The Rally attracts all sorts. Sure there are the stereotypical bikers, but they are actually far and few. That's the greatest thing about the Sturgis Rally, you can forget your regular life for a few days. It's the attraction, I think."

"If I offended you, I apologize," Gavin said.

"No need to. I'm not easily offended. As I said before, I think it's funny. So, Gavin-who-is-going-to-be-a-senior-next-year, any plans for after?"

"No, not really," Gavin said and looked at the ground. "School really is not my thing."

"Okay. School isn't for everyone. Skills? Talents?"

"No, nothing."

"I feel I've hit a sore spot. I should move onto a different topic, but that won't help matters. Now I can say that everyone has a talent or skill, but that is complete bullshit. The truth is that *most* people have a talent or skill. And of those most people, only a small percentage actually take advantage of that particular skill," Pipes told him. Gavin lifted his head and actually looked Pipes in the eyes. "You're young. Take advantage of that. What do you enjoy doing?"

"I like sailboats," Gavin said and then looked at Grandpa, almost ashamed.

"A sailor, huh?"

"I, actually, have never stepped foot on a boat. My father does not allow it," Gavin said and felt himself blushing. He didn't like having this conversation in front of his grandfather.

"It's because of an accident that happened when his father was seven," Grandpa said. Gavin had never heard his grandfather discuss what happened with anyone else before. Grandpa gave Pipes a shorten version of what happened. Pipes was quiet throughout the story. Grandpa finished it up with, "Michael still blames himself for Naomi's death. I could never get him to realize that it wasn't his fault. It was mine."

"Thank you for sharing that with me," Pipes told him. "But I must tell you that you're wrong. You are not to blame and neither is your son. It was an accident. Those that always look into how an accident could be prevented need to realize that it has already happened. If they are looking to prevent future ones, that's great. But if they're dwelling on what could have changed in order to prevent a past one that's a waste of time. It was a tragic accident. No one was to blame."

"I've been told that before. My wife told me that a lot. She never blamed me for what happened even though she was well within her rights. Belinda never did. My marriage could have been over. It has happened to other couples when tragedy strikes, but it didn't happen to us. For that, I will be forever grateful."

"Your wife sounds like she was a very wise person," Pipes said, and Grandpa nodded. Grandpa looked like he was about to cry, which made Gavin even more uncomfortable. He wiped his eyes with the palm of his hand and shed no more tears.

"She was. She was the greatest woman I have ever known," Grandpa said. "She's why we're on this trip. My memory has been a bit hazy lately. I can remember her face, her voice, but other memories are becoming lost. Soon what I have left will be gone. Before that happens, I want to revisit one of the happier places I spent with her to see if it will sharpen my memory some. Sounds silly, doesn't it?"

"No, not at all. I was married once, but I'm divorced now. There were some good times, and I do cherish those. Sadly, the bad times outweighed the good ones. Part of the reason we got divorced. Well this conversation has taken a turn to depressing," Pipes said and turned his attention back to Gavin. "I believe we started with your skills. I'm not going to let you off that easy. Sail boating aside, what else do you enjoy?"

"I like to mow lawns," Gavin said and thought that sounded lame. "I, well, mean I mow lawns in the summer for money. Mostly just neighbor's yards. They have to be within walking distance because I do not drive."

"Just mow. Do you do anything else?"

"Sometimes I will help with other areas of yardwork like where to put flowers and such."

"You're into horticulture. That's great. Any good at it?'

"My customers do not complain. It is just a hobby," Gavin said as he watched the ground.

"Could be more, Gavin. Sometimes a hobby can turn into a career," Pipes said.

"That's true. Never thought my skill in fixing cars would amount to much, but it did," Grandpa said.

The temperature was already hot, and Gavin wanted to continue to Mount Rushmore.

"Here you guys are!" a voice from behind called. Gavin turned and saw Roadkill, along with Janice, coming up from behind. Janice had on a gold necklace that she wasn't wearing before. It didn't add much to her already lacking beauty. "We're ready to go see the faces."

They walked back to where the van was parked, a long ways away. Roadkill and Janice were still holding hands as they made their way to the van.

Soon they were back on the road to Mount Rushmore. The monument was not far away, and as they turned a corner and there they were, all four presidents- Washington, Jefferson, Roosevelt, and Lincoln. Four of the most famous presidents in American history were immortalized in granite in the Black Hills. The white faces looked very stoic on the mountain.

As they got closer, the traffic got heavier. Most of the traffic, of course, consisted of motorcycles. The parking lot was so full, they had to drive down a ways to an alternative one and take a shuttle bus back to the entrance.

Gavin thought Keystone was teeming with people, but that was nothing in comparison to Mount Rushmore. Gavin was worried that the group would get separated in the mass. He stayed close to his grandfather because he did not want a repeat of the Mall of America incident.

"It's been a long time since I have seen this," Grandpa said as they were walking. The monument was directly in front of them and with every step towards it, got bigger. "Last time I was here was with your grandmother, father, aunt, and uncle. Haven't thought about that trip in a long time."

"Construction started on the monument in 1927 and unofficially finished in 1941," Gavin said.

"Thank you, professor!" Janice yelled from behind. Gavin ignored her. He figured she had been one of the jerks when she was in school, who had made fun of the smarter kids.

"Could pick up a book at the gift shop," Grandpa said. "You would learn more that way than getting it all on the Internet."

"Cool," Gavin said and stopped his history lesson for the moment. "Wow, that is unbelievable!"

"Hard to believe that dynamite did most of that," Grandpa said and winked at Gavin. "You're not the only one that can give a history lesson, professor." Coming from Grandpa being called *professor* wasn't an insult.

They continued walking until they arrived at the mezzanine that was below the monument. It was still a decent distance from the faces, and there was a path that would take people closer, almost directly below.

They took the path below, and Gavin was all eyes the entire way. By the time they were done touring Mount Rushmore, Gavin could tell his grandfather was exhausted. Back in the van after getting a book on the history of Mount Rushmore at the gift shop, Grandpa fell asleep.

"I think what you're doing for your grandfather is very noble. I worry that you did it without your father knowing, though. Your parents must be very worried," Pipes said.

"Yeah, but my father did not agree to take Grandpa. It was now or never. Next summer would have been too late and there was no way it was going to happen during the school year. My father has his first principal job coming up. He could have taken time away now."

"How do you know that? He has to be very busy right now. School starts in less than a month, I imagine. You and your father don't sound close," Pipes said, and Gavin grunted.

"I love my father. He just does not understand me. We do not talk very much about anything. I shudder to think about what is going to happen after my last year of school. I know he expects me to go to college, but I do not think that is in the cards," Gavin said and looked over at his sleeping grandfather. "I do not care what trouble I am going to get in when I get home. I had to make this trip. You know, you should have been a psychologist. I do not usually talk to people like I do with you."

"That's not the first time I've heard that. I like to know what's going on in people's minds. Philosophy professor, remember?" Pipes said with a hearty laugh. "So, after you get your grandfather to Colorado, what next?"

"What do you mean? I guess I will return home."

"I mean, what next for you? Even after getting home. Things won't be the same for you, not after this. Your relationship with your father, your grandfather and yourself will all change."

"What do you mean?" Gavin asked.

"That is something you will have to figure out." Pipes said and didn't say any more the rest of the way back to Sturgis.

They arrived back at the campsite at eight in the evening. It was requested that Roadkill make same recipe he did the night before, which he gladly did. Grills were fired up, almost in unison as meat was prepared. Beer cans also popped open in unison and the evening's festivities were at a start. Many of the campers went into Sturgis to join in the festivities that were offered there.

As the food was cooking, Gavin found himself sitting back in the same chair he sat in the night before. He realized he hadn't had a shower since two days ago. No one seem to mind that he was stinky, probably because they were in the same shape. They would get a shower tomorrow wherever they stayed in Estes Park.

Gavin was fully planning on getting to Colorado tomorrow. He didn't regret staying an extra day in Sturgis. It had been fun, but now it was time to move on and complete what he had set out to do.

The corn and burgers were good, and Gavin was able to procure another Sierra Mist. His grandfather was visibly tired, so after going to bathroom, he went into the van.

Roadkill was still by the grill. Janice was nowhere in sight, so Gavin went over to his friend.

"What's up, Gavy!" Roadkill said when he saw Gavin. Roadkill had been drinking again, and Gavin wondered how many he had consumed. "This has been a great day!"

"It was not too bad," Gavin admitted. "Where is Janice?"

"Back at her campsite. I'm going to join her in a little bit. Said she wanted to get cleaned up."

"You are going to spend another night with her?' Gavin asked. He was worried that Roadkill would sleep in too late.

"You bet! She said she wants to properly thank me for that necklace," Roadkill said.

"You bought her that necklace?" Gavin asked. He thought that the necklace was expensive, but maybe it wasn't. "How much was that?"

"Five hundred," Roadkill said and looked toward the three grills that were now cooling. "I'll pay you back."

"What! That money came from my supply!" Gavin shouted. He kept the bulk of the money on the bottom of his duffle bag in a sock that didn't have a match. "You took my money!"

"I'm good for it!" Roadkill said and looked back at Gavin. He was no longer smiling. "You know I don't have any money myself. I think I should get something for driving you around!"

"I have been paying for all the food, gas, and lodging! Roadkill, you know we have a limited amount. Fine if you want some reimbursement for driving. I can understand that!" Gavin told him. He made a mental check to see how much was left. "But it should wait until after we get back. We still need to get to Colorado and home again."

"I don't think I'm going home," Roadkill said quietly. At first Gavin thought he heard him wrong, but then the words processed in his mind some more.

"Did you just say you are not going home?"

"Yeah, yeah I did. This place, this place is great!" Roadkill said louder. "I have never felt so accepted as I do here!"

"This place is only for a few more days! The Rally will be over and then what?" Gavin could not believe what he was hearing.

"I thought about going back to Meridian with Janice."

"Are you out of your mind? You just met that girl! Did she ask you to go with her?"

"No, but we have been getting along, like, really good," Roadkill said.

"She is ten years older than you! How do you know this is not just a fling!"

"It's not! I think I love her. I have never felt this way about a girl before. She's so damned nice to me!" Roadkill said. Gavin's mind was processing everything that was going on, trying to find something that would convince Roadkill that this was the mother of all bad ideas.

"What about my grandfather? What about taking us to Colorado? You promised to drive us!" Gavin said, his voice rising.

"I never promised anything, Gavin. You have to understand that this was *your* journey. It was not mine. My part in this story is over."

"This is not a story! This is real! How am I supposed to get Grandpa to Colorado now?"

"There has to be a bus station here or in Rapid City. I'll drive you there, and you can get there that way."

A bus was not the answer. Gavin did not want to risk bus stations having his and Grandpa's name on some watch list. He didn't know that it was even possible, but did he really want to take that chance?

"We cannot take the bus. No, you have to come to your senses and realize that you cannot go off to Meridian. What happens if she does not want you to come with her? Then what? Return to St. Clair Shores?" Gavin asked, and Roadkill was silent for a moment.

"I'm not returning there. There's nothing there for me any longer."

"What about your mother?"

"Gavin, she could care less if I was there or not. You don't understand. Your parents love you. You don't know how lucky you are. You can complain about your father all you want, but the truth is that he cares for you. Maybe he could back off a little, but trust me, that's better than having parents that don't give a shit about you," Roadkill said and looked away. Gavin thought it must be the twilight because it looked like Roadkill was crying. "Janice has been so nice to me. I never had anyone that's cared for me that way. Take your grandpa and go to Colorado. It's been fun."

"Roadkill," Gavin said, but Roadkill had started to walk away. "Roadkill! This is not right! This is ridiculous!"

He was about to go after him when a hand gripped his shoulder and held him in place. He turned around and saw it was Pipes holding him.

"I have to go after him, please let me go," Gavin said.

"Going after him won't help. He's made up his mind," Pipes said. "I heard the whole conversation. Just about everyone in the campsite did."

"Then you know why I cannot let Roadkill do this."

"Why? Because of your trip to Colorado?"

"Well, yes because of that," Gavin said and paused.

"That's a selfish reason. What's best for Roadkill?"

"It cannot be this! This is just stupid!" Gavin said and shook loose of Pipe's grip. He didn't go after Roadkill since he was now out of sight.

"Perhaps it is, but it's his mistake to make. He feels that this is what he should do. How can you stop him? There really isn't a way. Gavin, don't just put up a fight because you need him to drive you to Colorado. If he truly is your friend, you will let him go and find another way."

"What other way is there? Will you drive us?" Gavin asked. He didn't really expect Pipes would really do that, however,

"No, I'm afraid I can't. You and your grandfather are really great people, and I've had a blast talking with you two, but no, I will not drive you. Gavin, if this is going to get done, then you must find a way to do it. It's now in your hands," Pipes said and started to walk off.

"But I cannot drive! We cannot take the bus! How?" Gavin called out to the professor of philosophy.

"If it's truly important, you'll find a way."

That was the last thing that Pipes said to him as he disappeared into a nearby tent, leaving Gavin standing by the grills. Gavin put his hands in his shorts' pockets and walked back to the van. What was he going to do? How would he get his grandfather to Colorado now? Chance the busses? That way didn't feel like it would work at all.

Arriving at the van, he got in the front so as not to wake his grandfather. When he closed the passenger door, he turned and was facing the driver's side. Something hanging from the ignition caught his eyes. Roadkill had left the keys to the van hanging there.

Chapter 16

I had my learner's permit, which would surprise a lot of people. I got it last year when I was 16. My father made me get it. He said every young man at the age of 16 learned how to drive, and I was not going to be any different. My father was trying to get me to be normal and more responsible. I told him that it was a futile effort in futileness. He just looked at me funny.

I passed the permit test with ease and was permitted to drive with a responsible driver. Of course that responsible driver was my father. Our lessons did not go well. I do not know if he thought he was a great teacher and I was just a poor student, but I could tell he was getting frustrated. We would come back from our lessons, and he would storm out of the car once I parked in the garage, one time almost sideways.

That was when my grandfather stepped in. He offered to give me lessons. My father said that Grandpa did not have a valid license any longer. Grandpa said that my father could sit in the back as long as he kept his mouth shut. My lessons went better after that. I think that made my father angrier. My grandfather just knew when to push and when to hold back. My father is all push and no hold. The only thing that I had trouble with was parallel parking, but who does not have difficulty with that?

I have to admit it was fun to have lessons with my grandfather, even though my father was in the back. After I logged in all the hours I was supposed to have driving with a licensed driver, I could have taken my driving test. My father expected me to take it, but I did not. I had no desire to get my license and drive a car by myself. He asked me why I went through all the lessons getting to the point where I could get it and not even take the test. I told him once Grandpa stepped in, the lessons became fun. I liked the time in the car with Grandpa. My father just threw up his hands and stormed off. It was like watching some cartoon character get mad. The only thing missing was the steam coming out of his ears.

End of Entry

+ + +

Hot Springs, South Dakota was now in the rearview mirror and it wasn't even seven in the morning. The van was heading west on Highway 18. Grandpa was in the passenger seat, taking everything in that they were passing by. Gavin was driving.

He had told Roadkill that he couldn't drive, but that wasn't being completely honest. He couldn't drive legally. Gavin didn't have a license but he knew how to drive, thanks to the man that was sitting next to him. It had been over a year since he was last behind the wheel and his permit had expired, not that it really mattered. Grandpa wasn't a licensed driver anyway.

After seeing the keys still hanging from the ignition, Gavin knew it was serendipitous that they were there. Fate had given him the answer he sought. At first he argued with himself about doing it. It was Roadkill's van and taking it would be stealing. Then he told himself that there really wasn't any other way.

As he was mulling it over in his mind, he checked his duffle bag for the money. The supply was down quite considerably. There was only $200 left. Gavin was quite surprised and disgusted. He tried to think about how much they had gone through getting to Sturgis and didn't think it was $2,100 plus the $500 Roadkill paid for that necklace.

Had Roadkill taken that much? Gavin knew he should have kept better track of the cash, but he felt there should have been more left. Roadkill must have helped himself to some of it. Two hundred dollars was not enough to get them to Colorado and back again. If they were lucky, it might get them there. That upset Gavin, and it also helped him make a decision about something that he kept going over and over again in his mind.

That morning, using his grandfather's watch as an alarm, he woke up at five. It had been a restless sleep, and he attributed that to what he was planning on doing. The camp was quiet, three in the morning seemed to be the camp's bedtime. He went to wake Grandpa up and found him already up. Gavin was glad to see that his grandfather was not having one of his fugues.

"We are leaving as soon as we are done with a bathroom break," Gavin told his grandfather.

"Roadkill?" Grandpa asked, and Gavin shook his head.

"He is not coming with us. He has decided to stay with Janice. He told us good luck." Gavin didn't tell his grandfather that Roadkill was unaware of them taking his van. After finding some of the money gone, Gavin's qualms about taking the van were gone. He had paid for it; it was just that Roadkill didn't realize it.

Gavin chose to get up early for one main reason. He wasn't worried about Roadkill getting up before they left. There was no chance of that. He wanted to leave before the camp got up and created more traffic. His driving skills were minimal and rusty. Trying to navigate the van through a sea of motorcycles just did not appeal to him.

As he left the camp, he felt a small pang of remorse about what he was leaving behind. Roadkill had been a good friend, no matter how it ended. He wished he could have had a better good bye with him. Also, he wished he could say good bye to the others, especially Pipes. They were a good bunch and treated him and his grandfather well.

What would their reactions be when they discovered Gavin and his grandfather were gone? He could imagine Roadkill waking up, walking back to the van, and finding it gone. Gavin had left Roadkill a parting gift; he left the remaining corn in a pile where van had been parked.

Because of the missing money, Gavin didn't think Roadkill would call the police. True, it would be hard to prove that Roadkill took the money, but he wouldn't see it that way. It was a tradeoff. Gavin thought he should have confronted Roadkill about the money, but if he had done that, he wouldn't have gotten the van.

Getting his grandfather to Colorado was more important than ever for Gavin. They had gone so far and come so close. When they finally arrived there, Gavin would figure out what to do to get them home.

"We'll be leaving the Black Hills soon," Grandpa said. "It was a nice stay. Did you have a good time?"

"Yeah, I guess I did," Gavin said and meant it. He had met some nice people, had a nice talk with a semi topless girl, and received his first kiss. All in all, not a bad couple of days. "We should get to Estes Park by this afternoon."

"Estes Park? What's there?" Gavin took his eyes off the road to look at his grandfather and saw a smile on the old man's face. "Just kidding. So, how do you think Roadkill will take us using his van without his knowledge?"

"You knew!"

"Didn't take much. I doubt Roadkill would just turn his van over to you."

"Well, you are right. I did pay for it. He just does not realize it yet," Gavin said and told Grandpa about the missing money. Grandpa shook his head in disappointment.

"He's a nice young man, but I worry about what life might have planned for him. He's heading for a sad ending. One similar to the father he so despises," Grandpa said.

"What makes you think his father had a sad ending?"

"What other ending can you have when you leave your family?"

The terrain was declining into smaller hills, and Gavin could see flat land ahead. He glanced at the rearview mirror and saw the Black Hills back there. Pine trees were in abundance, some were a pleasant dark green while others were in the process of dying. "It takes a real man to stick it out and make sure his family is cared for. Sure, he might get a divorce if things aren't working out with the wife, but if there are children involved, one doesn't just leave."

"Grandpa, am I a disappointment to my father?" The question surprised not only his grandfather but him as well.

"Well, that's a big statement. Your father loves you, you know that. I know that's not what you asked, but I wanted to get that out anyway. Your brother went to college, which your father holds as greatly important. College is important, don't get me wrong, but it's not for everyone. Your father is in education and feels everyone should be educated. He's not wrong there at all. It's just how a person gets educated is where he's wrong," Grandpa said and paused for a moment. "I want to say that you're not a disappointment to your father, but in truth I cannot. Nor can I say that you *are*, so don't jump to conclusions there.

"When a person imagines the children he or she has, there are certain things that the person imagines. When that person has a child that doesn't meet expectations, it can be quite shocking. Does disappointment set in? Maybe, but that's when the person needs to realize what being a parent is all about. Being a parent is loving his or her child. One doesn't have to like his or her child's decisions but that doesn't mean the child is a disappointment. I'm sorry I'm not answering your question. I just can't speak for your father. I can speak for me, however. You are *not* a disappointment to me."

"Thank you, Grandpa." Silence descended on the van, but it was a good silence as the two concentrated on the road ahead.

***

Michael had forgotten how beautiful the Rockies were. It had been a long time since he was last there as a child. He was now wondering why he had never taken his family on vacation here. It was almost nine in the morning, and he was looking out of the window of his rented cabin.

He arrived last night at ten o'clock. He had pushed hard and made it. Earlier that afternoon, he had gotten a call from Whispering Pines. When he saw the number he got excited, but the call wasn't about his son or father. They had called because an opening had become available, and even though there were others ahead of him on a waiting list, the manager decided to bump Michael up. So there was a cabin if he wanted it. Michael thought for a moment and said that he would take it. He needed to sleep somewhere, so why not there? Michael told them he would be arriving that evening around ten and was told that arriving late wouldn't be a problem.

The cabin had two bedrooms, a small living room, a bathroom, and a small kitchen area. The décor was on par with the name of the place with all the pictures of pine trees hanging in the rooms. There was a flat screen television in the living room with a couch in front of it. Michael had yet to turn it on.

After he got settled in the cabin, he called home and talked with Nancy for a while. There had been no news from the home front. Nancy was relieved that he had made it to Estes Park safely. He told her he would call again tomorrow.

After talking with her, he thought about calling Detective Wellington but decided against it. Wellington would call him if something came up. By now, Michael thought the only reason Wellington would call him was if there was bad news.

The following morning, Michael woke up feeling better than he had in days. It could have been the mountain air, even though he was still trying to get used to the change in altitude. Michael knew it would take a few days to get used to it and doubted he would be there that long.

At nine o'clock there was a knock at the cabin door. It was the manager, who asked if he could come in.

"Mr. Pierce, I'm Kevin Quincy, head manager here at Whispering Pines. I'm sorry I wasn't here last night to greet you." The manager was shorter than Michael and a lot thinner, and Michael thought Kevin was older than him by ten years.

"That's okay, Mr. Quincy. I got in around ten," Michael said and wondered why the manager would worry that he wasn't there when Michael arrived.

"Please, call me Kevin. When we first got your call about your son and father, we didn't think much of it. But the more you called, the more concerned we became. We've been keeping an eye out for them. I also talked with the police here and told them about the situation. You might want to go over there today and touch base with them. I was told they had some detective from Michigan already talking to them about your situation. It's quite the story," Kevin said.

"Thanks, Kevin. I plan on going to the police station today to let them know I'm here. I don't know what good it will do, being here, but I had to come."

"Of course you did. I can't imagine what you and your family are going through. Your son takes your father who has Alzheimer's and disappears with him. You haven't heard anything from them?"

"Not a word. For all I know, they might not even be coming here."

"You must be somewhat certain, though. I wasn't going to tell you this, but I arranged for you to have an open cabin. I was able to find another place for the people who had the cabin rented," Kevin said with a smile.

"You didn't have to do that!" Michael said.

"Don't worry about the renters, they are staying at a, well, more refined place for the same cost. I was drawn to your story and wanted to make sure you had a place here at Whispering Pines," Kevin said. They were sitting across from each other at the table that was in the kitchen area. Michael couldn't help but thinking that there was more to Kevin's hospitality.

"That was very nice of you," Michael said.

"Well, I wanted to talk to you about something. I have a friend who works at *The Denver Post*. I casually told him about your situation, and he is interested in your story. He would like to interview you if you're willing."

There it was. That was what the manager was really interested in. It probably would be good press for the Whispering Pines. At first Michael was going to say no, but then he hesitated.

"I'll tell you what, if my son and father do make it here, your friend can have an interview. As I said before, they might not even come here. My son doesn't drive and the person that has been driving them is, well, erratic with his decisions," Michael said.

If they arrived, then everything would be fine and a news story would be fine. He was kind of surprised that nothing had been made of it already. He supposed if something bad happened, then it would definitely make the news.

"Fair enough. Mr. Pierce, I hope everything turns out fine," Kevin said and stood up. "Please keep me updated on the search."

"Sure," Michael said and then the manager left.

Michael had mixed feelings about Kevin. He seemed nice enough, and it made sense that he would want positive press for his business, but there was just something about him that didn't set well. Michael waited a few minutes and then walked outside. He hadn't had breakfast yet because he hadn't had time to get any food. He planned on going into Estes Park to talk with the police and then get some food. Being unsure of how long he would be staying, Michael thought he would buy enough food for a few days.

Since he came in during the dark, he hadn't fully seen the mountains. Stepping outside, he was really able to take them in. The sky was clear, but that could change in a flash.

Michael remembered the afternoon storms that occasionally happened in the mountains.

The cabin faced south and there were mountains right across Fall River Road, where Whispering Pines was located. There were more cabins across the way, right in front of the mountains.

Michael knew that on the other side of the mountains there was another road with even more cabins and hotels. If he were to travel down that road, it would take him to Rocky Mountain National Park. He doubted he would be visiting the park on this trip. He wasn't here for a pleasure vacation, though he did wish that Nancy and Pauline had come with him. They would love it here.

Michael locked the cabin up and walked to his car that he had spent so much time in the past two days. He looked at it and couldn't believe that he had made 1,300 miles in two days. As he got in, he wondered where Gavin and his father were at that moment. He hoped that they would make it here. There was a lot he wanted to say to them.

***

Wyoming was nothing but an arid landscape. The van was traveling on Highway 18 still, but they had long since passed into Wyoming. What seemed really strange to Gavin were the towns that they passed on the highway. Some of the towns had populations smaller than 20. One town had the whopping population of seven. Gavin wondered why bother even having a town there? How could the town survive with such a small amount of people?

It was ten in the morning, and they had the windows rolled down because the air conditioning was not working. It had stopped just as they'd left South Dakota. Gavin hoped it wasn't a sign of things to come. Even with the windows open, it was getting hot in the van. He was worried about his grandfather and hoped the heat wouldn't cause him to have a heat stroke.

Gavin planned on stopping in Lusk, which looked like it had a population bigger than 20. There, they could take a bathroom break and purchase some bottles of water. Gavin was worried about the dwindling funds, but he thought they could spare some for water.

"Not much out here," Gavin remarked.

"It's Wyoming. The dust clouds outnumber the people," Grandpa said. "The part with Yellowstone is nice, but this part, not so much."

"What do you remember about Grandma?" Gavin asked as he kept his eyes on the road. He was still getting used to the driving aspect but had been getting better. His speed increased, and they were close to going the speed limit.

"I remember her face, of course, and the sound of her voice. There are other aspects I remember, but there is too much that's blank in my mind. The last few days have shown me that some memories have not been completely lost, only buried. I have been trying hard to remember my honeymoon with your grandmother. All I get is fog. I'm afraid that that one memory is lost. If it is, how many others are gone with it?" Grandpa said and sighed. He looked out the window at the passing scenery. "Getting old is not an easy thing to do. And the strange thing is, when did I get to be so old?"

"Grandpa, you are not old," Gavin said, and Grandpa laughed.

"You're kind, but I'm 75 and have Alzheimer's. That has to count for something. Perhaps if I didn't have this disorder, I wouldn't feel so old."

"Grandpa, this conversation is depressing."

"That it is. So let's change the subject. You told Pipes yesterday about having a skill in lawn service. Have you ever thought about looking into that?"

"There is no future in that."

"Grass always grows."

"In summer," Gavin said. "Where are you going with this?"

"Just making some conversation," Grandpa said, but Gavin doubted him. "Seems like you are better at other aspects of lawn care. Horticulture is a good career choice. You're outside most of the time, and you have the possibility to work on your own."

"I have no idea what goes into learning horticulture."

"That's what education is for. I'm not saying a four year college, but there are two year programs that would teach you what you need to know," Grandpa said.

"I think I liked the conversation about you being old better."

"You don't like to talk about your future, do you?"

"No, I do not."

"Why not?" Grandpa asked. Gavin was silent for a moment, and his grandfather seemed to know he was thinking about the question.

"Because it is so uncertain," Gavin finally said. "I do not like the uncertain or unexpected."

"This trip was uncertain. There were unexpected events that happened, but here we are."

"I planned this trip, the routes, the stops, and where we would stay."

"And how did that turn out?"

"We made stops that were unplanned and stayed at places that were not on the list," Gavin said.

"Did the unexpected happen?"

"Yes," Gavin said and his thoughts immediately thought of Courtney.

"And was it all bad?" Grandpa asked and for a moment Gavin thought his grandfather knew what he was thinking about.

"Some of it was."

"Yeah, yeah some of it was. But some of it wasn't. You cannot predict the unexpected. That's why it is called the unexpected. You just have to deal with it the best way you can. By accepting what you can't change and doing the best with what you can," Grandpa said. "Doesn't matter how much you plan, Gavin. The unexpected will always happen."

"So, I should not be afraid of the unexpected future?"

"No, but you can be a bit wary. It's okay to make plans but realize that those plans will change."

"Thanks, Grandpa," Gavin said but wasn't sarcastic. If those words had come from his father, Gavin would never have even listened. Coming from Grandpa, it was a lot different. "Lusk is coming up. I thought we would stop and take a break."

"Good idea. I have to tap the lizard something fierce," Grandpa said, and Gavin looked at him funny. "I have to go the bathroom."

"How does tapping a lizard equate to going to the bathroom?"

"How doesn't it?" Grandpa responded and laughed. There were times when Gavin didn't understand Grandpa's humor at all.

***

At first Bernie kept a wary eye on Gavin as he drove the van. Gavin had been visibly nervous and the van would weave slightly. The more he drove, the better he got. He seemed to be remembering the lessons Bernie had given him. As they got farther into Wyoming, Bernie stopped watching Gavin altogether.

Bernie was tired. That's all it was, pure exhaustion. After doing nothing for almost three years, the last few days had been very pressing on him. There was no way he would ever trade the past three days for anything, though. For the past three days he had lived for the first time since going to Lake View. There was a world out there that he had forgotten and part of the forgetting could not be attributed to the Alzheimer's. Too long he had been dormant at the home. It was too easy just to give up and go with the flow there. Bernie knew the place was nice and they treated him fine, but it was still a trap all the same, a trap where it was all too easy to just sit around and let life pass one by.

When he realized he needed to get out of Lake View, even for a little bit, he knew he wanted to try and reclaim what memories he could. Thinking that Michael would be the one to take him, he hoped for at least a pleasant trip. When Michael basically refused, and Gavin stepped in, Bernie accepted because he knew that it was his last shot.

Being on the trip with his grandson was a dream come true. The trip had stirred feelings he hadn't felt in a long time.

"Cheyenne is coming up," Gavin said. "I believe it is the biggest city in Wyoming."

"What, do they have a hundred people?" Bernie asked, and Gavin laughed.

Bernie liked to make his grandson laugh. It was like making Bucky Stevens laugh. There weren't many similarities between Bucky and Gavin, but both only laughed when something truly funny happened. There was no pity laugh just to be polite.

It was sad to think that he hadn't thought of Bucky in a long time until recently. Bernie was probably the last person on Earth to remember that Bucky Stevens existed. When the Alzheimer's claimed his memories of his friend, his friend would no longer exist. The world would move on. That was the cold hard truth of everything. Bernie could try and hold onto his memories as long as possible, but in the end it didn't matter. When he died, at least there would be those that remembered him. His friend Bucky only had a handful of people that ever remembered him, and all were gone except for one.

"So, if a person moves out of Wyoming, what happens?" Gavin asked. Bernie smiled, knowing the answer but didn't say anything. "The population of the state is cut in half."

"And if a person moves into the state, the population is doubled," Bernie finished.

Both laughed at Wyoming's expense. Bernie looked back out the window and saw that it was getting dark out. It was too early to be dusk, so Bernie looked in the rearview mirror. Dark storm clouds had arrived and had arrived in a hurry. He knew what those clouds meant. Heavy rain was coming and if they were lucky, that was all. "Gavin, you might want to pick up the speed."

"What? I am going the speed limit, finally," his grandson said.

"Yes, but we have storm clouds moving in. Perhaps we can get ahead of them where it won't matter."

Bernie felt the van pick up speed, but after a few minutes, he knew it didn't matter. The storm was going to overtake them no matter how fast they were going. The first drops started falling with big splatters on the windshield. Gavin turned the wipers on and thankfully they worked. The heavy drops remained but started falling harder. Soon the visibility was down to just the car in front.

"Should I pull over?" Gavin asked. His face was pale, and Bernie saw that his grandson had a death grip with both hands on the steering wheel. Gavin's question was a viable one, and Bernie thought about it.

"No, just concentrate on the car in front of you. And turn the lights on," Bernie instructed. They could make out the car in front by the taillights. Gavin searched the dashboard, found the button and pulled it out to turn the lights on. The headlights did little for visibility, but at least the people behind them would be able to know that they were there.

"Are you sure we should not pull over?" Gavin said, louder this time because the pounding of the rain was drowning out all other sound.

"I'm sure. There could be flashfloods from this torrential downpour. This land is too flat for any kind of drainage. Just keep driving, we'll get out of it," Bernie said, trying to sound confident.

They still had visual contact with the car in front, but it was getting tougher. The road looked like it was no longer, there as the rain had covered it in a sheet of water. Bernie's left foot was stepping on an invisible gas pedal. The red taillights were still there, and Bernie was thankful that the car's driver had the same idea of just getting out of the rain.

"Grandpa, we cannot keep going like this!" Gavin shouted over the pounding rain. They were passing road signs, but Bernie couldn't read them. They were just quick green blurs in his perpendicular vision.

"Just keep going, it should…" Bernie started out and just like that, they were out of the rain. There was no slowing down of rainfall, it just stopped abruptly. "It's over. You can slow down now."

"Good," Gavin said, and Bernie could feel the van decelerating.

Before slowing down, Bernie glanced at the speedometer and saw that they had been doing 90 miles per hour. His grandson, who hardly had any driving experience, had just driven 90 miles per hour through a pounding rainstorm. Either the kid was going to be a great driver, or they had been very lucky.

Another green road sign was coming up, which indicated their turn. During the storm, they had passed by Cheyenne without knowing. Bernie was about to mention the turnoff, but Gavin turned the signal on and started up the exit ramp. "We are an hour out of Loveland, and then it is about 30 miles to Estes Park."

"Would you like to find a spot and pull off? That had to be quite stressful on you," Bernie mentioned to Gavin.

"I can make it to Loveland if you can," Gavin said.

Bernie nodded and the journey continued. After four days they were close to the final goal. Bernie felt he would remember Belinda and the time they spent on their honeymoon, but how many of the memories would come back? Would they be the ones that truly mattered? How would he feel if the memories didn't come back? What would he do if those memories were lost forever?

Bernie didn't want to think of that possibility. If that happened, then the goal of the trip would have failed. If that happened, however, the trip was not a complete waste. This trip had been good for Bernie and for Gavin as well.

Bernie settled back in the chair and looked out the windshield. He knew the Rocky Mountains would soon be visible, and he didn't want to miss that.

Chapter 17

Writing Entry for Friday, June 4

I have mentioned that my grandfather had owned three automotive repair shops, the original one in St. Clair Shores and two in the surrounding areas. He was nervous at first when he opened his second store because he knew he would have to hand over responsibility to a manager. The first manager seemed quite capable of running the new shop. It was the third one that gave Grandpa problems.

Grandpa said that the guy seemed great when he interviewed him so he hired him. The trouble did not start until a month later when Grandpa started getting complaints from workers at the shop and customers.

Grandpa prided himself on doing quality work at affordable prices. He was an honest mechanic and made sure his employees followed suit. He said a happy customer was a returning customer. An unhappy customer did not come back, and there was a chance that the unsatisfied customer would reach out and make his or her gripes known, creating a reputation resulting in other people being less likely to come into any of the shops with the same name.

Confronting the guy did not work; he just denied it. Grandpa wanted proof that the manager was over charging for labor and charging for work that was not necessary. At the time, on the ABC Television Network, there was a news show that would run stings to catch people doing all sorts of illegal activity.

My grandfather was a huge fan of that show. So he decided to set up a sting of his own. My grandfather asked one of Grandma's friends to be the one to go in with her car. She agreed, in return for some free repairs. Kathy Polluck was her name, and she drove a 1977 Chrysler New Yorker. Grandpa said the thing was a boat. He checked it over from trunk to stern to make sure everything was running just fine. There was only one problem with the car, and Grandpa wanted it that way. The one problem would be what the car would be taken in for. Grandpa waited until his target was the one on shift and Kathy brought her car in.

As Grandpa was waiting to hear from Kathy, he was nervous. Grandpa bet that the ones that put on the stings on the ABC show did not sweat as much as he was. He worried that the manager would actually fix the car properly. He was not worried that the manager would figure out it was a sting because Grandpa felt the man was not bright enough.

Grandpa was in the shop when he got the call from Kathy. She said she had just received the estimate for the repairs. It was four times more than Grandpa would have charged, and the manager had also said there were several things wrong other than the actual reason the car was brought in.

Grandpa went over to his third shop and walked in. Kathy was sitting in the waiting area and another employee was behind the desk. He recognized Grandpa and stood up. Grandpa told him to relax.

After that, Grandpa walked back to the shop. The manager was the only one back there, and he was not even working on the New Yorker. He could not suppress his surprise at seeing his boss unexpectedly. Grandpa looked at the New Yorker and then at his manager. He then told the crooked man before him all about the sting. At least the manager did not try and deny it. He knew he was busted. Grandpa fired him on the spot.

Grandpa then went back into the records and looked at all the customers that the fired manager had personally helped. It took Grandpa over a year to fix what mess the manager had made. Grandpa refunded the customers' money, which set him back financially. He did not have to refund the money because the customers were not aware of any wrongdoings. He did it because it was the right thing to do. The manager had made a mess in Grandpa's name, which was something that could not be undone. Grandpa had never cheated anyone in his life. He believed in treating people with respect and hoping to get the same back. In this world today, that is a hard mantra to live by.

End of Entry

Loveland was a pleasant city. The mountains loomed to the west and the city surrounded a lake. It was three o'clock when they arrived there and stopped at a park to use the bathroom. Gavin stared at the mountains in awe.

"These are twice the size as the ones in South Dakota!" he said.

"Just wait until we are driving through them," Grandpa said.

He sounded tired. Gavin hoped to get going so they could rest once they got to Estes Park. He was well aware of his money situation but thought they had enough for at least one night at a motel. They had filled up before the ordeal in Cheyenne and had enough gasoline to get them to Estes Park. Since both had used the bathroom, Gavin figured it was time to leave.

"Shall we move on? We are only 30 miles away."

"And about to go on one of the most beautiful stretches of road in the United States."

They got in and Gavin turned the key in the ignition. Nothing happened. Gavin tried again. The car didn't start. The lights were on, so it wasn't the battery.

"It will not start," Gavin said.

"Pop the hood," Grandpa said and opened the passenger door. Gavin pulled the lever and got out himself. They both looked at the engine, although only one of them had an idea what he was looking at.

"What is it?" Gavin asked.

"Well since it's not the battery, it could be a number of things. Since the car sounds like it wants to turn over, my guess is the fuel pump," Grandpa said, still peering at the engine."

"Is that an easy fix?" asked Gavin.

Grandpa laughed. "Would be if I was in my shop with the right tools and parts," he said. "Sorry, kiddo. It's the end of the line for our ride."

"Shit!" Gavin yelled out. People, who were enjoying the day at the park, turned and looked at them.

"I do believe that is the first time you have ever sworn in my presence," Grandpa said. Actually, it was the first time Gavin had ever sworn.

"How are we going to get to Estes Park now?" Gavin asked.

He wanted to go over and kick the van but knew it was pointless. Were there buses that went there? If so, how much would that be? They had $115 left, and Gavin thought that even if there was a bus that went to Estes Park, they would not have enough. The thought of hitchhiking briefly entered his mind, but he had no idea how to go about it. Who would even entertain the thought of giving them a ride?

It was over. They were 30 miles from their destination, and that was as far as they would get. Had he been alone, he would have just walked, but there was no way his grandfather could make that distance. He sat down on the curb and put his head in his hands.

"Gavin, it's okay," his grandfather said as he sat down next to him.

"No, no it is not. I promised you that I would get you to Whispering Pines. How can we get there now? There is no way. We are stuck. Heck, I do not even know if we have enough to stay in a motel tonight," Gavin said, his head now buried in his arms.

"We can sleep in the van," Grandpa said. "Worked the last few nights."

"Yeah, but what about the next few days? We cannot spend it in this park. How can we come so close and not make it! It is just not fair!"

"That's life, Gavin. It's been a fantastic trip. I am still glad I went, no matter how it ended."

"I promised, Grandpa. You always kept your promises to me. Now I cannot."

"Gavin, from no fault of yours. You tried your hardest to keep it. That is what counts. Some promises can't be kept," Grandpa told him, and Gavin lifted his head. There were tears coming down from his eyes, and he was embarrassed.

"Did you ever make a promise you could not keep?"

"Yes, I did," Grandpa said. He was silent for a moment and then said, "I promised Naomi when she was a baby that I would always take care of her and keep her safe. That obviously didn't happen."

"But Grandpa that was an accident. That was not your fault."

"Neither is this yours. It just happened. We had a good run. We gave it our best shot and came up a little short. The question is what are we going to do now?" Grandpa asked.

Gavin had a feeling Grandpa already knew what they were going to do. It was just up to Gavin to make the decision. They sat in silence for a few minutes as Gavin mulled it over in his mind. He realized by the end that there really wasn't any thinking needed on the matter. He really had no choice. That was when he started to look around the park.

***

The police department was a waste of time, Michael thought. They listened politely and then said they would keep an eye out. Michael didn't expect anything huge to happen when he went there, but he was hoping to be better received.

It had taken him an hour to find someone who had talked to Detective Wellington. As Michael was talking, he realized there was little that police here could do. He ended the conversation by saying he just wanted them to keep an eye out.

After talking with the police, Michael went to the grocery store, which was very busy. There were a lot of tourists and campers stocking up. As Michael walked through the aisles, he thought about what he wanted to get. The problem was what to get and how much because he had no idea how long he would be in Estes Park. He originally had thought of getting enough for two days and decided to stick with that. The cabin he was at had a grill, so he thought he'd make use of that. He selected what he would need for a hamburger meal, and then decided to treat himself to a good New York strip steak.

He arrived back at the cabin at four o'clock and put the groceries away. He went outside and sat on the deck chair, just looking at the mountains. His cell phone rang, and he looked at who was calling. He didn't recognize the name on the screen and thought about not answering it. He thought again and then pressed the answer button.

"Hello, Michael Pierce speaking."

"Dad, it is me, Gavin," his son's voice said over the phone. At first Michael thought he was hearing things.

"Gavin, is it really you?" Michael said and realized at how stupid that sounded.

"Yes, it is really me. Dad, I, uh, need help," Gavin said.

"Is it your grandfather? Did something happen to your grandfather?" Michael knew something like this would happen. "How bad is he?"

"Grandpa is fine. We're stuck in Loveland. The van will not start."

"Loveland? Wait, where did you get a van? Is it Clarence's? Is he there with you?"

"Dad, slow down. It is Roadkill's van, but he is not with us. It is a long story. We are almost out of money. We need help," Gavin said and sounded close to tears.

Michael realized that Gavin must be out of ideas if he was calling him for help. Then it hit him about the money. How could they almost be out of money? They had started with close to $3,000. Michael decided to worry about that later.

"Where are you in Loveland?"

"At some park by the lake. There is a fake Statue of Liberty across the street."

"I remember the place. Stay put. Someone will pick up in a little bit," Michael said. "Just stay there."

"We really cannot go anywhere unless it is on foot," Gavin said. "We will be here."

"Good, and Gavin, we have a lot to talk about."

With that the conversation ended. Michael purposely didn't tell his son that he would be the one picking them up. He thought it would be best if he didn't mention that.

Michael took his keys out and headed to his car. It would take about 40 minutes to get to Loveland depending on traffic. Michael realized that the last few days' ordeal would soon be over.

***

Gavin gave the cell phone back to its owner and thanked her. The 20-something girl then walked off, leaving Gavin alone with his grandfather.

"That was nice of that young lady to let us use her phone," Grandpa said. Gavin just nodded. He was embarrassed because he had cried in front of the girl. It was probably why she let him use her phone. "How did the conversation go?"

"He is sending someone to come pick us up. The police, probably. He said to just sit here and wait," Gavin said and sat down on the curb next to the van.

He couldn't believe it was over. A part of him wanted to take his grandfather before the police arrived. But where would he take him? Where would he find someone that would take them to Estes Park? Should they walk along Highway 34 and hope someone would pick them up? No, they could not do that. Grandpa would never make it. He was tired as it was.

They were stuck. The police would arrive, take them to the station, and then either hold them or send them home on a bus. Would Gavin get charged with something? There were another thousand burning questions in Gavin's mind that wouldn't be answered until the police arrived.

"We had a good run, didn't we, Gavin?" Grandpa said. "You got lost at the Mall of America, peed on the side of the road, and attended a cat's funeral."

"Wait, I got lost at the mall?" Gavin said. He looked at his grandfather and saw him smiling.

"I knew where I was the whole time."

"Sure you did. So, looking forward to getting back home?" Gavin asked.

Gavin missed some aspects of St. Clair Shores, but he also felt he had grown so much. He realized that the Nautical Mile was just one beautiful place to visit. The world never felt so open to him. Going back home, he could resume his mowing job and start his routines up again. Would it be the same though?

"Yeah, about as much as I look forward to Howard farting after he eats the meatloaf. I'll just resume my boring existence until, well you know," Grandpa said.

Gavin did know. He wished there was something he could do, but he had already failed on his first attempt at helping his grandfather.

They sat there for another 40 minutes just watching the people in the park and looking at the mountains. Gavin wished he could go further into them but knew that it would not happen.

Gavin's stomach rumbled, which surprised him. After all that happened, he was getting hungry. He wondered if the police would at least feed them.

A car pulled into the park's parking lot. At first Gavin didn't take too much notice of it. It pulled into a spot next to the van. It was maroon and a Buick Verano. It reminded Gavin of his father's car. He saw the license plate and noticed that it was from Michigan. What were the odds of that?

The driver's side door opened and out stepped a man that looked like his father. It couldn't be him, because his father was 1,300 miles away. In addition, this man wasn't wearing a suit but shorts and a T-shirt.

"Do you guys need a ride?" the man said, and he even sounded like his father.

"Dad?" Gavin said as he stood up. "How? You are supposed to be in Michigan."

"So are you," his father said. They stood looking at each other for a moment and then his father moved closer. He grabbed Gavin by the shoulders and pulled him in for an embrace. It was the first time in a long time that Gavin and his father hugged. "I was so damned worried about you."

"I am sorry, Dad," Gavin said and he could feel himself crying for the second time today. "I, I…"

"Michael," his grandfather started to say. Michael ended his hug with his son and then hugged his father.

"Dad, I'm so glad to see that you're fine."

"Gavin took good care of me," Grandpa said. "Please don't blame him for this. I forced him to do it."

"Dad, if that was even true, I wouldn't believe it. You two have been out here for a while. Grab your stuff and let's go," his father said.

"Dad, how did you get here so fast?" Gavin asked as he walked over to the van.

"I'll explain when we get into the car," his father said. Gavin opened the back and grabbed their duffle bags. Everything they had was in those two bags. His father opened the trunk of the Verano, which Gavin saw was empty. He placed the bags in it and the trunk was shut with a loud bang.

"What about Roadkill's van?" Gavin asked as he looked at the vehicle that he had traveled in the last few days. He was actually going to miss that old van.

"I'll call the Loveland Police and let them deal with it," his father said. "The thing looks like it has seen the last time it would run. Where is Clarence?"

"Sturgis," Gavin said as he was about to get in the backseat. His father shook his head and indicated the front seat. Gavin guessed his father wanted to discuss what happened.

"Sturgis, boy this should be an interesting story," his father said and helped Grandpa into the backseat.

Once everyone was buckled, his father pulled out. Gavin looked back as the van fell away in the distance. He turned around and noticed that they were heading west, into the mountains.

"Dad, we are going the wrong way," Gavin said. He was still trying to grasp the fact that he was sitting next to his father.

"No we're not," his father responded. "We're going to finish what you started."

"What? Really? But, I thought you would take us home," Gavin said.

"I will but not until *after* we go to Estes Park."

"Thank you, son," Grandpa said from the backseat.

"No need to thank me, Dad. I should have done this in the first place," Michael said, and again Gavin was shocked. "Don't get me wrong, I'm still upset that the two of you endangered your lives, but I've had some time to think. And this is what's for the best."

"Well, I'm glad to see I didn't raise a complete asshole," Grandpa said and Gavin thought his father would be upset about that comment.

Dad just laughed. "Gavin, sit back and enjoy the view.

Enjoy the view he did. The ride was gorgeous. Highway 34 was winding around mountains and followed the Big Thompson River. Gavin was all eyes as he took everything in. None of the three talked, even though the other two had been this way before. His dad had just driven from this road, but his grandfather hadn't seen it for quite some time. The mountains went straight up and Gavin could see why they were called them the Rocky Mountains.

"Is that a store that sells cherry cider?" Gavin said as they passed some buildings.

"Yep. That place has been there for quite some time," Grandpa said.

"I remember passing that place when we came here when I was a kid," Dad mentioned.

"How old were you?" Grandpa asked.

"Seven," Dad said. The fact that Grandpa could not remember Dad's age did not escape either of them as they looked at each other. "We will be staying at the Whispering Pines when we get there."

"How did you pull that off?" Gavin asked. "That place took over when Cabins by the Thompson closed."

"You'll see how I pulled it off when we get there. It will be part of your penance for going on this trip," Dad said with a smile. Gavin wondered what that was all about. "When we get there, I have some phone calls to make. In fact, I'm going to make one now and you will do the talking."

"Mom, right?" Gavin asked.

"No, the president of the United States," Dad said. He pressed some buttons on the console, and Gavin heard a phone ringing over the speakers.

"Hello?" Gavin's mother's voice came over the speakers.

"Honey, guess who I have in the car next to me and in the backseat?" Dad said.

"It better be Gavin and your father," his mother said.

"Hi, Mom," Gavin said after his father looked at him.

"Gavin! It's about time! Are you all right? Is your grandfather okay?"

"We are both fine, Mom," Gavin said and felt the tears coming again. What was with him? He never cried this much. "I am sorry to put you through this."

"Damn right, you'd better be sorry!" his mother said. "You had all of us worried sick!"

"If I could have avoided that, I would have," Gavin told her. "That was never my intention."

"Michael, where are you now?"

"We're heading to Estes Park. I think we'll spend a few days there and then head back," his father said.

"So you get a vacation, huh?" His father smiled that smile when his wife feels like he had pulled something over on her. Gavin had seen it enough to know what it was. "I think you three had this planned all along. Explains why you found them so easily, Michael."

"Easy? *Easy!*" his father said, but the smile was still there. "I had to wait in that cabin for almost a whole day!"

"I want an actual vacation next summer, buddy. For the entire family," his mother said and his father chuckled. Gavin couldn't believe what a good mood his parents were in. He looked at his father, and it was like looking at him for the first time. It had been a long time since he had seen his father in this kind of mood. "Gavin, for now, have a good time in the mountains. But, when you return, we're going to have a long talk."

"Yes, Mom," Gavin said.

He had a feeling that the talk would just be perfunctory. Had his parents still been furious about this, he wouldn't be heading to Estes Park.

"I love, honey."

"I love you too, Mom," Gavin said.

"I'll call you again later," his father said.

"You better," his mom said and that ended the conversation.

"That went well," his father said as the line went dead. "Better than I expected."

"You got a good woman there," Grandpa said. "Told you that the first time I met her."

"Yeah, you also told me not to screw it up," his dad said and then laughed along with Grandpa. "Hey, there's a park ahead that goes along the river. Let's stop and enjoy the scenery."

"Sounds good to me," Grandpa said.

The winding road led them to a turnoff and then they went down a slope to the park. There were a few people there, taking pictures and hiking around. A path went along the river that led to a dock.

"I need to make another phone call. Business and all. Gavin, take your grandfather out and look at the Big Thompson."

Gavin nodded and exited the vehicle. The mountain air smelled fresh and the sound of the river was soothing. Gavin no longer had the 'how would his parents react when he saw them again' hanging over his head, but he didn't think that was why he felt so free. His grandfather would be going to Estes Park and that was what really mattered.

"So, what do you know about the Big Thompson?" his grandfather asked after he had gotten out of the car.

"Well, it starts in the Rocky Mountain National Park and flows into Estes Lake, where it is regulated by a dam," Gavin said, going off what he had read about before the trip.

"Damn, Gavin, you sound like a history book!" his grandfather said with a laugh. "What about the flood of 1976?"

"You know about that?"

"Came here with the family in 1981, so the damage was still somewhat fresh. It was a flash flood that ended up killing around 140 people."

"A hundred forty-three, actually. Five have never been found, which is a little creepy if you think about it. In 2008, a man who they thought was killed by the flood was found alive and living in Oklahoma. He had been staying at a cabin and left the morning of the flood without telling anyone. To be thought dead all those years!" Gavin said. He had been saving that nugget for a while now.

"Must have been thought dead only around here. Government had to have known he was still alive. Wires got crossed somewhere," Grandpa said.

"So, how's the view?" his dad's voice came from behind. Gavin still couldn't believe his father was wearing shorts. It had been a long time.

"Get your phone call done?" Grandpa asked. His father nodded and joined them at the railing of the dock. The water of the Big Thompson was rushing by next to them. Grandpa looked at the water and said, "Forget how powerful this river is, even if it isn't very wide."

"So, are we going to go look for the spot tonight?" Gavin asked.

"No, not tonight. Grandpa needs some rest, and you two need a night to get somewhat used to the high altitude. Tomorrow we'll tackle the spot," his father said.

"That sounds good to me," Grandpa said. "What's for dinner?"

"Thought we'd go to a nice restaurant in Estes. Then head to the cabin. I imagine it has been a tiring and interesting trip for you two," Dad said.

"You bet it has," Gavin said. "I even saw a biker babe's boobs!"

"Oh," was all his father could manage to say.

***

They ate at one of Estes' finer restaurants. Bernie said he would pick up the tab, and his son said he bet he would.

When they arrived at the cabin, Bernie hoped he would recognize the area. So far, he had only a vague notion that he had been there before.

"The cabins are different," Bernie said. "They seem better built."

"I can imagine the ones you and mom stayed in were not of the highest quality."

"Damn walls were so thin that I bet the whole area heard us!" Bernie said and laughed at the surprised look on both his son's and grandson's faces. "What? Can't an old man reminisce about the woman he loved?"

"Thanks, Grandpa, but you can keep that kind of reminiscing to yourself," Gavin said. They pulled up to a cabin, but there was already a car there. Despite that, Michael pulled into a spot next to the Jeep that was there. There was a man sitting in the Jeep, who got out when they stopped the car. "Who is that?"

"That is part of your penance," Michael said, getting out himself. He walked over to the man, who had a camera around his neck and was dressed in a suit. They talked for a moment, while Bernie and Gavin sat in the car.

"Well, I suppose we should get out," Bernie said. After they had exited the vehicle, Michael and the man walked over to the car.

"This is Riley Harding. He's a reporter for *The Denver Post*. He wants to do a story on you two," Michael told them.

"A story?" Gavin said. "Why would he want to do that?"

"Because of the human interest aspect!" Riley Harding said. "When I caught wind of this story, I knew it had to be done! My friend Kevin is the manager of Whispering Pines and was the one that clued me in."

"Uh, Dad, do we have to?" Gavin said and looked at his father. Bernie saw the look on Michael's face that said they had to do it and with no argument.

"We would be happy to discuss the situation with you Mr. Harding," Bernie said, putting on his best smile. "Although, I'm hoping it won't take too long. Both my grandson and myself are tired and haven't slept in a bed for the past few nights."

"I'm sure we can keep it under a few hours," Riley said, still with the same smile on his face. "Shall we go into the cabin and begin?"

"Sure, why not?" Bernie said. "The sooner we get started, the sooner we get done."

***

Gavin was beyond tired when he went to bed that night. He had to talk with the reporter for two hours. Halfway into the interview, his father came by and said that his grandfather should go to bed. Gavin thought the interview would be over then, but he was wrong. His grandfather said goodnight and went to get ready for bed. Gavin's father said that Gavin would be happy to continue the interview.

Gavin told the reporter pretty much everything, only leaving out small parts (namely Courtney, that part he was keeping for himself). They started with why his grandfather wanted to go and why Gavin decided to take on the responsibility. His father chimed in from time to time, but Gavin did most of the talking. It was the most he had ever said to a complete stranger. His father had said it was a penance, but it felt good to talk about it. Not only was he able to tell Mr. Harding the details, but he was able to fill in his father as well.

It was ten o'clock when Gavin finished up his story. His grandfather had gone to bed, and his father was sitting next to him.

"So, tomorrow you're going to find that special spot that your grandfather came for," Riley said.

"Yeah, we are," Gavin said back.

"I would really like to join you. It would be great to go along with the story we have already," Riley said and Gavin was alarmed. He didn't want any strangers coming along with them.

"I'm afraid that we have to pass on that. We would like to keep it a private family matter," his father said, making Gavin sigh with relief.

"I understand," Riley said but sounded disappointed. "Would you mind if I ask you some follow-up questions though?"

"I'll answer those," his father said. "Now, I think my son needs to get some rest."

"Well, thank you two for your time. And thank your father again. Remarkable story. I'm glad it turned out well."

Soon, Gavin found himself in bed, trying to get to sleep. He would be sharing the bed with his father. The cabin had two bedrooms, and his grandfather had the other one. Gavin could have slept on the couch, but his father said they could share the bed. His father was out in the living room calling Gavin's mother again.

As Gavin lay in bed, he thought about what the reporter had said about everything ending well. That wasn't exactly true, at least not yet. It all depended on how his grandfather did tomorrow when they went looking for the spot that he had taken his grandmother to when they went on their honeymoon.

Gavin wondered why the spot was so important to his grandfather. He hoped they would find out tomorrow when they went there. He closed his eyes, and still hearing his father's voice in the other room, fell asleep. He didn't even wake up when his father came to bed 15 minutes later.

Chapter 18

Writing Entry for Friday, September 7

My senior year started without my father working at my school. When he first got his new job, I was glad that he would be leaving. Now, I'm not. Since the events of the past summer occurred, the relationship has changed between my father and me.

Not surprisingly, I was assigned to Mr. Kubach, who has had me since I came to the school. Again he is having me keep a journal. At first I thought he didn't even bother to read the entries I wrote last year and just wanted to give me more busywork. That was not the case at all. He said he loved the stories about my grandfather and wanted more. He also had read the news story about my grandfather and me. Riley Harding wrote his story, published it for *The Denver Post* and it made its way to St. Clair Shores and beyond. Mr. Kubach said he would love to have my perspective with a more detailed version.

I do not mind writing it down. I feel that it will do me good to do that. I learned a lot on that trip with my grandfather. A lot about myself, and a lot about how important memories are. While it is great to keep memories in one's head, there are other places where they can dwell as well. Other places where they would be safer.

There are memories that happened during that trip which I think I will never forget, but I know that might not be possible. There are memories that I want to make sure I keep for

posterity. One of them was the day after arriving in Estes Park when my grandfather found that special spot he had been searching for a long time.

End of Entry

+ + +

The air was hard to breathe in. Gavin hadn't noticed it before, but now that he was hiking in it, it really was affecting him. They had been hiking for half an hour. It was eleven o'clock in the morning, and the sky only held a few clouds. Gavin noticed that in the mountains, the night air was cool no matter how hot it got during the day. It was perfect weather for hiking. His grandfather was in the lead because it was 'his rodeo' as Gavin's father put it. Grandpa moved at a decent pace, but Gavin could tell the elderly man was getting tired. If they didn't find that spot soon, Gavin feared his father would call it off.

"Grandpa, how are you doing?" Gavin called out as his shoes crunched on some dry pine needles.

"Never been better," his grandfather said. Gavin thought his grandfather was just embellishing the truth. He thought his grandfather actually *had* been better. "I think we're getting close now."

"That's what you said ten minutes ago, Dad," Gavin's father said. They had started hiking right behind Whispering Pines. Grandpa scouted the area out, and he thought he recognized the area where Grandma and he had started their hike. Their hike took them up the mountain right away, with only a few flat places to rest. "Dad, it's okay if you don't remember where it is. It has been a lot of years since you were here with Mom. I bet I wouldn't remember every exact spot I took Nancy on our honeymoon either."

"I would remember this, trust me," Grandpa said, and they continued. There were no trails where they went, and Gavin had questioned that. Grandpa said that sometimes a person doesn't have to stay on the trails in life, especially when finding the good things.

Gavin's inexperience in hiking showed through as he constantly stepped on loose rocks and sticks, sometimes making him trip. So far he had escaped a massive fall.

The terrain continued to slope upward and there were pine trees all over. The air smelled of the pine trees, which Gavin found pleasant. It was hard to believe that the human world was only a few minutes away. Gavin wondered what it would be like to be hours away from civilization.

"Dad, if we don't find it soon, Gavin's going to break a bone," his father called out. "Gavin, for crying out loud, watch where you're going!"

"Sorry, Dad," Gavin said as slipped on a small rock.

There was just too much to see. So far, they had only seen a little wildlife other than the usual birds. They had passed a fox a while back that watched as they passed by at a safe distance. Dad suspected that there was a den nearby, which was why the fox hadn't run away. Gavin was hoping to see some bighorn sheep, but so far had come up empty. They walked for ten more minutes when finally Grandpa stopped.

"Is this it?" Dad asked, but Grandpa was silent.

***

Michael had asked him if this was the spot, but now Bernie wasn't sure. He thought he would know when he found it. Now, he started to doubt himself. Had the Alzheimer's robbed him of that or was it just age?

He looked around and nothing seemed familiar. He knew they couldn't stay out hiking and looking around forever. They should have found it by now. Belinda and he hadn't been hiking for long when they came across the spot so many years ago. Bernie closed his eyes and tried to concentrate on retrieving the memory. It didn't work.

Maybe he would just have to accept that it had been a fun trip, first with his grandson, and then with his grandson and his son. Michael hadn't disappointed him when he showed up. Bernie felt he had raised the boy right after all.

If he could only find that spot! That spot had taken on mythological ramifications for him. It eluded him, and it worried him why it was so elusive. Going on this trip, he wanted to see how far his disease had advanced. It seemed to have not advanced that far because he had fared quite well. Except for this. Had old age worn away such an important memory?

'Oh, Belinda, what has happened to us?' Bernie thought as he looked around.

He turned around to tell Michael and Gavin that they should return to the cabin, when he stopped. There was a huge rock to the north of him. It looked somewhat familiar. Then he realized. He was on the wrong side of it! He took off towards the giant rock at a pace he didn't think he had in him any longer.

***

"Grandpa! Slow down!" Gavin shouted as he saw his grandfather take off. Michael followed without saying anything, and Gavin started up as well.

Grandpa made it past the giant rock that was protruding from the side of the mountain. By the time Gavin caught up, his father had already made up to where Grandpa was. The area where they'd stopped at was the shape of small triangle. In the middle of the somewhat curved triangle was a bare spot that was surrounded by pine trees and rocks. It was just large enough to hold about six people standing up, fewer if those same people sat down. It was kind of a weird balcony that jutted out of the mountain.

"This is it!" Grandpa exclaimed. At first Gavin thought Grandpa was talking to either himself or his father, but that was not the case. "Yes, this is it!"

Gavin was about to say something, but his father stopped him with a hand on his arm. His grandfather looked around some more, moved to the middle, and then stopped. At first he didn't do anything, and Gavin thought he was lost again. Then he dropped to his knees. Grandpa did it so quickly that Gavin thought he was passing out. Before Gavin could react, his father stopped him from going forward.

"It was right here, here in this spot!" his grandfather said excitedly. "Belinda, I remember! I remember everything!"

His grandfather's voice was loud and confident. It was a voice Gavin had never heard come out of his grandfather before.

"This spot is where you and I made love, Belinda!" Grandpa was still on his knees, looking at the spot. Gavin raised his eyebrows and looked at his father.

"We came 1,800 miles so Grandpa could sit on the spot where he had sex with Grandma?" Gavin whispered to his father.

"Someday, you might understand," his father said, but Gavin doubted it.

***

Michael told his son that someday he might understand why it was so important for his grandfather to come back and revisit a place where he and his wife had made love. When Michael realized that this was a spot where his father and mother had sex, he was a little repulsed by it as well but he quickly got over it.

Michael understood why. Of all the times his father had made love to his mother, this one time stuck out. Perhaps it was because of the strange location, or some other reason Michael didn't want to think about. Obviously Bernie remembered something, which was what drew him to this area. Once here, the memory came flooding back. Michael could look forward to making love to his own wife for many years to come, but all his father had were memories, memories that could be gone in less than a year or more. Michael did not want to think about that.

"Let's go down the mountain a bit," Michael said to his son. He felt he was intruding on something special.

"Did Grandpa and Grandma really have sex out in the open?" Gavin asked the question that Michael wished he would have left alone.

"It appears they did," Michael said.

"Did you and Mom ever do it somewhere risky?" Gavin asked.

"Do you really want to know?" Michael asked, looking at his son.

"Never mind," Gavin said, and the two of them retreated down the slope to leave Bernie alone with his memory for a while.

***

Although it had been 51 years, the memory was the sharpest it had ever been. Bernie was two weeks out from coming back from Vietnam, and with thanks to a loan from his parents, he was able to finally take his young bride on a honeymoon.

The mountains were a wonderful change from the jungles of Vietnam, not that he had actually spent any time in the jungles. When he arrived back in the United States, he wasn't all the way home yet. He had to go through the process of being honorably discharged and then taking a bus back to St. Clair Shores. Belinda had wanted to come to New Jersey to meet him, but he told her to stay at the Shores. He wouldn't really be home until he was in his wife's arms, kissing her.

He resumed his job at Al's Shop, and few weeks later went on a honeymoon. The morning after they arrived, they decided to go on a hike behind the cabin. It was a beautiful day out as they hiked up the mountain. They arrived at the triangle area and stopped to rest. Belinda, who looked stunning in her shorts and button shirt, took Bernie's hand and pulled him close to her. She kissed him on the lips and then gave him that look.

"Here?" Bernie asked.

She nodded and that was all it took to break down his resistance. They had made love many times since he returned from Vietnam, but none of them was anything like out in the mountains. Yes, it was harder to catch his breath, but at that moment, it didn't matter.

Even though the times they made love after that were all good, it would never be the same as it was in the mountains. That was the type of experience that Bernie would often look back on fondly, though in the past few years it had been getting fainter and fainter. Not any longer. Just being in the same spot had revitalized the memory.

Bernie knew how lucky they were not to have anyone stumble in on them while they were having sex, but at that moment, he didn't think they would have cared. They were two people in love and had been separated for too long. They were going to make the most of their time together.

Their experience on the mountain wasn't the one where Michael was conceived because unbeknownst to either of them, Belinda was already one week pregnant by then. She wouldn't figure it out until two weeks later when she missed her period.

The rest of their honeymoon had been wonderful as well, but it was the time on the mountain that Bernie enjoyed the most.

He had proven that his memories were still there, the important ones anyway. The trip was a success. He could hold onto the fact that his memories were still there a little bit longer. In a way, it was bitter sweet. The memories were there, but Bernie knew soon they would be gone, and he would never have another moment like this one again.

"Thank you for a wonderful life. I'll see you soon, sweetheart," Bernie quietly said and opened his eyes. He was back in 2015 and on his knees. Michael and Gavin were not in immediate sight, but he knew they were around. Michael and

Gavin still had a lifetime of memories left, and that made Bernie feel good. Bernie's life of making memories was over. Now, it was just a matter of time when the Alzheimer's really kicked in.

Bernie stood up, took one last look at the spot, and then started down the mountain.

***

Grandpa made his way down the mountain, and Gavin's father went up to help him out, which Grandpa let him do.

"Thank you, boys. I appreciate everything you've done for me. She was my only love. She also was my first, last, and only." Grandpa said. "We can go back to the cabin now."

Gavin found out that going down a mountain was trickier than going up one. His legs wanted to pick up speed, but he didn't dare let them. He paid more attention to where he stepped because he knew if he fell, he probably would tumble the rest of the way down. Glancing back, Gavin saw that his grandfather was being helped down by his father. Grandpa looked tired. He also had a look of happiness to him. Gavin realized they had achieved their goal. Gavin realized something else as well.

Chapter 19

Writing Entry for Friday, June 5

After coming down from the mountain, we went back to the cabin to let Grandpa have a nap. He slept for three hours. After that we puttered around at Rocky Mountain National Park. Then we made the journey back to St. Clair Shores. It took us a day and a half, which was a lot shorter than the trip to Colorado. There is so much I could write about from the result of that trip, but since this is my last entry, I'll write about what I realized as I was coming down the mountain.

I realized that things would never be the same for any of us that were making that journey down. For my grandfather, he would go back to the nursing home knowing that his memories were there, but for how long? For my father, things would be different with his relationship with me. For myself, a lot would be different. The world is a bigger place for me now, I know that.

I graduate next weekend. I cannot believe I will be done with high school. My future is still murky but not as murky as before. I am no longer dreading the unknown. Yes, it is scary leaving the safety of high school (I know I said I hated school but at least school had a routine to it), but there are a lot of good things out there in the world. My trip with Grandpa taught me that.

The year has gone well. My grades are up, possibly due to the fact that either the classes are easier or maybe I cared a little more. I even went to my senior prom with Sophie Kline. Granted, she asked me, but I did say yes. I had a good time with Sophie, and we date from time to time. I haven't seen her breasts like I did with Courtney, but I have kissed Sophie, so all is well there. Sophie still has a year left in high school, but I have a feeling that our relationship will not end when I graduate. Right now I have no after high school plans. At least my father has not been bothering me about that.

I have not brought up what happened with Roadkill, even though Mr. Kubach has asked me several times. I purposely put off his questions until now. The truth is that I do not know what happened to Roadkill. I have not heard from him since I left him at Sturgis with Janice. I went over to his house a month after returning and found no one home. There was a 'for sale' sign in the front yard. That made me feel bad seeing that sign. I hated how we left each other, but I still do not see how it could have been any different. As far as I know, Roadkill's van is still in the impound lot at Loveland. Or maybe it has been auctioned off by now. I wonder if it still smells like corn.

That brings up another point I have been saving for this final entry. I have my driver's license. I got it a month ago. I was even allowed to take my father's car to pick up Sophie for a date. She did all the driving up to then. I still do not have a car, but judging how slow I am at most things in life, maybe in a couple of years I'll have one.

I am walking through for my graduation. If left up to me, I would not do it, but my parents are insisting I do. Sophie also says I need to walk and get my diploma. I think it is a lot of pointless hoopla for a piece of paper. My parents are throwing a party and everything. My aunt and uncle are coming as well for the ceremony.

There is one person that will not be at the ceremony, and next to my parents, he is the one person that matters most to me. My grandfather will not be able to make it. His condition has worsened dramatically. He does not even recognize my father or myself.

It did not start happening right when we got back. It was about two months after when Grandpa's Alzheimer's really kicked in. He went from the end of stage one to stage two in a matter of days. He is no longer at Lake View. He needs more care than they can give them. He is at Johnson's Home for the Elderly. The name does not offer much creativity, does it? They treat him well there at least. I still go and visit him, and I am ashamed to say that I do not go every day. I just cannot do it. When I go, he does not recognize me, and I have to tell him who I am every time. He just nods his head and then stares at the television. Most of the time the television is not even on. We do not play chess anymore. The last time we played chess was in September, and Grandpa struggled during that game. Grandpa's body is strong, but his mind is what is weak. He even needs help going to the bathroom. The nurses have to come in and ask if he has to go. If they did not do that, he would dirty himself. A lot of times my father will come with me. My sister does not go there much anymore, and I cannot blame her. I go because I feel it is necessary. My father says it is good for my grandfather to see us even though he has no clue who we are.

Sometimes he will call out my grandmother's name, and that actually makes me feel good. Somewhere in his mind, he still remembers in a strange sort of way.

My father asked Grandpa's doctor if his quick mental decline was normal. The doctor said that it sometimes happens, but it is not usual. I sometimes wonder if the trip brought it on. Perhaps the trip put too much stress on him, and when it was over, his mind just broke whatever barriers he had created. Several times I am tempted to tell my father about my thought, but I chicken out. I think I am too afraid he will say yes.

Am I sorry I took my grandfather to Colorado? No, I am not. I love my grandfather and always will. He needed my help, and I gave it to him. There are things that happened on that trip that I regret, but overall, I am happy I went.

What kind of disease eats away at a person's memory and leaves him or her as a living husk? Seeing him that day in the mountains with that look of wonderment on his face really let me know how awful this disease is. He had to have known that the memory he so desperately wanted returned, would eventually leave him again. Of course, now my grandfather does not even know that he lost all those memories. It is for his loved ones to mourn that occurrence.

I think what really scares me is the fact that Alzheimer's can be hereditary. That means my father has a good chance of getting it, as do I. I cannot imagine what it is like to lose your memories and seeing people you have known all your life and not knowing who they are. That is what scares me the most, I think.

End of Entry

+ + +

Gavin rode in the passenger seat of his father's car. They were the only ones in the car and were heading to the nursing home to take care of Gavin's grandfather's belongings.

"He really was one of a kind," Gavin said as he looked out the window. St. Clair Shores still felt different to him and had ever since he had returned from the trip last summer.

"More than that," his father said.

"You know, Dad, I hope there is a heaven," Gavin said. "And that Grandpa is up there right now with Grandma. Perhaps they can go hiking together again."

"Amen to that," his father said.

Grandpa had died two days ago. He almost made it to another July Fourth. Grandpa's funeral was going to be on

Friday. Gavin's aunt and uncle would again make the trip to St. Clair Shores, along with his cousins this time.

Gavin helped his father make the funeral arrangements. His father hadn't asked him to help, Gavin had asked him.

Gavin and his father were with Grandpa when he passed away. His body had been shutting down the last month or so, and since Grandpa had a clause in his will, he was not put on life support. Gavin wished he could say that his grandfather opened his eyes one more time, looked at them with remembrance, but that did not happen. Perhaps he just paid too close attention to senior English class and the Romantic period. That just does not happen in real life. Grandpa hadn't remembered them for a long time.

"So, how are sailing lessons going?" Dad asked.

Gavin was finally allowed to go sailing, which had started last August. He loved it so much that he wanted to take lessons. To his surprise, his father said he could.

"They are going well. Sophie keeps bugging me to take her, but I do not want to until I have had more practice," Gavin said.

Upon starting the lessons, his father made him promise to wear a life jacket at all times, which Gavin did. His father also made it clear that Gavin still wouldn't ever get him on a boat. Some things can only change so much.

"I lied to you when I told you we were going to go and get Grandpa's things. I cleaned out his room yesterday," his father told him.

"Then where are we going?" Gavin asked.

"To the Nautical Mile," Dad said. Gavin looked at him and then his eyes got wider. "No, no it's not a sailboat. If you want one of those things, you'll have to buy one yourself. It's a surprise that Grandpa and I set up a while back."

"What is it?"

"It'll have to wait until we get there," Dad said and winked at Gavin. His father's first year as a principal went well.

They arrived at the Mile and went past the parking spots to an alleyway. "I had to arrange a spot to have this little production. I could have done it at the house, but I thought it would be more special here."

The alley was tight, but did widen some as they went further down it. Down a ways in the alley was a white, GMC Canyon pickup. Gavin thought they would squeeze past it, but instead his father stopped his car.

"Go on, get out," Dad said, and Gavin did.

"What is with the truck?"

"It's yours," his father said. Gavin looked at him in complete disbelief. "I thought it would help you out with your lawn service business."

"My *what*?" Gavin asked, still looking at the truck. It looked to be a 2015 model. Not the newest, but close.

"Your grandfather said that you wanted to start a lawn service business. I realize now that he probably meant that you needed to expand the one you already have. A truck is just the thing for that."

"That is *mine*?" Gavin said, his voice barely a whisper.

"Yes, it is. That is what Grandpa wanted. He told me last summer but made me promise not to say anything until, well you know," Dad said, and Gavin did know, his grandfather's death. "We can put the name of your company on the side. I think they have those magnetic signs that would work."

"Dad, I cannot accept this. It is too much. It is not fair to the other grandchildren," Gavin said, all the while wanting to get behind the wheel.

"I have already talked with your aunt and uncle. They agree that you are deserving of this, and more. What you did last summer took a lot of guts. To go against my wishes like you did and get your grandfather to the one place that made him happier than he had been in years, was a brave thing to do. I have said this many times since last summer, but I was wrong in not taking him myself. And you called me on that. The truck is yours. And so is this," Dad said and gave Gavin a piece of paper. On the paper was a number- 100,000.

"What is this?" Gavin asked.

"That is money to help with your business. Keep in mind that part of it probably should go toward your education. It has been sitting in an account that will be switched over to your name," his father said. Gavin was speechless. "Oh, and my name as well. I'm not about to give an 18 year-old access to a large sum of money like that.

"I know you loved Grandpa, Gavin. I did too. You were more than a grandson to him, you were a friend. Ever since that trip to Colorado, I have seen so many changes in you. Changes for the better. Yes, your grandfather regressed, but there was no changing that. You taking him on that trip didn't do it."

"I, I cannot believe this," Gavin said. It felt unreal. It had to be a joke. "Dad, I feel I do not deserve this."

"You do. Your grandfather said he wanted to invest in your future, even if he wasn't around to see it. He left your sister and cousins something too, but obviously not the same amount. Your grandfather was a wealthy man, even though you wouldn't know that from talking or looking at him. He built a business that did well and he did it with honesty. He just wanted to give you the same chance," his father said, and

Gavin could feel the tears coming. This time he didn't try to stop them, nor was he ashamed. He went to his father and the two of them hugged.

His grandfather had given him more than money. He had given him a much brighter future. Gavin wished he could say that he would never forget his grandfather and what his grandfather did for him, but in the back of his mind, he knew there was always that possibility. Was that possibility going to stop him from making as many memories as he could? No, it would not.

Acknowledgements

As a teacher I have dealt with many students that are like Gavin and each one were unique in his or her own way. Everyone face challenges, and when one has autism, even the smallest challenge can seem a giant obstacle. I want to thank those students I had and will have that have had autism for giving me challenges and making me a better teacher for it.

I also want to thank my wife Lynnae, who was my first editor on this venture. As usual, her suggestions were good ones. Another thank you goes out to Dr. Kevin Kremer, who edited the final version that you see here. Dr. Kremer runs the publishing company called Snow in Sarasota also was my sixth grade teacher. He is one of the reasons I went into education. It was great working with him, and he did an excellent job editing the novel.

Lastly, I want to thank Douglas Tiedman, who created the beautiful cover for the novel. Douglas did an amazing job, and I'm not saying that just because he is my brother.

www.ingramcontent.com/pod-product-compliance
Lightning Source LLC
Chambersburg PA
CBHW060542180626
46817CB00002B/682